Vampire's Demand

IMMORTAL PROTECTOR

BOOK FOUR

STEPHANIE FLYNN

Small Fish Publishing

USA

First edition
Cover design by Stephanie Flynn
ISBN eBook: 9781952372773
ISBN Paperback: 9781952372360
ISBN Hardcover: 9781952372780
ISBN Large Print paperback: 9781952372384

Also By Stephanie Flynn

Find my catalog at StephanieFlynn.com

Immortal Protector series

0.5 Vampire's Distraction

1 Vampire's Deception

2 Vampire's Secret

3 Vampire's Promise

3.5 Elf Bound

4 Vampire's Demand

5 Vampire's Destruction

6 Vampire's Conquest

Immortal Protector Side Tales

Deer Holiday

Depths of the Heart

Matchmaker in Time series

0.5 Minutes to Live

1 Seconds to Act

2 Hours to Arrive

3 Days to Hide

4 Years to Savor

Pirates in Time series

1 Pirate's Prize

2 Pirate's Treasure

3 Pirate's Plunder

Time Travel Romance Shorts

Fateful Time

One Crazy Time

If you like your urban fantasy without the romance, too, check out Stephanie Flynn's other name, Marie Flynn!

I
What's Wrong

Soren

I USED TO LIE across a quiet county road at night, waiting for an unsuspecting human to stop and offer assistance to a man in obvious distress. This used to be an easy strategy and minimized witnesses. After getting run over by people texting or driving drunk, my injuries weren't worth the extra effort. On occasion, when I wasn't feeling the greatest upstairs, I still resorted to it, but these days, I was feeling pretty good—better than good.

Under the cloak of night in the city park, I leaned against a tree in the shadows, waiting. Centuries ago, witches—basically fancy humans—created what I was down to the details of the bloodlust...on purpose. Since I appreciated not being in a pine box taking a permanent dirt nap, I had to accept the oddly cannibalistic nature forced upon me. The creative witches hadn't had the foresight to craft a cure, so here I was, still waiting.

Those witches sort of regretted what they'd created, and they've made it their life's mission to destroy my kind. That led me to why I waited quietly, patiently. My goal was to fill my stomach with as little risk of exposure as possible. Two options presented themselves. I could hyperspeed over and take a bite before my snack knew what was happening. Whenever I was irritable, impatient, or lazy, this was my go-to. As with all things, this option had downsides. For starters, the resulting flavor became bitter.

And secondly, the risk of my snack panicking, fighting, and making a mess dramatically increased. See, when choosing the ambush strategy, striking a moving target was difficult—exponentially more so with heavier humans. If my chomp on the carotid missed, the paralysis was slower to affect my snack. This guaranteed my snack would fight back in a panic. Now I risked tearing the throat clean out rather than making a nice pair of straw marks. Even worse? Convincing my snack that I was just as much of a victim in all this was nearly impossible.

Unlike my brother, I didn't have a ridiculous closet filled with endless options. So if I managed to bite my snack just right, and keep myself clean, there was still another problem. My brother's annoying rule of keeping the supernatural world hidden had some merit—see the witches' life mission above—so I'd have to pinch that cube of memory from the mind of my snack. For reasons I wished I could forget, I hated tampering with free will, but hey, sometimes survival meant doing things we didn't want to do. Tonight wasn't about survival.

After enough mediocre meals, a craving for the good stuff hit. Then I resorted to option two. A happy meal—not the kind that came in a paper bag—was far less messy and much, much tastier.

A man lazily jogged by me with earbuds dangling from his head and a glinting ring on his finger. The divorce rate wasn't so high because marriage was easy, but that ring meant it was a fair assumption he might be in love. And those endorphins were divine. Anticipating their flavor hitting my tongue, I salivated. I would've preferred a beautiful woman, but these days they tended to pair up. Perhaps the instinctual fear of the night and the recent chaos of 'animal attacks' had them spooked. If I tried anyway, I might succeed with the happy meal strategy on the first one, but then number two would by default become an ambush, and then I'd come full circle.

Having made up my mind on tonight's strategy and target, I used my hyperspeed to close the distance undetected, and I tapped on his shoulder. The sweaty man, slightly taller than me with baggy exercise clothes, startled and turned.

The jogger removed one earbud and frowned. "Can I help you?" His voice was uncertain, a tinge bit afraid.

That wouldn't do.

As the man assessed my inappropriate clothing—ferreting out my purpose—I smiled and pointed to his phone strapped on his arm. "What music app are you using? I keep getting all these ads, and they disrupt my focus, you know? I'm looking for something more...satisfying."

"Uh, I don't know. It came with the phone."

"Really? That's great. Technology these days...who would've guessed?" The jogger looked at me like I was nuts. In my defense, the rapidly changing tech was exhausting to keep up with. I'd thought about a short walk and a sudden drop in broad daylight to avoid facial recognition passwords. Seriously, how was I going to explain to my cell phone provider that no, in fact, I had not aged in the last two decades?

Or in the last two centuries...but they didn't need to know that either.

Seeing the man still on edge, I pointed to his ring, feigning friendliness. "Wife at home?"

"At work," he said carefully. But he stayed, perhaps willing to entertain a buddy. Making friends as adults was tough, even more so when one ate them on occasion.

"I've never been married. I don't think I ever felt the desire to stay with one fragile woman forever. Maybe I missed the signs in myself, or maybe I haven't met the right one. It's a big sea. What's she like—your wife? What made you decide this was the last catch you ever wanted?"

My brother had always been looking for the perfect catch. Of course, our circumstances weren't so bland as this jogger's, so rather than a fishing weekend, it was more like hunting for a great white whale that neither of us knew even existed. Fortunately for Oliver, and I meant that, my brother found his last catch. I actually respected Daisy—before she'd become a vampire—which was...weird for me. But I didn't expect a woman was out there for me at all, and as much as I enjoyed a weekend on the lake with beer, catching and releasing, I had no interest in traversing the northern seas. My niece wouldn't give up on me. Nicole Rockwell always tried to pry open my psyche to fix whatever she thought was broken. She wasn't going to find anything, because there was nothing wrong with me.

I was just a dude, surviving with a set of circumstances for which there was no cure. And since I wasn't being chased by pitchforks, I considered myself an unqualified success. No one had the right to judge me.

The jogger smiled warmly at my inquiry. "When I've had a bad day, she lifts me up. When I've had a great day, she's the only one I want to celebrate with. And when my day is just ordinary—the same old routine, day in and day out—there's no one else I could imagine waking up beside me. Can I give you a tip?"

"Why not? I've got time." Anticipating the flavor of his endorphins flowing down my throat, I beamed.

"Don't take this the wrong way, but I think referring to women as fish isn't a great place to start."

I wasn't a fan of criticism either, but I swallowed my urge to tear out his throat. He needed to simmer a little longer to be ready. I kept a grin on my face. "Choose metaphors that aren't misogynistic. Got it. But *why* is she the one? What made you say you couldn't live another day without her?"

He patted his almost nonexistent belly. "The first time she cooked for me, I knew. She makes the best lasagna ever, and that's why I'm out here most nights. I can't and wouldn't turn down her amazing food, but I gotta stay in shape, if you know what I mean."

That was my limit for the gushy, mushy stuff, and his blood sounded ripe. "Speaking of food..." I captured my snack's gaze, and with a dash of compulsion, I said, "Don't scream. You won't remember this."

The guy frowned. "Why are your eyes red?"

I added a new instruction. "Don't talk."

The jogger instantly obeyed, standing still and closing his mouth. Extending my fangs, I leaned into his throat with perfect aim and bit down on the pounding artery, calling me like a siren's song. As the sweet spray of endorphins flowed with the warm blood, I groaned. Swallow after swallow of the perfect mix of fresh O-negative and happy juice. There was nothing better on this earth.

Unlike my brother, with his unfortunate dairy allergy, I kept myself at maximum strength for times like when the witches had orchestrated another vampire barbecue. By always feeding on the freshest source possible, I'd saved his ass several times. Perhaps it was my laziness or perhaps the lack of social scorecards I could check before choosing the happy meal strategy, but I didn't discriminate—much. So, statistically speaking, I preyed on the innocent, sure, but also some not-so-innocent. The witches believed most humans leaned more toward the innocent side of the shades of gray. Hence, their life's mission to destroy my kind, but I didn't have time to delve into the nitty-gritty of a person's nuances before imbibing. To me, a meal was a meal. So the witches could leave all their judgment at their own doorsteps.

I pulled away and wiped my mouth, finally satiated. Without my support, the jogger fell to the ground while still in a trance. Blood trickled down his neck. His gaze was vacant. Easily capturing that gaze, I said, "A branch scratched you because you weren't paying attention to your surroundings, and it knocked you down."

The jogger met my gaze, but otherwise said nothing, as ordered. I used my hyperspeed and disappeared into the darkness.

Soren

I SET DOWN MY empty glass on the sitting room coffee table inside my brother's opulent bed-and-breakfast. I was gifted this place temporarily, and considering the digs I'd had recently, this place was nothing short of a palace. And with the limit-free credit cards I had access to, I'd installed a TV that, with the touch of a button, lifts and unfolds from a hidden compartment in the floor. Now I could enjoy my show in the proper way.

And I didn't think Nicole was complaining either. I was sure when Oliver returned home in a few months, he'd roll his eyes. But he'd insisted I deserved whatever luxury I cooked up until he returned from his globe-trotting honeymoon with his new wife. I had almost two centuries to figure out how to stash some cash, but I didn't have fat bank accounts like my workaholic brother, so why spend my own when someone offered theirs? Besides, I never knew from one day to the next where I'd sleep or whom I'd eat. After those damn witches turned me into their puppet, I'd lost decades of my own free will. Staying transient was safer. A moving target was harder to hit.

My several-times-over great-niece, Nicole Rockwell, limped over and sank onto the leather couch with a grunt. Gray sleek strands were pulled into a bun, and since the B&B closed to the public when my brother had returned for good, Nicole wore jeans and a blouse instead of her usual suit. The casual clothes aged her, a reminder that my time with her was limited. A part of me envied her finite life.

Knowing there was an end inspired a purpose—an urgency to accomplish...something, to become...something. I didn't have the desire to impress or be accountable to anyone. Since I'd earned my long-lost sun rung, I was free to come and go when I pleased. And now I was free to enjoy relationship drama in the form of a massive, folding TV. I lifted my feet onto the coffee table and leaned back to lose myself in my favorite show. Makayla and Kyle were arguing about the paternity of her baby, but they were wasting their energy.

I gestured at the screen as if Nicole didn't understand my reference. "These two people were meant to be together. They even have a child together, but every time they're in the same room, it's like a hurricane. They need to shut up and move into the bedroom already."

"There's more to a functional relationship than perfection in the bedroom," Nicole said dryly.

"Says the master of relationships," I replied back just as dryly. My niece took after my brother as a workaholic who never wanted to plant any roots.

"If you find the right person, you'll understand."

I made a dismissive noise and reached for my glass while rising off the couch. "Drink?"

She gestured in the affirmative, and I crossed the lobby to the bar, poured myself a refill and made her a glass. I returned to Nicole's side and handed her the drink, and my niece immediately brought the drink to her mouth.

Curiosity had me asking, "So what brings you down to my level of day drinking?"

"I'm not getting any younger, you know." She set her glass down, half finished.

"Clearly," I said playfully.

Nicole ignored the jab, which was unusual. Something serious was on her mind. I squirmed, hoping what I suspected wasn't coming. "One down and one to go."

And there it was. I snorted at the blunt answer.

"What?" she asked, astonished. "All these years I've wished my Rockwell boys would return home, find love, and be happy. You need something or someone to ground you, and I won't be around much longer. I want to see you at that altar, too."

I never believed humans and vampires could work, and I pushed that message too hard when I'd forced my brother to kill his first fiancée. Instead, she became a raging lunatic vampire. Oliver had much better luck the second time around. They were happy and bloodbonded—a ritual that afforded both lovers psychic energy and other useless stuff. I had no interest, no matter how much my big brother swooned about it. He had always been a sap.

Humans and vampires didn't mix...unless someone was hungry, naturally.

This conversation needed to rest permanently. "If I could materialize the perfect woman, who didn't run screaming at my fangs, who actually wanted to become a vampire, and who wanted to spend a literal eternity with me, then I'd be happy to." Not a single woman I'd encountered handled what I was without being compelled, so this whole rumination was pointless. "I've asked Allison Kincaid, before she went evil, and baby witch Lily Barrett if it was possible, but alas, the witches both said it was not, in lesser polite words. That means I'm a forever bachelor, licked, stamped and sealed. Toss me to the wind and let come what may." I rose and refilled my glass, not caring about what I'd grabbed from the vast selection.

"If not a human, then why not date a witch? They could handle what you are," Nicole said, twisting to face me over the couch.

I snorted at the ridiculous suggestion. Memories of the flames licking up our legs while witches watched with glee—there was no coming back from that. Although Lily had apologized, having been swept into the cult of Allison and Jamie's twisted beliefs of burning all vampires alive, I didn't trust a single other person with spellcasting abilities. "I'd be eternally thankful if a witch never touched me. And since I'm not gay, elves are out," I added before she could. "Their females have been extinct for centuries. That leaves my future a party of two: me and my freedom."

"That sounds incredibly lonely." Nicole smiled with a tinge of sadness.

Apparently, my logic hadn't been satisfying enough to drop this tired conversation into the grave for good. Only a woman clinging to my shoulder and licking my ear would convince her I'd found happiness in my life. But my niece was projecting her own fears and regrets onto me, which was why I remained respectful toward her. I wished I could let her die in peace, knowing her 'boys' were happy and cared for, but, as usual, I was the one to break her heart. That guilt dragged me straight back to my brother's bar, but this time, I dropped back onto his fancy couch with a full bottle. I could feel my niece's gaze.

Nicole climbed to her feet with a grunt. "If you're going to stay a lump on a log around here, I need enough space to vacuum around you."

I kicked my feet up onto the coffee table and swallowed down—I checked the label—a few swigs of Dom. Not bad.

She grunted with annoyance at my minimal effort. "People dream of winning the lottery. Even though the odds say it'll never happen, they still make plans, and have wishes and hopes. Sharing those can tell you a lot about a person."

I frowned, not following.

"Even with your brother's unlimited credit, access to cars, and three months of ownership of this place, you sit here, doing nothing all by yourself. Can you honestly tell me you'd rather do nothing than absolutely *anything*?"

And still the conversation continued. Well, that gave me a great idea. I got up and gestured my invitation to Nicole. "Go ahead and vacuum to your old heart's content."

"Where are you going?" she asked, both suspicious and with a lighter tone of bubbling excitement.

"I'm taking your advice, Nicole. I just figured out what I need to 'ground me'." It definitely wasn't the nonexistent white whale. "As you said, I happened to have access to lots of money and some boredom to cure. See you later."

Nicole's brows rose.

Since my niece didn't want me to lounge around here, I'd go somewhere else to keep a seat warm. Then I could watch my trash TV in peace without the never-ending guilt trips of disappointing her.

2

It's Fake

Indie

I'd fled my homeland with nothing but what I'd carried on my back. Whenever a threat appeared in my life, I'd packed my saddlebags and mounted up for an unknown destination. And I chose a new home based on a lack of unusual murders or 'animal attacks'. While I no longer slept under the stars with a horse standing guard, much of my life was the same. At least with a vehicle, I could carry more of my belongings, and I could sleep protected from the elements.

I never stayed in any single place long enough to forge friendships, but I had no place for entertaining, anyway. Today I had to make a special exception, and I should've sniffed the air freshener before she ducked inside the cramped quarters. Renowned witch Allison Kincaid pushed a lock of light brown hair behind her ear. She wore modern glasses that matched her shirt and accentuated her big brown eyes. She seemed young for the reputation that preceded her, but I was in no position to judge. Allison was willing, and I was in dire need of her services. Ironically, time was not on my side.

Allison had directed me to bring us here—a place called Fully Loaded, where humans indulged in lively spirits. I wasn't a drinker. Altering my mental status nearly got me caught once, and I couldn't let that happen again.

"What are we doing here?" I asked, uncomfortable being in the parking lot, even in broad daylight.

"I need you to track someone down for me, and with their help, we can do as you ask."

I stiffened. Opening up to one witch was risky enough, but now she wanted me to bring someone else in. If she'd lied about her capabilities, what did that say about her trustworthiness? I couldn't compel my identity from her memory. As magical beings themselves, witches were impervious. And I didn't have time to start all over. Witches didn't exactly have websites with amazing SEO leading me right to their doorsteps. I'd traveled the countryside searching, avoiding crowds, and great care had to be taken when inquiring about the hidden world. The wrong person could summon the enemy in droves, and I had to assume my capture would result in a great reward—not because of my vanity, but in spite of it.

"Finding a witch is no simple feat." I protested, uneasy with this change in plan.

Allison gave me a reassuring smile. "Someone in there can help you."

Surely, a witch could inquire about a witch more effectively than I could, and I was safer here in my car. "If you're so sure, why do I have to go inside?"

She gazed at the exterior of the building with lips pressed thin. "Some memories need to stay buried. Understand?"

I understood avoidance better than most. I followed her gaze, dreading the memories of the night I'd drunk too much and nearly got caught. Considering how crucial this deal was for my survival, I said, "I'll be back shortly."

All I needed was a second witch. No problem. I exhaled deeply and climbed out of my car.

Indie

As the warmth of the sun cocooned my face, I smiled. Sunlight meant I was safe from one of my many enemies. Personally, I didn't loathe vampires. They served their purpose, but I couldn't trust them.

I glanced at the ring on my finger, a gaudy old emerald bauble, and it flickered like a severed live wire. Time was breathing down my neck like a bloodthirsty, mindless...vampire. A car horn honked at the stoplight nearby. Buildings in the downtown area were quaint, still maintaining that charm of yesteryear, but across the street and down the block, modern chain gas stations drew traffic. This small town—Marinette, Wisconsin—was busier than I preferred.

I didn't like attention.

I wanted to run for cover, away from eyes that could see me, but this wasn't a place I'd consider without hesitation. I didn't know who would be inside. Stalling only meant more waiting, so I steeled myself and pushed through. The bar was surprisingly modern, cool, and sophisticated—steely gray with neon green accents. There was a dance floor in a room off to the side, dartboards, and billiard tables. Electronic slot machines jingled and flashed in the corner. There were only a few customers present. To my enhanced eyes, vampires were indistinguishable from humans unless they purposely outed themselves or burned in the sun. To find my own kind required the removal of my protection, which I couldn't do. So I used the basic intuition I'd been using and scanned the couple of daytime patrons. I believed was safe, but I made a note of the exit at the back.

A man sat at the bar, dark wavy hair blocking his face, lost in his thoughts on his phone, nursing a drink. A riveting plump woman with cherry red lips and long black curls pulled into a messy bun worked behind the bar. I settled onto a stool in front of her, ignoring the customer a few seats over on my right. He was playing a kind of word game.

I glanced at his screen out of curiosity. In small backwater towns, the lack of cell signal was definitely an issue. I'd spent countless hours with word puzzle books found at gas stations.

"Hey, honey. What can I get you?" the bartender asked, stealing my attention.

"A seltzer water is fine."

The bartender lifted an eyebrow. "Who goes to a bar during the daytime for water?" Her critical eyes skimmed my attire as if seeking her own answers.

"I'm not a drinker."

"Well, I insist you give me something to do," the bartender said with a crooked smile. "I'm going crazy over here cleaning glasses."

Since I didn't want further attention, I chose a simple mixed drink just to take up the space in front of me. "A mimosa then."

"Make it on the house," the man next to me said.

I turned to him to reject the needless offer, but his brilliant green eyes met my gaze, so stunning they looked fake, and my breath froze in my chest. His mouth quirked into a smile, sending small lines crinkling around his eyes. The man's dark wavy locks were longer than my short blond cut, and he sported a neatly trimmed beard. A bright white T-shirt strained over thick arms and a broad chest. But there was a look on his face that sent my heart pounding in my chest.

Thankfully, humans couldn't hear that.

If I had to guess, he was a healthy upper twenties, early thirties. But like all humans, this beautiful specimen was too young for anything but a fun time. I raked my hungry eyes along his very pleasing shape, and at once, I blushed. This was ludicrous! I had never responded like this to anyone, and I needed to cool down before I started sweating in front of the guy. Out of necessity, I added, "Extra rocks, please."

The bartender placed a hand on her hip and addressed the sexy miles of man next to me. "You don't get to tell me who gets a free drink."

"Oh, but I do," he said while still staring at me. His voice was deep and smooth, and I wanted to find out just how deep he could go.

I always had a bad feeling about places like this, and I should've listened to my instincts. Just as I was about to dash for the exit and beg Allison for somewhere else to ask for help, the sexy human tore his gaze away, giving me a moment's reprieve.

"Cora," he said with a small lift of his amused lips, "I insist you give this woman a free drink."

"Says who?" Cora the bartender frowned.

"Allow me to introduce myself." He puffed his chest with an importance apparently only he knew about. "I'm Soren Rockwell."

The name didn't register as familiar to me, but Cora's eyes bugged. "You're Mr. Rockwell? I'm so sorry, sir. I had no idea you're the new owner. Like me, I don't think all the employees know about it yet, and now I'm rambling. One drink on the house, coming up." The bartender set to work mixing the alcoholic drink. From assertive to nervous. Despite her change in behavior, this sexy human didn't intimidate me. No, there were several very specific words he did to me instead.

And all of it was simply foolish.

The new owner slid himself over a few stools. "As I said, Soren Rockwell. May I ask the name of the woman gracing me with her presence on this fine morning?"

As his scent—likely a cologne I could never name—reached my nose, my heart pounded harder, and my cheeks heated. What on earth was wrong with me to respond like this to a *human*? The urge to run returned, but I couldn't make myself move.

And it had nothing to do with the free mimosa.

Seeing as I'd encountered zero elves since I'd arrived in town, I believed I was safe to give him my name, and I wanted him to know it. "My friends call me Indie."

He reached out a hand to shake, and mine met his. Thick, strong fingers wrapped around mine. The warmth and softness of his touch sent sparks of lust roaring through me. My heart pounded even harder.

He slowly released my hand. "Just Indie?"

"Indiara Niskatar, but only my family calls me Indiara, and I don't prefer it."

Soren made a face—not one of recognition, thankfully, but one of confusion associated with long-winded and unusual names. I hated my full name. Every time I heard it, I shuddered at my father's stern voice reprimanding me.

"I know it's a mouthful," I added.

His eyes sparkled with amusement. "Well, Indie, you don't appear to be the day-drinking type, so what brings you here?"

This guy was the *new* owner, likely not who Allison had in mind for help. I glanced at a flash on his phone screen, and I noticed a ring. A bright ruby wrapped in white gold, surprisingly feminine, adorned his left ring finger. This human was taken.

That was a relief.

But I wasn't going to be able to kick him out of his own building to get a private word with the bartender. Since the daytime patrons were few and mostly drunk, and I trusted Allison's lead, I said, "I'm looking for information."

"You're in luck," Soren said playfully. "I happen to know stuff. For example, you are the most beautiful woman to have ever crossed that door."

Cora made a swooning noise while working on my drink.

I made a point of glancing around at a few shaggy men hunched on their stools. One hiccupped, leaning into his drink, and the other mindlessly slapped a button on the slot machine. Giving Soren the benefit of the doubt, I said, deadpan, "Your sample size is lacking."

Soren laughed. "Don't be so humble."

He'd compared me to middle-aged human men who were in desperate need of showers and shaves. Humble had nothing to do with it. I said coolly, "That's not appropriate, Mr. Rockwell."

He switched his tone at once, finally getting I wasn't amused. "Please call me Soren and pardon my forwardness. I assumed your ring-free finger meant you were single."

My emerald rested on my right hand, but his wasn't. "Just as I assumed, your ring-adorned one means you're not."

Soren looked at his ruby and removed it. "This?" I gazed upon him with utmost interest as he positioned the ring snugly on his middle finger, but I noted no magical changes. He was an ordinary human. "Does that clear things up for you?"

I had my friend waiting in my unfortunate car, and I couldn't lose her assistance or patience. I had no right to be entertaining a flirtatious human. "Actually, that's not necessary." Since mainstream society was aware of witchcraft but relegated it to a meditative religion, I hoped asking for the magical version would give me one real answer. Keeping my voice low, I said, "I'm in search of someone who practices magic. You know—herbs, candles, chanting. That sort of thing. Sound familiar?"

"You're looking for a witch," Soren said simply.

I was on the right track. "Do you know one?"

"Allison Kincaid used to work here," the bartender said, eavesdropping. "Rumors are she's a witch, if you're into that kind of thing."

Clearly, Cora was on the 'meditative religion' side of the practice, so she wasn't who Allison had in mind when she'd sent me in here. "Anyone else?"

Soren grimaced. "I don't blame you for passing on Allison's help."

And the helpful lead wasn't him either. I was curious about what he knew of her, but I had more pressing matters than to indulge in gossip. "Do you know of another? Or is there someone else here...?"

"You know, boss," Cora started, injecting herself into the conversation again. "If Allison were still around, she would insist on a grand reopening to celebrate the change of hands. I think we need a party to remind the locals where the best place is for drinks and dancing."

I blinked and looked around the room again. One of the old men belched. This was the best?

Soren brightened. "Cora, how fast can we swing a marketing campaign and some decorations?"

Cora beamed, settling my demink in front of me. "If you bring the décor, I can get the crew to spruce this place up for the weekend."

"It's settled then." Soren's brilliant green eyes sparkled. "Indie, I can introduce you to a witch."

Finally. I smiled. "Point me in the right direction, and I'll be on my way."

The flirty human gazed into my eyes with a mischievous smile, and my stupid heart fluttered. "Not so fast. I need something in return."

My home was on wheels, and keeping it moving was critical, but not even the air to inflate the tires was free anymore. Favors always had strings, and I shouldn't have been surprised by the delay. "Like what?"

"I have this...aunt. Nicole's getting up there in age, and she worries about me. A lot. Too much, really. You would do me and her a big favor if you could show up as my date."

Perspiration rolled down the glass just as it rolled down my back. A flash of heat tore through me. As much as I could picture a very sweaty, very naked, long night with this sexy human, it was impossible. "I can't."

Soren didn't falter. "No date, no witch."

I gritted my teeth. "Will you accept cash?"

Soren leaned closer, and his scent filled my nose again. I refrained from inhaling deeply, but it took effort. "Cash is easy to come by. My niece can smell a paid date a mile off. You'll convince her. You're properly motivated."

I needed that connection more than anything, but crowds weren't safe, and going out with a human was pointless. They were too weak, and their lifespans were crushingly too short, for starters. "This sounds like extortion."

Soren sensed my hesitation and added, "How are your acting skills?"

I tipped my chin up, fully confident. "Most excellent."

"Perfect. A fake date then."

Fake? He didn't actually want to spend time with me. I couldn't help but be a little hurt. "People do that?"

"Like I said, this is for Nicole. Fake it for me, and we have a deal. But you have to be convincing."

I looked at the flickering emerald on my finger.

"And I promise you a very good time," Soren said, and flashed a steamy grin.

I wouldn't mind having his hands on me for an evening, all for the sake of his aged aunt. During one evening in this small town, what could really go wrong?

"Are you going to drink that?" he asked.

A chilled drink wasn't going to fix my reaction to his human, only make me less able to listen to my own reason. And I wasn't changing my stance on beverages just because it was free and from him. "Like I said, I only wanted water."

He gazed at me, not offended at all. As if his gorgeous eyes could see right through my protective spell, I wanted him to look anywhere else, so I rose and said calmly, "We have a deal. I'll meet you here this weekend for the party, and I'll convince your aunt it's real."

"It'll be a night you'll never forget." Soren's steamy gaze sent my heart pounding again.

"The word you're looking for is 'hypnotic.'" I pointed at his unfinished puzzle and headed out without looking back. Naïve human. I'd make him forget.

But I wouldn't.

3

A Favor

Soren

When Indie had walked out of the bar, the air went with her like a vacuum, a black hole from which I might never recover. She was taller than most women, maybe five-eight or nine, and as a solid six feet myself, I appreciated the extra height. Made things easier to reach. Her short blond hair exposed her long delicate neck, and the wisps over those stunning blue eyes were mesmerizing as they shifted in the gentle breeze of her movements. She was simply gorgeous, and her voice was a siren's call to my cock.

"Mr. Rockwell, your tongue is lolling," Cora said with amusement in her tone.

Women pawed at me for attention wherever I went. That was part of being a vampire—pheromones and seduction were part of the hunt—the feed. But I had to make an enticing deal to convince Indiara Niskatar to be my date. Me—Soren Rockwell. Me! I couldn't believe it. Having lost my wingman brother to the fate of nuptials, I was truly embarrassed at how far off my game was. I could've compelled her into submission to save the mortifying chuckle from my employee, but I couldn't stomach rooting around in people's brains for something so frivolous.

And then, with a glance at my game, she'd solved the puzzle that had me stumped. I was impressed. Speechless. But the most puzzling piece of the Indie pie was her heart rate jumping for me. Despite her objections, she wanted me too.

That damn fine woman twisted me up in ways I hadn't ever felt before. I lived with a lot of regrets, but this was one I could prevent. After Allison Kincaid had attempted to murder several of my kin, I wouldn't track her down for anything or anyone, but her newest recruit had flipped sides. I texted my sister-in-law's sister, Lily Barrett. The baby witch was all that stood between me and showing that woman the stamina of a vampire. *I need a favor this weekend.*

Little dots of a reply bounced, and I stared at the screen with impatience. She finally replied, *I'm busy.*

Ever since I'd survived the bloodbath at the Menominee campground, I took advantage of the vacation offered by my brother. Maybe instead of being a bump on a log or a bum on a couch, I should've been more welcoming to my newest family member. Now I needed to convince her I had something worth showing up for. *I'm throwing a party.*

No response, but...I didn't wait very long.

'Open bar?' I texted, trying not to let the desperation bleed through my fingers.

Another stretch of silence followed before the dots returned. *'What kind of favor?'*

That wasn't a 'no'. I smiled to myself in relief. *A friend needs some witchy woo.'*

I could picture Lily rolling her eyes. I added more politely, *'She needs your expertise, please.'*

More silence.

"Do you want me to dump that, boss?" Cora asked, nodding toward the abandoned, sweating mimosa.

I needed a blast of cool liquid, so I lifted the glass and downed it fully before sliding the empty to Cora. "Tastes great."

Cora beamed at the compliment. "So, do you want me to make some banners or something? I don't mind a little overtime if it means I can flex my artistic muscles. You'd need to supply all the materials, of course. Bartender's wages and all."

I glanced at my phone again. Still no response. "Hold that thought."

Cora washed the glass. "Sure thing, boss."

I lifted off the stool and pocketed my phone. Lily showing up was more important than decorations, and I wasn't above bribes.

Indie

I couldn't say the last time I'd been on a date. Now I had to pretend to have a good time with a very attractive human all for the sake of his aging family member. It was sweet, really, and a little pathetic. The closest thing I'd had to a night out lately was when I'd had the close-call at the bar, but that incident had been unplanned and unwanted. I suppose that left me just as pathetic.

Why I'd ruminated about the human when a far more important revelation was at hand surprised me. I slipped behind the wheel.

Allison immediately asked, "You're back. What happened?"

"Your information was correct. I have a lead, and we're meeting this weekend." I started up the car.

"Who's the witch?"

Allison clearly didn't like surprises, and neither did I, so I wished I could tell her. I hadn't even thought of asking. "He'll tell me this weekend."

"He?" Allison asked, genuinely confused.

Soren hadn't been the contact, but Cora didn't seem knowledgeable, and she hadn't offered any information.

Now, I didn't know what I should do. "Soren Rockwell traded a 'fake' date for a meeting with the witch. Am I misunderstanding the trade, or is a 'fake' date actually done?"

Allison snorted and laughed. "Soren negotiated a fake date like some business transaction? What a deplorable ass, needing to bargain for a date, like some scrawny teen lusting after his best friend's mom. I can't blame you for turning him down. Seriously, who does that?"

On the contrary, he wasn't deplorable in the slightest. Images of those thick biceps flashed before my eyes—no, not deplorable at all. But I didn't know Soren, and Allison's reaction had me concerned. "He's throwing a party, and we won't be the only ones attending. If he's as awful as you say, would you run interference for me?"

Allison made a noise somewhat resembling indigestion. "Soren and I aren't exactly friends."

By her description, I'd figured that, and I was curious about what had happened between them. Since I had no intention of accepting a second fake date, no matter the favor involved, and since I wasn't staying in town much longer, the fascinating drama mattered not. "You're declining?"

"I wouldn't be welcome." Whatever had happened between them appeared to have ended poorly, and since Allison had laughed at Soren, I suspected she harbored no feelings for the man any longer. Which...I shouldn't have even cared about. "Go meet Soren at the party. Make contact with the witch, and when you identify her, I'll tell you the next step. Sound good to you?"

I've handled worse. An evening with Soren was...easy, maybe even fun. "Yes."

"Can I ask—do you live in here?" Allison pointed at my boxes in the back seat. Where she sat was half my bed.

"When the occasion calls for it," I said simply. I didn't feel the need to impress anyone with my possessions. When I had to focus on staying hidden, such matters were trivial.

"This is going to take time. You should probably find a comfortable place to stay."

Time. The magical word that once held no weight at all. I wanted to envy those days, but they hadn't been rosy either. At least now I had my freedom, but to keep it, I had to stay on the move. "How long do you think?"

"I can't say for sure, but it depends on whether Soren can pull through for us, so I'm not holding my breath."

I was afraid of that. I needed to find somewhere safe, and a human would be my first choice. The idea of going back inside, picturing Soren at the bar and casting me that enchanting smile of his, sent my pulse ripping through my veins. "I'll wait until the crowd thins." More like until Soren left. "I don't need witnesses."

"That's wise."

I hadn't remained invisible all these years by being reckless, but I declined to state the obvious. I turned the car out of the parking lot, heading toward Allison's house to drop her off before returning for a different human's help. Because there was no way on this earth I would ask to borrow Soren's couch. His intense green eyes had burned into my mind, and a flash of heat tore through me. No way at all.

Soren was dangerous to me.

4

More Help

Soren

The baby witch had taken up residence in the old Barrett house on the bay after her father was killed and her mother had skipped town. Lily Barrett's car was in her driveway, but she was ignoring me. With my enhanced vampire hearing, I discerned two distinct heartbeats, some shuffles, and frustrated mumbles inside. With the distortion, I couldn't recognize either voice, but the one clearly not Lily's was male.

The elf Pierce Evansson had been pursuing my sister-in-law for months, but when he'd finally conceded to my brother, Pierce had set his sights on her sister, Lily. Around that time I had been under a witch's spell, so my priorities were elsewhere, but now Lily was family, and no one deserved what that featherbag wanted from a woman.

Elves, man.

As much as I hated tampering with free will, I accepted it as part of my survival. And a quick sip-and-erase to feed didn't harm my snack in any meaningful way, but elf compulsion was...I wouldn't say evil. Doing what was necessary for the sake of survival could hardly be coined as evil, but there was definitely a scale. Elves were incessant, disease-spreading pests who could slip through the back door and catch their victims when least expected. I wouldn't wish an elf's fate on my own worst enemy. I couldn't imagine that the life of a female elf had been much better. Shit, they were extinct, for God's sake. What the hell did the males do to them?

Whenever I indulged in a live meal, I was doing women a favor, because my bite rendered them useless to elves. See? I could be altruistic and selfless. And I could also rest easier knowing Lily's witchy side, alive and kicking, meant she was immune to the elf's mind control. But humans were fallible. Hopefully, whoever the brave soul was behind that door, he could defend Lily against a determined elf.

Shamelessly, I knocked on her front door again. "I know you're in there. I need to talk to you."

A gentle muffled argument on the other side. Whatever it was, it could wait, but I couldn't. "It's important, Lily."

The door finally opened a few inches with Lily's body blocking my view of the interior. She wore clothing, so I wasn't interrupting anything essential. "Now's not a good time."

I held out a bottle of wine with a friendly smile. "I brought you this."

"Did you *buy* that for me?" she asked, unimpressed.

"Courtesy of Oliver's extensive collection. I don't keep up with his business dealings, but this one is older than me, so I'd wager it was a gift."

Lily frowned.

"Look, he has plenty, and I'm sure he won't miss one bottle."

"You're offering me alcohol?" She hardly glanced at it. How could she be unimpressed? Oliver only liked the finest things, so this had to be worth something.

"Think of it as a payment for future services. I need you to meet my friend at the party, and I'll do anything you ask to make it happen."

Shuffling came from inside, and a male voice cleared his throat. Lily turned back toward her visitor and frowned before returning her attention to me. She was annoyed at either me or her visitor, but since I brought her the oldest bottle of wine my brother owned, it couldn't be me. In which case, I was concerned for Lily. Perhaps her chosen date wasn't up to the task of taking care of my newest family member properly. If that were true, I'd kick his ass.

I lowered my voice. "Are you okay?"

For only a flash, Lily's eyes widened as if confused by my interest in her well-being. "I'm...fine. It's a bad time."

"I need this," I pressed. "Just promise me you'll be there, and I'll owe you a favor."

Lily turned her head again as if asking permission from the mystery man of the hour, and she faced me with less enthusiasm than I'd hoped. "Can I bring a date?"

I was a business owner now, and I had to make sure my place profited. I couldn't explain to my brother I blew a bunch of his money on a business, only to watch it crash and burn because I couldn't hack it. And I looked forward to judging the shit out of the brave soul behind the door. "The more the merrier—within the city's occupancy limits, naturally."

"We'll be there." Lily took the bottle and closed the door in my face.

I sighed with relief. Soon I was going to have Indie eating out of the palm of my hand, begging me to please her in ways humans couldn't.

Indie

Darkness had arrived before I managed to return to Fully Loaded, and the parking lot was packed. I had probably been avoiding Soren because I didn't know what to think about him. I found him appealing in ways that I should ignore, and Allison despised the man. But I was stuck in this small town familiar with the hidden world for however long this process required. I needed a place to stay, and I knew only two humans in these parts. One of them was not an option, and I hoped he wasn't still here.

I pushed through the door, and now I believed Cora when she'd said this was the best place for drinks and dancing. The difference from day to night was as literal as it could get. Laser lights flashed around the place, and I squinted. Humans and their weak vision could ignore the laser lights blinding their retinas. But I didn't envy them. Music thrummed from a side room, and some people gyrated to the rhythm, but most held drinks and chatted in small groups. Young humans squeezed beside each other at the bar. There was laughter and the sloshing of liquid.

I appreciated the protection and speed of my vehicle, but most of the time I missed the simpler years. Before modern technology captured every moment. Before anyone could find anyone else with a few touches of a button. When the décor had been animal skins, woven rugs, and pine boughs—functional and naturally pleasing to the eye. We'd worked harder to survive, yes, but we could also cherish our peaceful time together. We'd engage with one another in titillating subjects—not argue facts and lies in front of a virtual crowd of meaningless voices who drowned your opinions in noise. How an inferior species managed to take over the Earth and relegate us to the shadows truly baffled me.

The winds had certainly changed.

I moved through the crowd. There was glitter. So much glitter I felt like I needed a respirator. Thankfully, any landing on my wings became included in the spell protecting me. I was going to have to vacuum my feathers after this, but pulling up at a car wash to vacuum invisible parts of my body would raise too many eyebrows. My sparkly conundrum only confirmed Allison had been right about my need for a temporary home.

As I made my way toward the bartender, I maintained awareness around me, seeking signs of those who hunted me. Cora spotted me through the throng and smiled—friendly and professional. "Indie, you're back!"

I leaned on the bar so she could hear me over the eardrum-rattling noise. "Can I have a private word with you?"

Cora settled a drink on the bar nearby and moved closer, drying her hands on a towel. "I can't leave the bar unattended, honey. Tell me what you need to say. The drunks won't hear you, and if they do, they won't remember."

She asked for it. "I was wondering if you were single."

Cora's steamy gaze dipped to my chest and back to my face. "Single as sliced cheese and straight as a ten-spot sliding into the cake machine, but for you, honey, I'd make an exception." A drink request interrupted us, and Cora serviced the customer and returned her focus to me. "But I'm sorry, Indie, you and the boss have a thing, fake or not, and my paycheck can't get between that."

I didn't want to be reminded of my upcoming date. "That's not what I meant. I'm looking for a place to live, and I wanted to know if you live alone."

Cora began filling a frosty mug from the tap, friendliness cooling rapidly. "Look, honey, if you're not here to order, you can see yourself out, friend-of-the-owner or not."

I needed more time, and to avoid wasting more, I ordered the same thing I didn't want before. "I'll take a mimosa, then."

"That's more like it." Cora mixed the drink and settled it in front of me.

I needed to convince her to help me without being seen. I looked over my shoulders in an exaggerated, paranoid way, and I leaned closer. "Did you see that guy?"

Cora squinted at every person around me, and I played into her instinct. I rushed around the bar and ducked behind it.

Cora bent down next to me. "Is someone after you?"

This was a risk I had to take. I glanced up to check no one could see us, triple-verified I had my natural glamour fully in place, and I slipped off my malfunctioning ring. Using a convenient ability to suggest a human's subconscious guide her consciousness, I captured Cora's gaze. When her eyes widened in confusion, I knew mine were glowing an inhuman shade of green. "Tell me, Cora, do you live alone?"

Cora's face softened, as if in a trance. "I do."

"You want me to be your roommate. You're going to like it, and you're going to give me privacy." I kept my glowing gaze tightly on my mark. "And you won't remember me behind the bar."

Cora blinked, and I returned my ring to my finger, cutting off my magical abilities. I shuffled back toward the crowd, rose to full height, and waited to see if anyone would question me. But no one paid me more than a passing glance. I returned to my drink and found Cora already handing out another order.

She returned to me with a broad smile, friendliness returning. "Indie, I'm looking for a roommate, and I hear you're in need of a place to crash. I think you should move in with me. I promise to give you all the space you need."

I smiled warmly. "That sounds like a lovely offer."

"I can tell you're a great friend," Cora added. "Your mimosa is on the house. I'm sure Mr. Rockwell won't mind. Besides being close to the owner pretty much makes you a princess around here."

That word had been thrown in my face for years as an excuse, and with it, brought nightmares of what I'd escaped and still ran from. Some days I wished I could compel myself to forget.

But then I'd get caught.

5

Sprinkle of Unease

Soren

I carried a pile of shopping bags to the lengthy dining room table of my brother's B&B, and my niece followed me with curiosity. Retirement bored her entirely, but since Oliver was out of the country, it wasn't my place to open up his residence for business. Besides, he'd promised me full use of this fancy pile of bricks, so I was making the most of it. Nicole should be excited.

"Don't take this as discouragement, but what is all this?" my niece asked.

I glanced at my mountain with pride. "How steady is your painting hand these days?"

Nicole leaned on the doorframe and lifted her gently trembling hand. "As long as you're not asking me to pluck a splinter out of your heart, I'm probably capable. Why?"

She listened eagerly as I told her about my spontaneous purchase of a business. "I'm throwing a celebratory new ownership party, and naturally, you're invited."

Nicole waved her hand as if swatting the idea away. "At my age? The music alone would give me palpitations. I've seen what you can do when you're properly motivated, like when you decorated for your brother's engagement dinner for the promise of a sun ring. And believe me, I understand the gravity of your ring. But this—this goes beyond hanging lights and lanterns. I have to say, I'm impressed." Nicole beamed with pride. I was on the right track toward what she wanted, what she needed, to stop nagging me.

But if she skipped the party, I wouldn't get full credit for my efforts, and I suspected that, no matter my charms, I only had one shot with Indie. "I have someone coming whom I'd like you to meet." I gave her my best cheesy grin.

Nicole glowed with excitement. "I had an inkling. Why didn't you just say so?" My niece approached the table and eyed my spread. "In that case, nothing but the sweet release of death will stop me from getting to this party."

Although in jest, the idea was horrible. I had so little family left these days. "Don't joke about dying."

Nicole dug into the first bag and retrieved a paint set. "There are only two guarantees in life, and I don't look forward to taxes. No one ever knows when Death comes for them, but as each year ticks by, he's getting closer to paying me a visit. Someday I'll welcome his arrival, but not until

I see you happily married. This is the closest you've ever gotten."

"Closest? Nicole, it's a first date." And I had to make a deal to get Indie to show up. If Nicole knew that detail, she wouldn't be so impressed. Obviously, I refrained from offering it.

"So, who's this special lady who caught your picky eye?"

I unloaded brushes from another bag. Not only was I willing to wet her whistle to further enforce her coming, but a part of me liked seeing my niece so damn happy. And…I kind of wanted to talk about my date. My…fake…date. Well, before the night was over, Indie was going to know nothing about our date was fake.

"Her name's Indie, and she's like no one I've ever met before. Tall, blond, smart as a whip. And she doesn't even drink. Isn't that weird? I'd go nuts if I didn't take the edge off occasionally."

Nicole shot me a look of disbelief.

"Daily," I corrected.

Accepting that response, she added, "She sounds lovely, but you met her in the bar?"

"She was looking for a witch." I unrolled the plain white banner across the table.

Nicole's excitement dimmed. "What is she?"

Having never considered it, I frowned. Vampires could sense each other, like an undead version of gaydar. "If she's looking for a witch, then she isn't one, and I didn't get any vampire vibes off her."

"A human then." The amusement returned to Nicole's lips. "So you changed your mind about them?"

After forcing my big brother to kill his first human love, and my almost killing his second, I suppose I'd learned a lesson: the heart wanted what the heart wanted. Daisy had been a human, and she'd saved my life when I didn't deserve it, and for her forgiveness, I loved her like a little sister. But I still didn't believe humans and vampires could mix. My proof—Oliver's love became a vampire, and now they were truly happy and bloodbonded.

I lifted the corners of my lips. "I'm not proposing, Nicole. It's just a date."

My niece made a dismissive noise that I promptly ignored. "Well then, do you want me to take over the planning and preparations?"

There was a lot to do and not much time. As much as I hadn't minded helping with the decorations in exchange for my sun ring, I wasn't the artsy type like my brother. Nicole must've gotten it from his side of the family line.

"I don't know if 'grand re-opening' sounds better. Or maybe something like 'under new ownership' or 'welcome and drink yourself into a happy place' is the best option here," I said, staring at the blank canvas. "If you know what's best, have at it."

Nicole lifted a brush. "I'll take care of the banner. If you need any more help, you know where to reach me."

I thanked my niece for her eagerness, and I headed to my bar with a massive pile of balloons and a rented helium tank. Everything was going to be perfect, even if for one night only.

Indie

In Menominee, across a busy four-lane street from a gas station and a convenience store, Cora unlocked the door to her apartment. Apartment was defining it loosely. Her home was a tiny house in a row of identical tiny houses with varying shades of colorful paint. Each had a pair of windows with shutters and a front door between shrubs. It was so cute and convenient, but from the outside I could tell it was very small.

Cora let me inside. It was messier than I preferred—clothes draped all over, dishes piled on the coffee table in front of the TV, unopened shipping packages on the floor, and closed bottles of nail polish had been tipped over onto the couch. There wasn't room for me.

"So, what do you think, honey? It's not very spacious, but I didn't plan on having a roommate." As if she'd made a blunder, Cora backpedaled almost in panic. "Not that I regret our little arrangement. Living solo can be lonely, and I'm glad you're here." Cora went to the couch and swatted crumbs off the fabric and collected the dishes, stacking them precariously in her arms.

I'd grown up in what modern humans called a castle—stone walls, tapestries, and turrets strung along the perimeter for the inevitable time when a conflict reached our gates. I had spacious quarters and a handmaiden who tidied my room, brought me food, and tended to my dressing. It was luxurious at the time, although I'd taken it for granted. No more so than now.

For Cora's sake, I should've gotten a hotel room, but I avoided them because they drew crowds. Securing a room without a credit card was getting trickier these days, and I didn't want to risk compelling a human where cameras were. And on top of all that risk, not having a human living in the room with me meant I also lost a layer of protection. After being in my cramped car, I yearned for space, but I reminded myself to be grateful for this human's service. I set down my bag on the cleared coffee table. To fix my protective ring, I could manage for a short while. "I promise I won't interfere with your life any more than necessary."

Cora chuckled. "That's a weird thing to say, but okay." She moved into the kitchen and unloaded the dishes into the sink. Then she turned and collected papers strewn on the dining room table. "I'll have space for you soon."

I wanted to help, but touching her things and moving them just felt wrong. Standing here and watching was awkward. "I'm going to head out. I'll be back later when you're ready for me."

"Oh, nonsense. My place is so small. This will take only a few more minutes. A good host would give you my bed, but I'm not that nice, so you can have the couch. The bathroom's that way. Look around and make yourself comfortable."

To ease the guilt, I headed into the hallway. As I'd expected, this place was very small—arm's reach from one room's door to the next. The left door was her bedroom. I strolled inside to gain some insight into my protection. I glanced at photographs, abstract art, knickknacks with meaning I couldn't begin to guess. A filled vase caught my eye. My limbs stiffened with each step as I approached the bouquet on her dresser, and I frowned.

The glass didn't have water, as the pale lilac flowers on lifeless spikes had been dried for long-term display. Or later use.

"Cora?" I called, unease in my voice.

My roommate approached, arms full of dirty laundry. "What's up?"

"Where did you get these?" I pointed at the vampire allergen—vervain. It was off-putting, almost threatening, as if a human had displayed a loaded gun for their guests to fear and respect. Cora didn't seem like the type. Was my temporary roommate afraid of my enemy? Or was she something more?

"They were given to me. Kind of dark and creepy, huh? Why?"

The tremble subsided. Despite the fatal dose of vervain right in front of me, she was innocent. Still firmly in the 'if you're into that kind of thing' disbeliever's camp. Whoever gifted it was either just as naïve or someone who knew exactly what it was.

"No reason." I smiled reassuringly. "They're beautifully creepy."

Cora smiled and returned to her work.

I returned to the living room, where Cora had pleasantly finished picking up. She turned on the faucet and pumped squirts of soap into the stream.

I couldn't get to that witch friend of Soren's fast enough, but until then, I'd had to face a crowd. I needed to blend in. "You're going to the party at Fully Loaded, aren't you?"

"I'm an employee, so of course, but I wouldn't miss a Rockwell party for anything."

I hated to learn what that meant, so I skipped asking. "I need pointers with regard to the dress code. Is it formal or cocktail?"

Cora laughed. "Dress code? At a bar? Honey, all you need is sexy, and since you'll be in the arms of Soren Rockwell, you better be hot."

So my reaction to him had been…normal. It was such a relief I allowed myself to reminisce about Soren's gaze and crooked smile. I wanted his hands on me. I wanted to kiss him, and I wanted to run my fingers along every inch of that human's body. My heart fluttered with possibility, but if I surrendered to the surging lust, I'd break him in half.

That would ruin the date.

6

Party in the USA

Soren

Humans and their dull senses. They loved this stuff, and sure, the open bar helped. But I considered this a marketing investment. Humans in glittery skimpy clothing packed Fully Loaded. Music thrummed my eardrums, but long ago I'd learned to shift my focus from the onslaught. Streamers twisted and hung along the walls, balloons dangled like enormous raindrops from the ceiling, and laser lights flicked around the room and reflected off the disco ball in the center. Not bad for short notice. Nicole did well, and so did my staff. The news crew had been here earlier in the week to run the story, and that was likely the reason for the unexpected turnout.

In the corner, safely near the bar, Nicole smiled blankly, rocking completely off rhythm, earplugs in her ears. Her eyes shimmered in the laser lights, as if the experience of young people partying was too much for her old senses to handle.

But she sipped a drink, enduring the pain for a chance to see a woman on my arm. I couldn't disappoint her now, but Indie hadn't arrived yet.

I shifted my stance and nervously adjusted the tie I'd borrowed from Oliver's vast closet. Normally, I was a T-shirt and jeans kind of guy, but as the new owner of a widely respected and successful establishment—with a prospective date—I'd felt a suit would be appropriate to display the right message. I'd mirrored everything my brother was, but I wasn't like him in the slightest. Where he fit the clothing, I was a wolf, a predator, in the sheep's clothing of an attractive, harmless human. But the suit was too short on me, as if screaming I was a fraud. I hadn't the faintest idea about running a business. My brother had always run things from behind the scenes, and yet here I was thrusting myself into the public, increasing my risk of exposure exponentially. I had enemies. I shouldn't drag Indiara Niskatar into my treacherous world. The gorgeous human deserved better than me, but since she wasn't here yet, maybe she'd figured that out.

I knew she was smart.

A brunette woman appeared out of nowhere, and she offered me her spare glass. "Hey there, handsome. Want a drink?"

The last time I'd been to a bar with a young crowd squeezed in like sardines, I'd been elbow-deep in women. And when I'd needed my brother to go to bat for me, he killed the mood with his brooding. Oliver was always a shit wingman. The murders that night hadn't helped any. Now these humans treated me like royalty—no wingman required—and I used every ounce of restraint not to laugh. No wonder Oliver had always worn a suit. If I wanted, I could have my elbows or fangs fully inserted in women once again, but right now, I'd take a bat to keep them off me.

"I can't believe I'm saying this, but no, thank you," I said while skimming the crowd.

Still no Indie.

"I get it's an open bar, but I wanted to dance. Join me?" the brunette asked with a sultry tone and a flirty gaze aimed right at my cock.

I'd moved my sun ring to my left ring finger, but it had no effect on any women approaching me tonight. Only Indie had accepted the boundary. Maybe I should switch back into my jeans and T-shirt. Or maybe I should try brooding. That kept the women away.

Maybe I should flash my fangs. That would definitely work and be oh so satisfying. When I was in a cruddy mood, I'd skip the sneakiness of the ambush and the effort of the happy meal and go straight for terror. My wolf, my baser, animalistic side concealed in innocence, loved a good game once in a while, and this insistent human was testing my patience, but she was slightly tipsy and only reacting to my predatory nature. Humans were so oblivious to the dangers around them. How they managed to control the world while I skulked in the shadows was...baffling.

"Not a dancer, huh? Can I offer you something else instead?" the brunette asked, trying hard to send me a very obvious message.

I'd already turned her down. Now, I ignored her. I skimmed the crowd, looking for the leggy blond with stunning blue eyes. The longer I waited, the more I started to believe Indie was a figment of my imagination. A dream.

"You seem distracted," the brunette said and pawned her spare drink on a confused passerby. This woman clearly wasn't used to being turned down. Eventually she'd get the hint that being a pest wouldn't work. "I can fix that. I can fix just about anything."

She squeezed my cock. I lifted my eyebrows at the sudden and unwanted sensation. That was enough. I removed her offending hand with a tight grip on her wrist. I gazed into the brunette's vacuous eyes as she bit her lip in steamy anticipation. For too long I'd considered the fang flash. Instead, I calmed my wolf and conjured up my ability to tap into her conscious thoughts, like a mechanic shifting her gears. This wasn't a quick and necessary snack for survival, but if I didn't wrench around with her free will, I was going to make a full meal out of her. And my wolf was always hungry. Giving her a stern and controlled face, I said, "You are not interested in me. Leave me be and don't touch people without permission."

The flirty nibble of her lip fell away. After a couple of blinks, the brunette dipped away, following a trail of confusion. I should've eaten her just on principle. While scowling at the brunette, my bartender caught my eye. She'd just come through the front door, and she smiled at me.

I moved through the crowd toward her, and I leaned into Cora's ear. "You remember the woman I chatted with the other day? The blond who asked for a witch?"

"I love what you've done to the place, Cora. How is your back, Cora? You look great, Cora," she said, pointing out my rudeness.

Technically, I had all the time in the world to find Indie, so I could spare my employee some kindness. "You look fabulous."

Cora preened, satisfied. "Of course, I remember Indie."

At least she hadn't been scooped out of my imagination and dangled as a tease. "Have you seen her? Is she here?"

Cora turned and stretched to search for her, but my employee was shorter than most here. "My roommate was just behind me. She's around here somewhere, but since I'm off the clock and it's an open bar, excuse me, boss. I have some drinking to do."

Indie and Cora were roommates? Since when and why?

Cora smiled at the dumbfounded look on my face and patted me on the shoulder. "You look fabulous yourself."

The crowd quickly swallowed her, and I scanned the sea of faces again, trying to find the leggy blond. While moving through the crowd, I spotted Lily. After all my begging and the bribe, dragging my sister-in-law's sister out here might have been for nothing. If not for the open bar, I might've felt guilty. I headed toward her when the moving laser lights blinded me. I squeezed my eyes shut and rubbed them, and while looking for Lily, I squinted. For a split second, Indie was framed by the door, glancing around shyly as if searching for someone.

Hopefully, looking for me.

Bodies shifted in front of her, and Indie moved, disappearing into the undulating crowd. I combed the guests. Most of the partygoers were human, but I think an off-duty Kevin was roaming around. The vampire paramedic surprised his best friend and partner by never disclosing his fanged status. I got a chuckle out of it. Surely no one, especially not Kevin, would take their fangs to my date under my own roof.

I moved efficiently through the crowd, not quite at the speed of a vampire, since I didn't want to tip anyone off to the danger in front of them, but quicker than an ordinary human would. I was on the hunt, not for a meal, but for a dance. At the bar, I found Indie seated, trying politely to brush off a man's advances. A surge of unusual possessiveness overcame me, and I rushed to his side and pressed a hand on his shoulder in warning.

The human looked up at me in anger, assessed my suit, and relaxed a bit. Maybe there was something to these sheep clothes. They almost controlled human responses, and far more cleanly than my fangs. He said, "You're Rockwell, right?"

"I am." I squeezed.

Unlike the brunette, this man understood the clear message. He lifted a drink in cheers and said, "I'll see myself out. Nice party."

I released my grip, and the human skedaddled into the crowd.

Indie smiled at me with amusement, and I took that as an invitation. I lowered myself onto the vacated stool. My date wore a sparkly top cinched at the waist and hip-hugging jeans. Her short blond hair was curled around her face. I wanted to glide my hands through her locks and down her body. And since she was here, that was a possibility instead of a dream.

Indie

While wearing my slowly malfunctioning and nearly drained emerald, I couldn't see elves. Vampires were invisible regardless, but they tended to have a confidence and posture that made them stand out to anyone who knew what to look for. Since I would absolutely not remove my ring again, even to compel myself a temporary home, I had to be sure I was safe here. I'd made a perimeter sweep, using my plain eyes to seek danger instead of my supernatural senses. They weren't as reliable, but that was the sacrifice I had to make, and why I'd rather avoid crowds entirely.

But this was far too important for me to run...yet.

I found nothing to cause me concern, only nausea at the overwhelming sensory input, so I headed for the bar to close myself off from invitations and to wait for my date. Not only did the enticing human twist me up inside, but I had to pretend to want him. 'Pretend' was the problem. To me, there was nothing pretend about this date, but for self-preservation, I had to give him those acting skills I'd honed while protecting myself from his charms—his very convincing charms. I wasn't here to play. I was here to save my life.

A drunken patron dropped beside me, and I grimaced. His efforts to pick me up were slurred with drink, and he reeked of stinging booze. To warn him off would take an easy squeeze of his overzealous hand, but to use that strength required my removing the only protection I had. So this was a chance to practice those acting skills, except I didn't get that far. Soren appeared, as if hearing my thoughts of discomfort, and shooed the man away. It was sweet, but there was nothing this human could do to keep me safe.

Soren lowered himself onto the empty stool, so close I could feel his presence. I'd thought he'd looked ravishing in jeans and a T-shirt with his messy hair, but in a suit with his hair tamed but for a little wavy tendril on his forehead that I yearned to touch...I exhaled slowly as heat spread through my body. My hands trembled.

"Are you okay?" Soren asked as if I were some fragile flower upset over the man's advances.

The only thing that upset me was Soren's pretend. "I can handle myself."

"Well, I need to be sure my date is comfortable and safe in my establishment. Pardon my intrusion."

The word safe sent a flush of heat through my chest. It was all I ever wanted, and Soren tossed it out there as if it were no effort at all. He had no idea. My stomach was in knots, and I couldn't do this. I couldn't get through this night without some relief. I flagged down the bartender on duty and ordered a mimosa.

"Not that I care—or I wouldn't be offering an open bar—but are you going to drink it?" Soren asked, confused.

The orange drink slid in front of me. One drink was enough to course through my body and give me the buzz of relaxation I needed. I did trust Soren to block unwanted advances, so I didn't have to. So I didn't risk a judgment call that threatened to expose me. I gazed at Soren as if challenging him, and I drank it down in large swallows until it was gone. The alcohol warmed my veins.

It actually tasted pretty great.

While I was still plenty capable of using skills of concentration, I touched Soren on the wrist—a simple gesture that commanded an order. "Let's do this."

Rather than sense my urgency and immediately acquiesce, Soren casually flagged down the bartender and ordered. He turned to me. "The night is young, Indie. What's the rush? You know what they say about 'all work and no play'."

He was delaying me, painfully dragging this out. If I could explain to Soren what drove me, he'd be helping instead of inhibiting. The urgency of finding the witch gnawed at me, but once my business was settled, I could enjoy myself a little more...if Soren was willing. Of course, I'd still have to be careful. Humans were delicate things. I tried to explain without worrying him. "Homework always gets done before playtime."

Soren's beautiful green eyes glittered with excitement. "Well, I'm not a parent or a teacher. I'm the boss, and the boss says screw the homework." His gaze rested on my lips. My heart pounded, and my restraint softened.

That was the mimosa whispering in my ear, showing me such wonderful things could happen with only a single touch. In my fear of harming a human and drawing attention to myself, I'd refrained from imbibing for so long I was what humans called 'a lightweight'. I was running out of time to uphold my end of the bargain.

I touched the soft, exquisite lapel of his fine but slightly ill-fitting suit, wanting to tug him close and capture those lips of his. For long, painful beats of my pounding heart, I considered showing his human what a supernatural being could do to his body, but I stopped myself and dragged the finger down. "Even the best bosses need wise guidance."

Soren beamed at the unintended compliment. "You think I'm the best?"

I wanted to know what he could do to me in turn. I wanted to know if he would be my best. Now I trembled for a different reason. "That remains to be seen."

Soren leaned close to my ear to be heard over the loud human music. His breath tickled, and the warmth of the drink pooled low and brought out a different kind of pounding—more like...a throbbing. "Does this mean you're sticking around to find out?"

Stay...the most terrifying concept and not possible. Unless...I glanced at the ring on my finger. If I could find what I needed, there was a possibility I could enjoy the human a little more than these painfully inadequate minutes. The urgency returned, but not so I could flee—so I could enjoy a little Soren. If he weren't completely faking this red-carpet unrolling invitation of what I wanted to beg for. Oh, that mimosa.

I needed to think clearly, so I lifted off the stool to show him this order wasn't negotiable. "When I'm finished with your witch, I'll have a little time."

Soren rose and stood inches from me. Was it the dull human sense or did he want what I'd been silently begging for? I wanted his hands on me. I wanted those lips all over my body. He leaned into my ear once more, and I shivered at the tickle. "One dance."

If his hands were on me, they weren't coming off until I was satisfied. "After," I insisted.

A flicker of disappointment crossed his beautiful face, but my offer registered slowly, and his mouth curled in anticipation. "Is that a promise?"

Such a simple word held such strong connotations. There were no guarantees in life. I'd learned that lesson as a young woman when I'd been betrayed by those who loved me most. But Soren, a beautiful human who only wanted to please his old aunt, wasn't threatening my dreams. He asked only for a dance. What came after was entirely up to me, and my resolve, my focus, was fading fast. Trying to claw back my clarity, I opened my heart to show him the smallest piece of my real life. Perhaps this would finally register my urgency. "I've spent a long time moving around, being invisible as much as possible and when forced to interact with others, pretending to be someone I'm not. I'm comfortable acting, and I'll give you a fair performance, but we must do this now."

The relaxed flirtatiousness drained away, and Soren immediately returned to the possessiveness I found admirable if misguided. "Who frightens you so?"

My world had to remain hidden—the only rule of my father's I obeyed. "It doesn't matter."

Soren leaned into my ear once more. I wanted his arms around me. I wanted him to tell me everything was going to be okay and that I'd be safe forever. His breath tickled my ear as he said, "As long as you stay by my side, no one will hurt you."

I gazed at his serious features. If only he knew what that simple statement meant to me, but he wasn't capable. "I appreciate the offer."

"She's right this way." Soren took my hand and guided me through the tight crowd toward the end of the bar near the back room. I suspected the elderly woman, with her head tilted against the wall and open mouth, was his aunt. I smiled as I picked out her gentle snoring. Human senses were dull to begin with. I couldn't imagine having the ability to sleep through this chaotic noise.

Soren shook her shoulder gently, and the old woman startled and glanced around, confused. Her tired eyes landed on her nephew, but when she spotted me at his side, she brightened immediately and rose with a wince. The old woman removed ear plugs and held out her hand. "You must be Soren's date, Indie."

All I had to do was convince the woman I was here to spend time with Soren because I wanted to. Such a thing had never been easier. Acting was not required. I shook her hand gently. "I am."

"I'm Nicole Rockwell, Soren's niece. It's a pleasure to meet you."

The confused old woman called herself his niece. I pitied the end of human life. What started out clueless and weak grew into strength and wisdom, but without exception, humans always reverted. "Pleasure's all mine."

"There's a decent man beneath the rough exterior, even if he doesn't believe it." Nicole picked a hair off the shoulder of his suit, preening him like a mother.

She was still confused. Soren's exterior wasn't rough at all. He was very enticing, but Nicole's description of what lay beneath had me curious. She believed he was a good man at heart, and I was certain he was, in fact, good. Why would Soren not believe the same? What had he done?

There were deeper layers to this human that I had yet to uncover—not that I needed any more reason for him to intrigue me.

"Nicole," Soren said sweetly but with a hint of warning.

Nicole's attention never left me. Youthful excitement permeated her. "And he's a great dancer."

Not one to waste an opportunity, and not needing to act at all, I wrapped my arm around his middle. Soren pulled me closer with an arm around my shoulders. Sparks of heat tore through me as my body touched his. My heart fluttered, and I captured Soren's gaze. With a flirty smile, I said, "I intend to find out just how great he is."

Soren's mesmerizing green eyes held my gaze. I'd told him exactly what I meant. As soon as our business was concluded, I would dance to the wild music, so our bodies could gyrate together as one. I wanted to feel his touch and press against him again.

"When I was young, there was this club," Nicole started, but Soren and I only gazed at each other. "Many disco biscuits were consumed, but, through my Swiss cheese memory of that decade, I remember Soren taking the dance floor and capturing the adoration of every woman in the building."

"That's enough, Nicole," Soren said gruffly and cleared his throat. "We've got things to do."

We certainly did. I looked at his aunt and said, "If you don't mind, I'd like to test how well he can move his body. It was nice to meet you, Ms. Rockwell."

"Call me Nicole," his aunt winked, and I couldn't help the comfort in having his aunt's approval. She rooted for us.

Soren took my hand and moved us away. His posture wasn't steamy or possessive. He whispered politely in my ear, "That was good work. I'm convinced."

There was the punch I'd been dreading. My chest squeezed at the rejection—the confirmation this had all been truly fake. I shouldn't have let him affect me so. I shouldn't have told him anything real about myself. He didn't deserve it. His aunt would be heartbroken, but that was Soren's fault. One night was all I spared him, and he chose to end it this way. My half of the deal was complete, and now I could get what I'd come for and get the hell out of here. "Where's the witch?"

A thought flickered across his face, and he cooled off even more. "Okay, fine. I'll get her. Just stay here."

The crowd swallowed Soren, and a chill settled over me. This pain wasn't my fault. Had I been in control of my faculties, I would've accomplished my mission without trouble. The damn mimosa did this to me. Made me vulnerable and then crushed me. I was never going to drink again.

7

Secrets Concealed

Indie

Life was a series of forked decisions, each one steering a person down a path, like the branches of a tree from the broad trunk toward the new growth buds. A path that couldn't be undone. Sometimes those decisions were arbitrary, like which breakfast sandwich from the gas station sounded the most appetizing today. I typically chose bacon, but opting for ham wouldn't leave me with regrets and haunted thoughts.

And I could remake that decision the next day.

The turbulence in my life was a result of my own choices. I was hurtling toward an unseen bud, from which I couldn't reverse course. When I reached the end, would I bloom or would I wither and wilt, lost to the cold of winter? The path ahead remained obscured. Past decisions that brought me to this particular branch were far easier to see. In my copious free time agonizing over puzzle books in my car and turning on the engine to warm myself, or in situations where I believed I'd made an incorrect, unchangeable, choice, I couldn't help but wonder how different my circumstances could've been.

Had I obeyed my father all those years ago, I imagined I'd be standing behind my mate, Evan Logonson, young prince of the enemy elf clan. I suspected we'd have several offspring to be groomed for different purposes in life, none of which I'd have a say in. And while my mate made decisions for the clan, I would be relegated to my mother's role—to be seen and not heard. My mother had refused too late. I'd refused and escaped.

Now, I stood in a packed nightclub with glitter sticking to my wings while I desperately awaited a mystery witch to protect me. And instead of being subjugated by my family, I'd been rejected by a handsome human. I'd made the right choice. Days of pain were far more tolerable than decades—centuries.

Soren Rockwell had everything I didn't—a means of supporting himself, respect among other humans, and a loving family. He could forge relationships without concern for his safety. His aunt was sweet. Just how I imagined a mother would dote upon her son, embarrassing him. Soren had the most valuable intangible thing in the world—freedom. Something I could never have.

I'd wanted a night of fun with a sexy human. Instead, sadness tugged at my heart. I envied Soren.

A tap on my shoulder pulled me back to the thrumming club. Soren had returned with a woman at his side. She was slightly shorter than I, with dark brown curly hair and deep blue eyes. She was beautiful and attractive, so I already questioned Soren's choice in this witch, but she was also...young, and I doubted her as well.

"Lily, this is Indie. Indie, my witch as promised."

We shook hands briefly. I couldn't speak about the hidden world in plain view of the public, no matter the level of sobriety. "Can we speak somewhere privately?"

Soren gestured with his head and took my hand, leaving the witch to navigate unassisted. I refused to read anything into that. He brought us to the far corner of the bar and opened a nondescript door matching the wall color. I followed him inside with the witch behind me. Soren flicked on the lights in a stifling storeroom filled with boxes. Immediately I sought a back door, an exit, but it was farther away than returning in the direction we'd come.

Away from the overwhelming noise, headache-inducing scent of sweaty humans, and painfully blinding lights, I sighed at the reprieve. Human senses were so murky they enjoyed such sensory overload. To me, I wanted to claw my own eyes out and deafen myself with a screwdriver. For another flash, I envied Soren...and briefly the witch as well. This was one of the few times ignorance was truly bliss.

While I tried not to trip on boxes and Soren closed the door behind us, the witch said, "It's weird to see Soren made a friend."

Of all the thoughts running through this witch's mind, likely about her purpose and my need, she'd chosen to jab at Soren's character, and I had been right to question her age. I didn't believe she had the maturity to accomplish the weighty task before her.

"Lily, where's your date?" Soren asked. Intrigued about whether he was changing the subject or about to jab back, I listened and paid attention to their special relationship. "I gotta meet the guy willing to stand between you and Pierce. He must have the biggest *cojones* north of the rust belt. You did tell him about...things, right?"

When someone looked forward to their date, a warmth filled their face at the thought of that special someone. My reaction had been so strong, I needed to physically hide from Soren until the time had come. Lily's features were cold, perhaps a pinch afraid. At a minimum, she wasn't interested in her date, whoever he was. If I didn't like my date, I wouldn't stay.

To save precious time and to ease the awkwardness, I redirected the conversation to where it needed to be. "Lily, I must apologize for my abrupt request to see you."

Shifting her gaze away from the awkward conversation, Lily warmed. "It's no problem. I'm happy to help, but Soren was lacking in the details. What favor did you need?"

"Assistance with a protection spell."

Soren stiffened. He'd claimed he could keep me safe as long as I was by his side, but this human had no idea what lurked in the shadows. He couldn't save me from anything but a thirsty vampire...by being bait, and right now, the fanged ones weren't my main concern.

"You should know the spell is...vintage...by today's standards," I added. I had to be careful in how I explained the gravity of the situation. The less these people knew about me, the safer all of us were. And by nature of the hidden world, I only gave the necessary information. Nothing was volunteered.

Lily frowned. "That's code for 'extremely difficult'. Are you a witch? Is that why you're asking for help—you need a second pair of hands to pull off the spell?"

Soren opened the back room door and gazed out with concern on his brow. I hoped that meant someone's sober status was interfering with his wiser judgment.

But I focused on the witch, my only hope. Her less than enthusiastic response had desperation igniting anxiety, desperation, and soon...begging. "I do need a second set of hands, and I can pay you handsomely."

Lily's eyes widened briefly, her cheeks paled, and she blinked a few times, as if daydreaming about what the dollar signs could do for her. I shifted my weight uneasily. I hated when witches gazed intently at me, regardless of the state of my ring's magic. After what felt like an eternal pause, she said, "I'll do it for a favor."

"Anything." And I meant it.

"What's going on in here?" A strange male voice asked from behind us. Lily and I turned.

Filling the doorway—the exit—stood a bulky, blond-haired, green-eyed man. He was easy on the eyes...for a human, but I didn't react to him the same way I had with Soren, which was a relief. Something—physiological or magical—hadn't gone terribly wrong in my head, but my anxiety over the dwindling magic in my gaudy emerald spiked. I wanted to press my urgency, but this blond man was delaying my critical meeting. At least Soren was blocking this man's entry into our small room. Perhaps he'd remove the interrupter.

"Pierce," Soren said with a dark tone. "What are you doing here?"

"It's an open bar, and that's my date." This Pierce fellow had a lighter, playful tone. He easily brushed aside the handsome bar owner and strolled up to Lily. He wrapped his thick arm around her shoulders possessively.

That chilly, almost afraid, countenance returned to Lily. I hadn't been imagining it. She didn't like this man at all, and by the sound of things, Soren didn't either. These people had developed their own hierarchy, like a flock of chickens.

Soren immediately closed the distance to the witch, fully capturing the attention of the blond man. "Lily? You brought..." Soren hesitated, complete disgust twisting his fine features. "...*him* as your date? What the hell...? Why? God, why *him*?"

The history here sounded fascinating, but it wasn't my business.

"I did," Lily said in a clipped tone, and she turned to me. "Indie, give me your number, and I'll contact you."

I couldn't believe I was being dismissed from my own meeting because of this blond brute. I glanced at Soren, still in disbelief, and he nodded. Disappointed, I swapped digits with the witch. These three had a history, and apparently their poultry drama was more important. Perhaps I hadn't properly conveyed the importance of my precarious situation. That was on me. And I needed privacy with the witch, so I removed myself from the claustrophobic space. I had a name and a phone number. Next time, we'd meet on my terms, where I'd be comfortable.

With awkward gazes watching me leave, I headed back into the bar proper, and I looked around for the only familiar face I knew—Nicole Rockwell. I'd like to hear more stories of Soren's escapades and then finish where we'd left off. I needed that dance, and I wanted the unspoken promises of what came after. The interrupting brute would not ruin my whole night.

Sensory overload assaulted me, but I focused on individual voices to drown it out while I scanned the bar for the sleeping elderly woman. Instead of chatter and laughter, instead of pleasant—if baffling—snores, I caught an unmistakable and alarming series of sounds. A dry gasp, a dull *thump*, and a grunt in pain. Then a thud of someone dropping to the floor. Someone had been stabbed quietly. I shouldn't involve myself in their quarrel, but I needed Lily, and I wasn't sure what I would do if she were harmed. Squaring my shoulders, I wove my way back toward the back storage room.

Pierce marched by, brow set firmly, with Lily at his side. I couldn't tell if he was dragging her, but she wasn't putting up a fuss for the public's assistance. If these two were fine, that meant...

I rushed into the claustrophobic back room and stopped short. Soren was kneeling and hunched forward. Something protruded from his back, and he was attempting and failing to remove it himself. Quiet curse words rolled off his tongue. Instinct ordered me to free the object, toss aside my magic-blocking protection, and heal him. I'd honed the ability to ignore that shrieking voice. Instead, I said what any other human would say. "I'll call you an ambulance."

Soren chuckled and grunted in pain. "Please don't."

Remembering what country I was in and its healthcare system, I hesitated. "I can drive you instead, but you can't get blood in my car." I didn't need my primary residence to be a vampire target.

"Just...pull it out, please. I'll be...fine." Sharp gasps punctuated his words.

He was in immeasurable pain, likely suffering from a collapsed lung, and the urge to heal him was overwhelming. I couldn't bear Soren to suffer when I could make it all go away with the wave of my hands. I could make him forget about the stabbing, the pain, and—my ability to heal. "You don't look fine, and removing an embedded object will cause you to bleed out without immediate medical assistance." I kneeled at his injury. He hadn't bled externally, but internally was likely a different picture. The weapon's handle—the knife's handle—was homemade. Carved. *Whittled*. The weapon wasn't a knife at all.

Abruptly, I rose and backed up. My mouth opened. How had I not guessed this? A human would've been unconscious or screaming for help, begging for an ambulance and not once concerned over the cost. The mix-up with Nicole's position in his family—aunt versus niece—was a dead giveaway, and I suspected she'd told the truth.

But how was it possible? He'd never made a move to drink from me, and he never tried to compel me. I'd first met him during the daytime. Soren could bend the known rules. What else was he capable of?

The old me would already be out that door, in my car, and heading down the road to find a new witch in an entirely new city. But the gaudy, flickering emerald on my finger reminded me I didn't have time to start over. I couldn't heal him, and I couldn't compel him to forget me or anything that had happened.

Soren craned his neck. "Indie, please pull it out. I swear I'll be fine afterward. It's not what it looks like."

What he said was true, but an ordinary human wouldn't have figured out his identity, and a human would follow requests that sounded reasonable. I had to play along. "It's not? From here, it looks like that Pierce guy tried to kill you, and now you need a hospital. I'm going to call the cops. They'll send the ambulance and catch that man." I feigned a gesture toward my phone.

"Don't, Indie, just pull it out. You have to trust me on this." Soren struggled, partially incapacitated, and he grunted in pain with each of his own attempts.

I'd warned him enough about his critical condition—had he actually been a human. Now I could reasonably follow through. "Hold still." I firmly gripped the stake and ripped it from his back. I tossed the bloody weapon onto the floor with a clatter.

Soren groaned in relief, and that sound...so deep, throaty, and full of husky pleasure...was distracting. After a few moments of supernatural healing, he sucked in a breath and slowly climbed to his feet. He stood in front of me, so close his scent filled my nose and sent my heart pumping wildly. Instead of ignoring my reaction to him, now I hated it—not just because I knew he could hear it. But if my magic malfunctioned in his presence...

I had to get out of here—without arousing suspicion.

"Thank you," Soren said, bright green eyes gazing back at me. After such an extreme injury, he had to be hungry. If he lost control or simply decided I'd make a convenient meal...

I *really* had to get out of here.

"I think you're in shock. That's why you can't feel it. You should lie down, and I think I should call an ambulance. I don't want to take responsibility if something were to go wrong." I motioned once again for my cell phone and started to head for the exit.

Soren captured my hand with an iron grip, and I was startled. The lustful gaze he used to give me was gone. I suspected he'd be furious with his attacker. On the contrary, Soren seemed...in high spirits. "For a paramedic, Pierce sucks at anatomy. At this point, I don't think he's capable of a proper staking."

I blinked, completely dumbfounded. "The man who stabbed you is a healthcare worker?"

Soren chuckled. "The irony, right?"

A human would never have gotten the upper hand against a vampire's speed and strength—not without the element of surprise, like a sniper. A witch would've chosen magic—and distance. Another vampire could use a stake, but it wasn't common. Vampire blood wasn't as nutritious, but they didn't waste meals. That healthcare worker had the proper tool on hand, the mandatory strength, and the ability to do the job with no need for surprise. That left one reasonable option.

I trembled. Soren's grip was so tight I couldn't budge him while my magic was smothered. My heart adjusted its rhythm in response to this terrifying revelation, which I knew he could hear. My voice rose with each horrifying thought. "We should call...really. We need to call...the police. He stabbed you. He can't get away with...assault and battery? Attempted murder? What if he comes back? What if he hurts Lily? Why...are you still holding me?"

"Indie, look at me." With his free hand, Soren tipped my chin up. He gazed into my eyes, but this time, his eyes glowed red. "I hate to do this to you, but you're not going to remember anything about my injury."

I'd never been compelled by a vampire before—I'd never gotten this close to a vampire before—so I wasn't entirely sure what to do. Since my blood would instantly give away what I was, I was relieved he'd chosen compulsion over feeding and healing himself, and even more relieved that he absolutely didn't know what I was.

Vampires didn't age after they turned. Despite Soren's handsome twenty-something face, he could be much older than me, and therefore much stronger. Calming myself and pretending I didn't see anything, I said repeated softly, "I won't remember."

Soren released me, his eyes returning to the previous stunning green. "It's for your own good."

There were far more dangers lurking in this small town than I'd realized. The vampire, the witch, and...Pierce had a complex history. Staying was beyond dangerous—stupid, even. Could I risk staying for Lily and Allison's help? Or should I get out while I still could?

I turned and forced myself to walk at a normal pace away from Soren, as I assumed someone who'd forgotten the danger would. It was the hardest acting I'd ever done.

"Indie, where are you going?" Soren called after me.

I hadn't decided.

8

Not Lost

I PUSHED THROUGH THE B&B's door and headed straight for the bar. Gritting my teeth against the healing pain, I shrugged off the suit jacket and tossed it onto a stool. I removed my not-so-white shirt and poked a group of fingers through the destroyed material. Oliver was going to be pissed. But that was his fault for blowing so much cash on clothing. At least I was still alive for him to be pissed at—the silver lining. I tossed the damaged shirt over the coat and moved around the bar. I poured myself a much-needed healing drink—bagged blood with the bitter flavor concealed with wine. Not my favorite, but it felt appropriate.

My niece appeared from another room and limped over. Nicole hadn't slept well these last few years, and I wasn't sure how much of that was worry or standard old age—something I would never experience. Although I never envied the gradual decline of the human condition, having a time limit seemed to add a meaning to life I didn't have. My purchase of the bar was to please my niece. It was a pleasant distraction with easy drinks—both fresh from the tap of the keg and the vein. Sometimes both at once. But it didn't drive me to care about life. It didn't fulfill me in any meaningful way. To me, it was simply convenience.

"I thought I heard some commotion. It's not even midnight. What are you doing at home so early?" Nicole joined me at the bar, lowering herself onto the stool next to the damaged clothing. She sighed heavily, as if removing the weight from her hip afforded her relief. I wished I could heal that for her.

"Date's over." I'd tried to get into the mood to party after healing enough to be passably alive, but the hunger was a bit much, and after the fourth question about my bloodied borrowed suit with the gaping hole in the back, I ended the party early.

"And here I thought your coming home early meant you were finally acting your age."

I mock laughed.

"Indie didn't work out?" Nicole asked with a tinge of the usual disappointment.

Damn. I thought the bar purchase would've given me a reprieve for at least a few more days. In answer, I asked, "Want a drink?"

Nicole gestured in the negative. "I'm too old for a buzz at this hour."

I grinned, unable to let that one go. "Then what does that make me?"

"Well-preserved."

I chuckled and lifted my glass in cheers before downing it fully. The hunger drew me to satiate the need to heal. The subpar mix wasn't enough to fully regain my strength. No wonder my brother was always so weak, comparatively. He actually lived off this repulsive stuff. I ducked under the bar and made another blood-wine mix, cursing the taste. While weakened from injury, hunting humans sucked, but I'll admit I was just being lazy tonight.

"You're awfully thirsty. Should I be concerned?"

I gestured at the clothing. "The elf got me."

Ever since the attempted vampire barbecue, I'd carried a folding, discreet blade to give the elf a taste of his own medicine when the situation called for it. Otherwise, I'd take the high road. I might be a feral wolf among sheep, trying to blend in with my brother's restrictive and stupidly expensive clothing—I mean seriously. I lost so many articles of clothing in day-to-day life, I couldn't fathom why Oliver spent so much just to have them tossed out. He was probably hiding behind deeper issues. Anyway, that damn featherbag was a fox—a big, lumbering hulk of a fox—with a broken moral compass. If an enemy wanted vengeance, which...he might be owed...then get the job done quickly and cleanly.

All I could figure was that the elf leaned heavily on his extraordinary—and unfair—healing ability to hold down his job, or he relished in this petty torture.

At my massive party, celebrating me, no less, I'd assumed we were going to be cordial, and after our little threaten-the-enemies-again chat, I had every intention of returning to Indie. Pierce had to ruin it all. The smug bastard.

Nicole inspected the damage and frowned. Concerned, she gestured at me. "Let me see you."

I offered her my bare back, uncertain if she could figure which injury was the newest one. I flinched at her touch of my marred and angry, but rapidly scarring flesh. That was the one. We healed like humans but faster than the normal rate of time passage, and nothing more. Elves could heal away wounds on others like...well, like angels, but they were far from it, and they didn't deserve that mistaken identity. Even if the elf felt bad enough to heal me on his own accord, he couldn't. Call it some incongruity between the living immortals and the dead immortals, or that elves were natural and vampires were bastards of magic, but their healing didn't work on us.

The only elf I ever wanted to suck on was one whose immortality had been stamped as expired. Otherwise, gross, plus they tasted worse than a terrified human cowering in fear. And remembering my vegetarian days—worse than a deer whose primary diet was nasty corn. My tongue wanted to shrivel up like a snail dropped into a salt bath.

"That elf deserves a whipping."

"No kidding. I need another drink." I moved around the bar. "Is the fridge downstairs restocked because I'm going through this pretty fast?" I grabbed a blood bag from the wine fridge under the bar and poured out another mix.

My niece ignored the question. She held the damaged fabric close to her face, and she squinted at it, shifting the lines on her motherly face.

"That's a pretty big hole. Do you need readers?" I teased.

Nicole quietly fingered the gaping, bloody hole in the fabric. She moved it over her lap, assessing its location maybe. Something was bothering her. Before I could prod further, she finally said, "I think Pierce Evansson has caused more than enough harm to this family, and yet you boys insist on letting him live." Nicole released the fabric and glared at me with her serious face.

I drank the next glass down, and finally the hunger began to ease. "I sense a question in there."

"Can I ask why?"

"Why did we let Pierce live?" She continued glaring. All right then. "For a while, we had a truce."

"Truce, goose. Don't give me that excuse."

I lifted my lips in amusement and clawed up another reason. Really, I had to think about it. "Well, I suppose he's

Daisy's friend, and Oliver doesn't want her to suffer that loss."

Nicole scoffed.

Alright, something else. "Pierce leans heavily into showing his opinion instead of speaking it...I mean, what do you expect from an elf? Oliver and I keep him in line."

"This says tonight he wasn't. An inch to the right and he would've hit home."

I frowned and fished in the fridge for another blood bag.

Nicole continued, "He's staked you and your brother countless times, and yet you let him live. If it were anyone else, you would've drained them dry and covered the attack by making humans believe it was animals. You've done it before. Why does he get the exception?"

I poured my mix and leaned toward her on the bar, suddenly feeling the need to defend my lack of response toward him. "You know vampires are hated, considered monsters. So, Oli and I have been taking the high road. Maybe the elves will change their minds about us someday. Maybe the witches will leave us alone if we prove them wrong. We just want a peaceful home, and that's the truth." A truth I'd never admitted before and didn't know I had. I wanted a home, safe for those I loved.

I mean, it was short list.

"You said yourself vampires are hated. If your reputation is shot anyway, then why do you care? I certainly know the real you, and I don't judge. In fact, I encourage many of your shenanigans."

She didn't know everything I'd done while under Newton Reed's spell, only the highlights. Still, to lighten the mood, I smiled. "You're biased, but thank you for being the best cheerleader."

Nicole was firmly stuck in serious-face mode. She tapped the damaged shirt. "This chased off Indie, didn't it?"

I slammed down my next drink in two swallows. "Has anyone ever told you that you'd be great at interrogation?"

"You're avoiding the question."

My staking had shaken Indie terribly, and I'd felt awful, but I would've made any witness forget for self-preservation. "I compelled her to forget all of it."

Nicole's tired eyes widened. "The whole date? What did you do that for?"

I sighed. "Only the attack. Indie doesn't need traumatic memories like tonight. She doesn't need me rooting around in her head, messing with her free will. What kind of life is that?"

"Soren, I love you. I don't mean to pressure you—"

"Yes, you do," I interrupted.

"Oliver found his love. If there's hope for him, I believe there's someone out there for you."

"Daisy is different. She's a spitfire to Oliver's broodiness. Indie is nothing like her. She's reserved, calculating, cautious." But she could be awfully sexy and playful when I got her to loosen up. But Nicole's help wouldn't be as useful if she didn't know what really held me back. I could imagine the fear in Indie's eyes and that flightiness of hers taking wing. "I don't think she can handle what I am."

Nicole's eyes glittered as if that were an easy hurdle to overcome. "If you have a little faith in someone, they might surprise you. Soren, I only want you to find someone who can ground you before I leave this mortal coil."

I beamed at the perfect loophole she'd given. "Perfect. When you're taking your last breaths, I'll turn you. Then you'll be around forever. Case closed." I was only joking, and Nicole's face projected her understanding.

But it also showed me something else familiar. She was disappointed—the one thing I excelled at. "If she doesn't remember the attack, what really happened? I want to help you fix it."

Early in the night, I'd asked for a dance, and she'd said after. I might have...shortcomings, but lying was where I drew the line. How could you trust someone whose every word could be a deception? And she'd lied to me. The beautiful woman I'd run circles around just for a single date and—I might add—enthusiastically fulfilled her obligations, dropped me like a rotten, hot potato. "It's not something that can be fixed."

"Oh, nonsense. I don't want to pull the 'old' card on you, but I have more experience with loving relationships than you do."

I gave her a side-eye and a crooked grin. "Watching customers vacationing at a bed-and-breakfast, who were mostly honeymooners, doesn't count."

Nicole bristled, clearly offended that her life's work was meaningless in my situation. "Regardless, you have more to offer than you realize, and I know you can sweet-talk your way back into her life. This time, don't screw it up. Take her somewhere safe, secluded, and romantic. Open your heart, and she'll see the real you like I do."

Nicole insisted I chased her down, so Indie had pleased my niece—clearly. Even though Indie didn't get to finish her spell business, I'd introduced her to the witch, so our deal had been done. There was one piece missing. She owed me a dance. Tonight, I literally got the short end of the stick on this deal. Heh, pun intended. I wasn't looking for a commitment—God, I didn't want one—so what did it matter if she'd lied?

Needing to placate my niece while I wallowed in my inadequacy, I dragged my cell phone out of my pocket. I'd gotten her number from Lily before the unfortunate events, just for this reason. I sent her a simple text, pleading to her prominent business side. *You owe me.*

Nicole waited.

I waited, certain I was more nervous than she was. I drummed on the surface of the bar. My heart pounded in my chest. Possibilities funneled through my mind as if our future were on fast forward. Dancing, getting naked, finding out what made her tick inside...and out. Time ticked by. I set down my phone and made another drink, wondering who threatened her. Who chased her? I wanted her to feel safe. Human drama was so much easier to solve than elf drama.

No reply came back.

I had to admit that hurt. "There's your answer. I'm not." I showed her the screen as proof, and I realized that was an argument I didn't want to win.

Nicole's excitement deflated like a balloon, but then as a new angle reached her mind, it came back. "She seemed so sweet. Does she know your number? In that text, you didn't tell her who you are. It could've gone to spam, or she might've just deleted it. There's a lot of scammers and creeps out there."

That was optimistic but misguided. Indie had shut me down. Only the deal got her to deliver a performance, and she was the best actress I'd ever met—well, as far as I could tell. But now that my niece was in a better place, I didn't want her to lose that hope. "You might be on to something."

"Before you bring her back into our world, stake the damned elf."

I lifted my shocked gaze dend smiled. "You are good at surprising me."

Nicole patted the bar and rose with a moan. "Here's another surprise for you—I believe in you. Now, I'm off to bed."

"Good night, Nicole," I said.

"Good night, dear. If anything weird happens, you'll have to yell really loud. These old ears don't hear like they used to." Nicole limped away.

Staking Pierce once and for all would allow me the chance to have a life with Indie. But every decision came with consequences. This one would incite a new war. I had a few assets I could pull—Kevin the paramedic, Stacey Barrett who'd actually left, and I could recall Oliver and Daisy from their honeymoon. But we weren't equipped to fight an entire elf clan. We'd barely survived a skirmish with two dozen elves, and they weren't even pissed at the time.

I couldn't take that chance.

And as far as Indie? If I continued pushing her, she'd file a restraining order, and I still had some dignity left somewhere. That text was my last olive branch. She needed to choose me, but I wasn't holding my breath. Instead, I held another blood-wine mix.

9

Protection

Indie

For Lily Barrett's help, I'd agreed to a favor. I hadn't known I'd be walking into the worst environment imaginable. Otherwise, I would've negotiated. An hour south of town, in Green Bay, Wisconsin, Lily led me into a four-story, glass and stone building encompassing everything I avoided—cameras, crowds, and enclosed spaces. Nerves fluttered through me as we moved beyond uniformed security guards stationed behind acrylic sheets, doors with badge-swipes or keypads, and through a final locking door I had no hope of tearing through.

Lily explained witch Newton Reed and research scientist Dr. Greg Barrett had perished for their noble cause—whatever it was—down here. Working with witches and humans was safe, but the unusually high mortality rate stayed at the front of my mind. Long after the windows had disappeared, the cameras vanished, and the staff were missing, we stopped at a secret underground lab. I didn't see any emergency exits. Allison needed another witch's help, and Lily was the only option I had, regardless of her confusing history with Soren and Pierce.

The text *You owe me* from a mystery number I'd received not long after I'd given my digits to Lily still echoed through my mind. Since she hadn't done anything for me at that point, she wasn't the author. Very few people had my number, so I narrowed down my suspects to Soren. I considered my end of our deal complete. He'd gone through an awful lot of trouble to please his aunt—more likely the slip of 'niece' had been the truth. Not just any vampire would care so much, and that spoke volumes about Soren.

He was...adorable.

So, his demand must refer to the dance he'd made me promise—less adorable, far sexier. The corners of my lips lifted. When I'd thought he was human, I'd wanted to be in his thick arms, to press against his tight body, and to feel the pounding of his heart, and there it would end. Human lives were just too short, and my concern over breaking him in half was legit. Spines were so fragile.

Turned out, he was immortal like me, and I should've been thrilled there was a possibility for more than a single night, but that was also the crux. I knew my worth. With a single drop of my blood, he could smell or taste what I was, and female elves were believed to be extinct. Soren could bargain for untold benefits, so that belief had to remain. I couldn't risk what little freedom I had for a dance. The entire idea sounded preposterous.

The stark, eye-watering scent of bleach burned my nose—humans and their weak senses. Before us were rows of microscopes, stacks of petri dishes, and workers in white gowns, studiously working on their tasks. Lights above commercial refrigerators blinked their status updates, protecting trays of test tubes. Mechanical fans filtered air throughout the bright, stifling space. A faint something else lingered in the air...blood. What were they hiding down here?

Lily proudly swept her hand across the lab. "This is where the staff collects and tests the samples. The analysis is done by scientists who are trapped under boulders of legal documents to keep this quiet, and they only know pieces of the absolutely necessary details, so even if they wanted to, they don't have anything of substance to leak."

Although I was immune to human diseases, the aroma of blood in the air and the unusually high mortality rate suggested this place wasn't entirely safe, and I didn't believe they were curing cancer down here. Until she helped me, I needed to trust this witch with my life, and her disclaimer didn't bolster my confidence any. "What's your role in this?"

"I'm not a scientist like my dad. Medical stuff gives me the squicks, so I avoid most of the...goings-on...down here. I'm more of a staff manager. Come with me."

I was not familiar with the term 'squicks', but I surmised unpleasant things happened, and I wanted to avoid them too. I followed Lily around the central processing area. On the opposing wall was a series of white unmarked doors, and on this side, Lily stopped us in front of a windowed door. It wasn't locked. She led us inside, and the nostalgic scent of musty old books filled my nose. Lily flipped on the light switch. A too-large table with a green banker's desk lamp and a pair of padded wooden chairs made the room feel tight, and books covered two walls. It wasn't animal skins, woven rugs, and pine boughs, but it was close. This room, in such stark contrast to the sterility beyond the door, was almost comforting.

Lily closed the door behind us and said proudly, "This is your office. Have a seat."

I respected the effort she'd extended for me, so I did. "What kind of favor do you need from me?"

Lily lowered herself across from me. She clasped her hands on top of the table. "You need help with a spell, but so do I."

"I'm not a witch," I protested, feeling like all her preparations carried impossible expectations.

"If I knew one I could trust, she would be here instead, but you have a different, arguably more valuable skill set."

Witches were as rare as I feared, and that confirmed Lily was my only hope of assisting Allison. And now I realized this selection of antique texts wasn't for personal enlightenment or entertainment. They were grimoires. "What are you looking for?"

Lily beamed. "A spell that's going to change the world."

Was it for the greater good or something selfish disguised as the greater good?

"That's ambitious," I said cautiously and likely a monumental task. I had a sinking feeling I wouldn't be bringing my two witches together within the next few days.

Lily smiled proudly. "I know, but it's going to be worth the effort. I brought you here because my source material isn't written in any of today's languages. Can you help with that?"

Nerves skittered down my back, but I gave the witch a friendly, innocent smile. "I bet you already tried an online translator, and since I'm not a witch, I don't know why you expected I could be of use."

Lily looked at the table bashfully and softened her shoulders, as if to make herself as benign as possible. "I feel like I need to give you a disclaimer, and I don't want you to be scared. Okay? I'm not going to hurt you. I would never do anything to hurt you."

I stiffened. That was just about the worst thing she could say. I glanced at the doorknob. She hadn't locked it. "Why do you think I'm scared?"

Lily glanced up at me with gentleness on her face. "I know why you want my help. Whatever spell you had protecting your identity malfunctioned...*very*...briefly. If I hadn't been looking at that split second…" She trailed off and whispered, "Indie, I know what you are."

My heart pounded in my ears, and my breath caught. The cameras, a crowd of witnesses, and enclosed spaces…with no exit. I had been so desperate for help that I'd ignored my instincts, which had served me well. I had to get out of this unsettling secret underground lab, and I rose from my seat. If my ring had failed, I would discard it and use my full strength to break through those secured doors.

Lily rose too, standing between me and the door. She gestured to placate my rising panic. "I won't tell anyone, Indie. I won't, and I haven't. I swear you're safe with me. We can help each other."

Despite the alarm ringing in my ears, her offer kept me still. "What do you want to translate?"

"Many of the grimoires on these shelves are millennia old."

I frowned at the implication. "How old do you believe me to be?"

"Old enough, and I mean no offense."

My age meant I was a survivor. I was concerned that her expectations were too high, and if I couldn't please her, she wouldn't help me. "You want me to translate an ancient spell that's meant to change the world?"

Lily's proud smile returned. "I'm looking for the original spell that created vampires."

Centuries ago, north of the Baltic Sea, before war tainted our lands, neighboring humans and elf clans coexisted peacefully, but like them, we grew our armories and trained more soldiers. I'd wanted to be one—a soldier, fighting to preserve our kind and our way of life.

During my years on the run, I'd extrapolated the truth. With their greater senses, their greater strength, and their ability to fly, long ago elves dominated humans. And my father had wanted to join our clans to defeat the humans once again. His plan for me was not to be a soldier at all, and that grave mistake cost him his life.

A vampire bite injected women with a protein that wasn't compatible with elf procreation, and watching elf numbers dwindle over the centuries was a small piece of justice.

The possibilities behind her mission were so heavy, I dropped back onto my seat. I asked breathlessly, "You want to destroy all vampires?"

Lily smiled at me, glowing with pride in her misplaced altruism. "No, not at all. If everything goes according to plan, any vampire exposed to the cure would lose the magic freezing them in time. They would resume their previous life spans as normal, fang-free humans."

Humans had clashed with elves, and the flighted-ones had severely underestimated their foes. Humans had been more vicious, more selfish, more greedy, and they procreated almost as rapidly as rabbits. After their victory, they'd erased elves from the oral stories told through generations. They'd erased or mistranslated the writings on purpose. Soon elves became myths. More recently, they'd become a joke in their affiliation with a character named Santa. Humans were cruel.

All of that was why I'd obeyed one rule from my father: keep the supernatural world hidden from the humans. Not because I had pride in my kind or that I held animosity toward humans. I'd obeyed simply for self-preservation, and eliminating the vampire threat would tip the balance I relied on for survival. But if I declined, I'd lose the help I needed to survive.

With a witch sitting across from me at this table, I could adjust my long-term plan later. My short-term survival was precariously urgent. Bringing out the acting skills I'd honed once more, I said gleefully, "And vampires reduce the elf population. That sounds like an amazing plan."

Lily beamed at my response. "With that settled, how can I help you?"

I reached my hand toward her, displaying the gaudy emerald. "It's magic is almost gone. It needs a recharge."

Lily gestured for it. "Let me see it."

I glanced out the window in the door. Anyone who could see me was completely engrossed in their own work, so I slipped off the emerald, and dropped it into Lily's palm. I expected her to tell me the same thing Allison had—the spell was too complex to restore alone.

Lily gazed at me, eyes widening in wonder. I didn't like the attention, so I cleared my throat. Lily's stare broke. "Sorry. I didn't mean to... When I said briefly, it was brief. I also thought I'd hallucinated, but you are beautiful, angelic, ethereal. All of you are."

I glanced at the table. "Thank you."

Lily closed her eyes and cupped her hands over the ring, concentrating. Her eyebrows rose, and she returned the jewel to me as if a vampire had gripped vervain. I immediately returned it to my finger, cutting off the witch's ability to see my wings through my glamour.

"Can you repair it?"

"You're lucky you're down here right now. The spell is gone."

I looked at my gaudy bauble, stomach clenching with a fear I'd dreaded for centuries. "Fully depleted?"

"Completely, and the spell that used to be there was so powerful there's no way I could've restored it." At least Allison had been honest. Lily added, "But I can give you something else that will work just as well."

That was unexpected. "Like what?"

"It's still a protection spell, but with side effects. You'll appear human to anyone who sees you, including witches, vampires, or elves."

Exactly what I needed. "But?"

"You'll also have the strength and abilities of a human."

I was confused. That wasn't any different from what I had, but required only half the effort. Perhaps magic was like technology—more convenient as the years progressed. "I can take it off when I need to, so I don't mind."

"No," Lily said evenly. "The spell imbues *you*, not the ring."

So I wouldn't have the option to flee easily, and I'd have to give up all my defenses until my ring could be restored by them both working in tandem. I could manage...for now, but I needed to know more before I'd accept that risk. "Is there a way to break it?"

Lily shifted uncomfortably. "I don't know, but I wish I did. I'm not in good graces with the witch who gave me the spell. And that's why I need your help. So here, if you can translate the rest of it, have at it." Lily opened her phone and swiped and dragged. Finally, she turned the screen toward me.

Lily had a photograph of the spell's original page. Skimming through the ingredients list, I slowed down as the text devolved into an old language. Just before the image cut off, the ancient language read, "A mar of the flesh shall break the seal."

"Well, there's your answer, and now I know you can translate old spells." Lily gave me a wry lift of her lips.

Keeping tabs on a delicate and ugly bauble had been frustrating, while preventing a mar of my flesh sounded easy.

Temporarily being fully human wasn't ideal, but it wouldn't be the worst thing I'd experienced.

"As long as you stay down here, surrounded by the safety of people, no one's going to hurt you, I promise," Lily said, as if trying to persuade me to accept her trade.

I'd heard that many times in my life, but never once had anyone pulled through for me. The bottom line was I couldn't leave this lab without protection.

"Do it," I said.

Lily grinned.

IO

Hidden Behind

Indie

Behind me in my library-style office were bookshelves full of tomes waiting to be combed. Stacked on the table next to me were the ones I'd already eliminated. Wearing white cotton gloves, I delicately turned the page in the next ancient text. The crackling of the paper made me clench my teeth in concern for the preservation of the pages.

I'd underestimated the young witch. With the impressive ease Lily had cast a powerful spell on me, I believed she could craft a cure from the original vampire-creating spell. Lily just needed me to find it, and I owed her a reasonable effort. The spell pre-dated me by—as she'd said—millennia. Without meticulous preservation methods, like witches re-copying it over the centuries, it simply couldn't stand the test of time. Unless...was there a spell that could spell another spell with longevity? Even thinking it sounded preposterous.

So how long was a reasonable effort before letting the witch down gently? Having a safe place to go to, where I was safe to be my new self, and given a purpose perusing texts was the opposite of what I'd been living lately. So, I determined I'd keep up the ruse until I was bored. Unfortunately for Lily, these books were fascinating. Witches didn't just write their ingredients and instructions. A literal 'cook' book would be so very dull. Witches had added thoughts, feelings, mishaps, warnings, and drama. Lily's favor delivered me to familiar, nostalgic worlds I hadn't had the time to visit in ages and other worlds I'd never had the opportunity to explore at all. I hadn't felt this young in a long time. Recognizing the language, I delicately turned another page, seeking words of key relevance while getting lost in the history.

Who would've thought that accidentally meeting a handsome vampire would bring me to such a fantastic place, where I could feel...free, safe, needed, and young? I couldn't have asked for such circumstances, let alone believed them possible. What if such an impossibility could happen for Soren? Would he want the freedom that came with being human?

I was enjoying my 'humanity' because the alternative had been horrible. But if I had what Soren had—ownership of a business establishment, a wardrobe of fine clothing, access to an iron, and copious friends and family—I wouldn't trade. Not for a second. I sighed. Luckily, the spell in question didn't exist—

A scream made me jerk, and I tore the page.

I frowned. That was loud, even with my new, weaker human hearing. I glanced through the narrow window in my door. None of the lab workers appeared disturbed. I got up and opened my door cautiously. No one paid me or that scream any attention, but I hadn't hallucinated it. I made my way to Lily's office and knocked. She called for me to enter, and I did.

Lily looked up from one of the many computer screens, eyes hopeful. "Did you find it?"

"Not yet. I heard a scream. Why isn't anybody bothered by it?"

The light in her eyes dimmed. "Close the door."

I sheltered us in privacy and lowered myself onto a chair in front of her desk.

"I don't want you to worry about the screams. They're routine blood draws, okay? But I want to tell you how important your mission is, and impress upon the importance that this remains between you and me only. Understood?" Lily said darkly.

I had only just begun to feel safe down here, and now a twinge of alarm crawled through me. "Understood."

"I was thrilled to have brought you on board. Our interests are aligned, and by searching for that spell, there is hope."

"Hope for what?" I'd already determined that if I were in Soren's shoes, I wouldn't want the cure. I couldn't see how she'd believe otherwise.

Lily rested her hands together on top of her desk. "Most vampires don't know the story behind their creation, and since they haven't been teaming up for centuries with witches around the globe to hunt for that spell, I'd wager most don't care or can't get a witch to see their side. But I do. The perpetrators, for whom the spell had been created, long ago served their sentences. Every single vampire inflicted since is an innocent victim of a greater crime—one of both personal horror and a perpetual curse—to inflict torture and death on other innocents until the end of time. These vampires didn't ask for it, and they can't escape it. You understand the unfairness of it?"

I pictured the process of an innocent being hunted by a vampire who had been a victim himself. A perpetual cycle of fear, a bloody mess, the...repeated coercion of it all. And I picture Soren having survived such trauma, and inflicting such trauma against his will. It was appalling. "I understand wanting the choice."

"Witches started this. It's my duty to stop the cycle—to free them from the curse. What I'd said was true. I'm trying to save vampires by returning them to their lost humanity, but not everyone agrees with me," Lily said quietly.

I had valid reasons for not wanting to hand over the spell, if it existed, but my reasons weren't nefarious. That safety I'd felt briefly, and trembled along with the scream, had begun to slide away from my grasp. "Who doesn't approve?"

Lily cast her solemn gaze to the floor. "I'm working on finding out."

The young woman in charge had led me to believe I was perfectly safe down here, but she knew someone opposed her. Had she discovered the saboteur was me? I didn't want to leave so soon, but my guaranteed safety was on the brink. "You're trying to undo centuries' worth of damage. It's a noble cause, but there are many other, far more attainable, ambitions. Pardon me for asking, but what do you personally get from this?"

"I just want my family back."

I blinked. Lily was me. Where she used magic, I'd tried with a sword. I had been thwarted, imprisoned, and I'd lost them all. If I were to destroy that spell, thwarting her efforts to save her family, I would be no better than *him*. Guilt squeezed my chest and, unable to sit still, I rose.

"I didn't finish," Lily said, puzzled. She rose to meet me or block me, concern written on her face.

"I need air."

Soren

I'd sent a second text telling her who I was, just in case, but I still received no response. At all. Not even a middle-finger emoji. I found myself spending extra time at my bar, keeping my folding knife close in case the featherbag decided to make an appearance and gloat. These long daily appearances weren't for the exquisite selection of alcoholic beverages, although their presence had been the perfect excuse, nor for the supervising of my staff.

Despite knowing in my bones she'd rejected me, I showed up each day, waiting, wishing Indiara Niskatar would decide I was worthy of a dance. I was pathetic, really. I could compel any woman I wanted to satisfy me. But that wasn't right. It wouldn't satisfy, and she wouldn't be *her*. I wanted to feel Indie's curves pressed against me while we moved to the rhythm, and then I wanted her body beneath mine. My mouth, my hands, would explore her like uncharted territory. I couldn't let go of the daydream of what could've been.

"I'm starting to think you're bored," Cora said with a chuckle, mixing me a drink in broad daylight on a Wednesday. "Don't you have anything else you could do?"

Shred all my dignity with a string of texts? "That's the glory of being the owner."

"Don't take this the wrong way, boss, but if I wasn't on your payroll, I'd be all over you." Cora said with a playful huskiness. "A man like you shouldn't be lonely."

"I'm flattered." I swiped letters to add another word to the puzzle and swigged from my drink.

"What about Indie? You two looked awfully steamy at the party."

I lifted my head. "Did she say something?"

"Didn't she?" Nicole asked with a look of disbelief.

I assumed Indie wasn't interested. Nicole had assumed my ignored texts had been sent to spam. What if there were a more nefarious reason I was being ignored? Like Lily had given me a bogus phone number on purpose. As much as it hurt the witch didn't trust me, I wasn't surprised. Lily and I had a tenuous alliance, mostly built on a family member in common—one I had threatened and kidnapped under orders from another witch...and attacked on occasion. But we were past that now, or at least, I was.

My employee was her roommate. "I must've gotten her digits mixed up. Do you have Indie's number?"

"Actually, I don't."

"Would you share your address so I can visit?" I asked very gently. That was something not likely to go over well. But I didn't want to go digging in the employee files for it.

"Sure. While you're there, get her number for me, too." Cora wrote her address on a napkin.

Risking a restraining order, I drove down the main thoroughfare through Menominee, and pulled into a parking lot for a strip of tiny rental houses. These buildings were smaller than the bed-and-breakfast's sitting room. I couldn't imagine such stifling quarters, but since I'd been a drifter for years, I couldn't judge. At least these people had a home. I was merely borrowing mine.

I approached the correct tiny house, and nerves tingling in my gut. Since Indie wasn't a drinker, instead of the standard bottle of wine, I brought her a word puzzle book and a fancy, fluffy pen. They weren't bribes, just thoughtful gifts. Hypnotic, indeed. Would she like them or think they were cheesy...cheap? Only one way to find out. I knocked and waited.

After a few more knocks, I tried to see through the curtains, but I couldn't. I waited and knocked some more. Then I stared at the curtains trying to pick up curious movement, but there wasn't any. The neighbors coming and going were sending me weird looks. If not a restraining order, then I risked a suspicious stranger doing suspicious things visit. I waited perhaps a little too long. I was truly, embarrassingly, pathetic.

That was my last olive branch for real. I should've listened to my gut. Indie was an amazing actress who ignored my texts. She'd never returned to the bar because she had no interest in me. I tossed the gifts into the shrubs by the door and headed back to my bar.

The only thing I looked forward to was tasting the rainbow of alcoholic fruity drinks.

II

Tenuous Alliance

Indie

After calming myself, I'd realized that comparing myself to my despicable father had been inaccurate. I hadn't done anything wrong, and I wouldn't, because the spell didn't exist. So I returned to resume my entertaining task, and Lily's alternative spell, the humanizing cloak, had been working splendidly. No one even sniffed in my direction.

I had no reason to request Lily and Allison join up and repair my gaudy bauble's spell. I would accept my new human life. And just as I resettled in my office, another scream tore through the lab.

When I'd first been introduced to this secret underground lab, Lily had told me the workers were collecting samples for research. The witch must've used a spell, so they'd forget and return each day, but I never noticed a steady flow of volunteers receiving a blood draw. Why would the test subjects scream over a blood draw at all? Didn't humans subject themselves to such as part of their routine healthcare? Lily was secretly trying to find a cure for vampires to restore their humanity, specifically their freedom from inflicting torture on other victims. But those ear-curdling screams sounded like torture.

This lab appeared to be where questions waited to die, but truthfully, none of it was my business, and I was perfectly content to continue in my mission.

A knock on my door lifted my head, and I called, "Come in." Down here, behind all this security, those were safe words to use.

Lily swooped in and closed the door behind her. She was stiff, pale, and alarm was written on her face—that same alarm from the night I'd met her, when she'd been Pierce's date.

My spine straightened, and for the protection of the grimoire before me, I released the delicate page. "What's wrong?"

"I have someone coming to the lab, and I need you to know this changes nothing for you or us."

That was...vague and distressing. "Does this someone object to what I'm doing? Do you want me to lie to them?"

"I expect he wouldn't approve. If you're asked, say that you're assisting with the vampire weapon. But the reason I'm here is to let you know he'll get the tour just like you did and be in and around. You know, a new employee."

I removed my cloth glove and frowned. "Why is this new employee worrying you so?"

Lily exhaled. "Look, I don't want you to...overreact. I promised you that spell is ironclad, and I stand by my word. Our deal is my priority above all else. You are safe here. You are a human to everyone, and I mean everyone."

A subsequent string of warnings about my safety and the spell cloaking me. That same terrified face from Lily having to be Pierce's date. Before I could dash past her, a knock at the door stopped my heart for a few beats.

Lily startled as well. The witch gazed at the visitor in the narrow window and opened the door wide. Her features weren't warm or welcoming. This had to be the one she'd warned me about, and this visitor was not a lab employee at all. Instinctively, my breath hitched, as if not breathing would make me invisible. My safety—my freedom, my life—hinged on the witch's skill. A trust I dreaded imparting to any witch, let alone an overly ambitious young one.

A tall, blond brute filled the doorframe—the hunter, who'd staked Soren so effortlessly. The...presumed elf. His wings and ear tips were invisible to me now, proving Lily's spell was working, but my heart pounded in my chest, and my limbs trembled. I fought to remain upright and calm. My place of safety became a place of horror.

"Hey Lily, they said you were in here." The elf faced me. "Indie, right? We sort of met the other night." He held out his hand to shake, but I ignored it, and his attention drifted back to Lily.

I should've shaken it to blend in better, but all I knew was a mar of the flesh would break the seal, and I had no idea how the ancient witches defined a mar. A scrape from a callused handshake? A scratch from a rough fingernail? I wasn't going to find out like five minutes after getting the protection. And certainly not while in another claustrophobic room with an elf and the exit so far away. I exhaled a shaky breath.

Lily shifted to the elf's side and smiled. And like before, it was fake. She was terrified of him, and a useless urge to protect her overwhelmed me. "Pierce is a friend."

I didn't believe that.

"Lily tells me you know of our world," Pierce said.

I smiled politely and said as I'd been directed, "I'm here to assist with the vampire weapon."

Pierce wrapped a meaty arm around Lily's shoulders, and they shared a friendly smile, which was far more genuine on the elf's side. "It's a strange new world out there, and I'm glad you're part of it. We need all the help we can get against those fangers."

A lump caught in my throat, and I tried really hard not to choke.

"Well, I've got places to be, but I'll see you around," Pierce said and waved before leaving. The door closed behind him.

I glared at my business associate.

"I know what this looks like," Lily said, genuinely apologetic. "I don't have a choice, but he means well."

"He's here for a vampire *weapon*?" No one I knew would ever describe a spell as a weapon.

"It's not as bad as it sounds. I mean, elves like to exaggerate the importance of their work," Lily said nervously.

"That didn't help," I said curtly and brushed past her and out to the main lab...and nearly crashed into a passing lab tech, but at the last second, I dodged the woman carrying a tray of glass test tubes. Luckily, she managed to preserve the tubes. After all the screams, I'd hate for the test subjects to be forced into extra blood draws on my account.

"Sorry," I called after the poor tech. She sent me a terse glance.

I should've listened to my instincts telling me to avoid this building, and now I had to flee before I was caught. I scurried through the lab as fast as I could without turning heads, weaving around equipment and cases of supply orders yet to be unpacked, and I rounded a corner in haste. In all the visual noise and my rising panic, I bumped into a firm chest, and my stomach leaped into my throat. I slowly looked up at the handsome face of my worst enemy and sucked in a breath. Was a bump enough to 'mar' my flesh and break the seal?

I swallowed a lump, hands trembling. The elf smiled at me, and nerves fluttered through my stomach.

"Indie, you look good." The sparkle in his eye was ordinary, so a bump didn't break the seal on my spell. Even knowing that, I didn't relax.

"Thanks," I said softly, trying to keep my voice even.

"What brought you to the dark side of the hidden world?" he asked.

Dark side? Vampire *weapon*? What brought me here had been self-preservation, but I never would've agreed to stay had I known the real mystery behind these walls. I feigned a smile. "Trying to make the world a better place."

Pierce beamed, showing off brilliant white teeth. "You'll fit in just fine around here. We're glad to have you."

He had no idea how extreme those statements were. I could never fit in down here, and if he saw the real me, he'd be far more than glad. "I have to get to work, you know, figuring out how these fangers tick." I swallowed back the obnoxious verbiage used down here.

Pierce laughed. "Don't let me hold you up. Jab them a little extra for me, okay?"

My fake smile drifted off, and Pierce's bright green eyes studied me. With the scrutiny of my enemy mere inches from me, I darted into the nearest unmarked door, fingers-crossed it was an emergency exit. Closing myself inside the dark room, there was no glowing red sign showing a way out. Well, I could catch my breath in a broom closet and escape after the immediate danger had passed.

I leaned my back flat against the door, panting, trying to ease the trembling in my body.

That was close. Way too close.

"Hello?" a croaky feminine voice said in the darkness.

Indie

With just one word, I'd forgotten my fear. I felt along the wall for the light switch and flicked it on. Despite having seen plentiful carnage and suffering, I gasped. A weakened woman wearing nothing but a torn patient's gown was kneeling on the cold tile floor. Her raw wrists were chained to the wall behind her, and the nest of dark brown hair on her head had long since matted. Her exposed skin, coated in bloody pokes, cuts, and bruises, told a gruesome story.

"Like what you see?" her raspy voice asked with a lift of her lips. I could only guess the hoarseness was from screaming.

"You don't look like a volunteer." I did not agree with whatever was happening inside this room, and I couldn't believe she had.

The woman snorted. "Oh, no, I asked for the chains. They make a musical sound when I rattle them in just the right way."

I'd spent time in a prison cell myself, but this...she couldn't defend herself. She couldn't fight. She couldn't move around. Despite all that, she still had...spirit. "What's your name?"

She studied me with big, empty blue eyes and a disassociation from spending too long in conditions like these. I recognized that look. I'd seen it on my fellow prisoner. This woman, like that courageous man before, had lost hope. "Why do you care? Stab me and get out."

I grimaced. She didn't beg to be released. She didn't plead for mercy. This tortured woman had already resigned to this fate. "I thought the workers drew blood. A needle wouldn't be called a stab."

The woman chuckled sardonically. "You must be new, but your ignorance doesn't work on me."

I frowned. "I don't understand."

The patient sighed with exaggeration annoyance. "Someone recruited you to work here, or you applied for the job opening. That says plenty about you, so no offense, but I'm not going to help you do your job."

Recruited for a *secret* underground lab filled with mindless—compelled—humans, a witch, and an elf. A test subject, to whom humans did unspeakable things all in the name of...Lily's noble cause. No, that wasn't right. I was working on Lily's cause. I slid down to the floor, my heart breaking for this poor woman. "How long have you been in here?"

"Forty-ish, I don't know. I lost count."

"Days?" I hoped it was only days.

The patient laughed. "You really are new. I'll give you a hint—it hasn't been weeks either."

Dumbfounded, I stared. The battered woman looked younger than Lily. Either she was a female elf, and Lily's humanizing cloak prevented me from seeing her true self, or what had Lily told me to say? *Vampire weapon.* "You're a vampire? But why aren't you healing?"

Chains rattled as her thin arms moved. "It's all part of their process, princess. If you wouldn't mind coming closer, I haven't had a drink in a while. Little parched here."

Even if I wanted to, a pair of fangs would definitely mar my flesh. "I can't."

The patient—prisoner—deflated as if she'd expended all her energy to educate me. Red and gristly wrists chained by heavy cuffs rattled. "That's why I said, get your sample and leave me alone."

"I only wanted your name," I said softly.

Her head snapped back up. "Did a lab tech screw up the labels again? If you're going to double up today's draw, then you have to give me double the rations."

I leveled my gaze at her. "I'm not one of those people, and I don't trust any of them."

The woman eyed me critically. "What do you want?"

"Moments ago I'd determined this underground lab was too dangerous, and I was in the process of fleeing."

The vampire lifted a bloody, crusty eyebrow at me. "Too dangerous...for *you*?"

She had no idea. The elf had been so close he could touch my hair, and at that thought, I squirmed, fighting the urge to resume rescuing myself. But this vampire's condition—whatever its reason—gravely worried me. "I was honest when I said I'm not one of them, but I had been recruited, as you suspected. I was lied to about the screams—your screams. I was told you were here of your own accord, and I'd assumed reimbursed handsomely for the...troubles. I want to help you."

"How can I trust you?"

I held out my empty palms. "I'm not here for any samples."

"I've seen that trick before."

Showing her my true self wouldn't help either of us, so I'd tell her something that would be detrimental to me. "They don't know I intend to thwart the mission they'd given me, if it's possible to complete it. My name is Indie."

The vampire glared at me suspiciously, but the tiniest flicker of hope passed across her features. After a long pause, the vampire said, "Della. Are you going to break me out?"

Like Lily had said, all vampires were innocent victims of callous witches, but I had selfish reasons for discovering the truth in this dark prison. If I broke her free, I'd never be able to return.

"I can't, but I promise you, as long as you keep my secret, I'm going to stop whatever they're doing, Della."

It was the easiest promise I'd ever made, but in making it, I'd have to do the hardest thing I'd ever do, pushing my seasoned acting skills to their limits.

12

A Gift

Indie

With my key turning in Cora's apartment door, a flicker of something pink in the shrubs caught my eye. Trapped in the boughs was a fluffy pen, and beside it, a new word puzzle book. I collected them both and pushed my way inside. My roommate had spruced up the place even more while I'd been gone.

Cora emerged from the bathroom with curlers in her hair and a robe around her thick middle. She had a full face of makeup, likely getting ready for a shift tonight. "For wanting a place to stay, you aren't here much."

"I work long hours." I didn't want Cora to think I was exploiting her too much, and I truly wanted to be in the lab.

"I hope you have all the privacy you need, honey." She moved to the kitchen and started a batch of drip coffee.

I'd compelled her to give me just that, but I hated having to tamper with her mind.

"I found these in the bush. Do people frequently litter around here?" I lifted the puzzle book and pen. I couldn't imagine why someone wanted to toss these things away. They looked new—at least donate them, or find a recycle bin for the book.

"Candy wrappers and empty pop cans, sure. Not stuff like that. The boss stopped by." While the pot burbled, Cora leaned against the counter.

I had to direct my initial grim thoughts away. Cora had said the boss was off limits because of her paycheck. "Soren was here?"

"He asked for my address, looking for you." Cora sent me a saucy smile. "I assume he brought you those, but I don't know why he tossed the gifts away like that—like garbage—but I bet it has to do with your date."

The puzzle book was a mix of word searches, crosswords, and scramblers. Similar to the ones he'd been doing on his phone when we'd met. He remembered, and he still wanted the dance I owed him. But he threw them out. "Why do you say that?"

"You are cute as a button. That slice of man cake wants you bad. Can't you see? He's been moping at the bar, watching every customer who enters the door, but not once has he got up for anyone."

I'd spent plenty of time daydreaming about how I wanted that night to end. But he was a vampire, and now I was a human who couldn't be bitten or scratched... Even being near a vampire was a massive risk to my life. Della was in chains, but I still couldn't trust her without them.

"He was moping at the bar when I met him. That doesn't prove anything."

"He doesn't bring them presents. It's clear he doesn't think your date was fake."

After I took care of the lab, I had to leave. Staying in one place wasn't safe. "I can't commit to anything right now. I'm only here for a little bit."

"No one said anything about commitment. If I had a man like that fawning over me, I'd show him my...appreciation. If you catch my drift."

Her enthusiasm lifted my lips. "I got it. Thanks, Cora."

"Anytime, honey. Anytime." Cora returned to the bathroom.

I had been so focused on that protection spell, and then the mystery of the lab that I couldn't focus on anything else. But now, as long as I didn't touch anything sharp, I was safe to be human. But that left me all kinds of vulnerable. If I approached Soren as a human with the strength of a human, I'd be helpless to stop him from feeding on me. I wouldn't be strong enough to defend myself against his attack. He was still a vampire—a sexy, predatory creature perfectly crafted to hunt and kill humans.

But a vampire wouldn't go through the trouble of buying me a thoughtful gift.

And then throw it away like garbage.

He'd given up.

Indie

I took a bite of my bacon-filled breakfast burrito, keeping the grease far from the delicate pages of the engrossing grimoire on my office table. This one was more difficult to translate than prior books. In the Middle Ages, witches crafted a spell to protect villagers against Christian raiders. I'd survived raids—not in the name of religion, but for our fertile lands. If such a spell would've worked, my clan—my family—would still be alive. I suspected this book was authentic to its time, but, like many of the books behind me, I believed it was counterfeit, crafted solely to swindle troubled customers of their coin. Which was another reason finding the original vampire spell was so lofty. Even if my eyes discovered the correct writing, the value of such a spell could've inspired forgeries.

Lily knocked on my doorframe and strolled into my office. She'd finally returned.

I finished the last bite and scrubbed my greasy fingers clean with the wet wipe I'd brought. "What brings you here, Lily?"

"Don't you want quiet in here? The screams can be jarring." Lily gestured at my open door.

Instead of tearing pages when I heard screams, my human-spelled heart leaped into my throat. I wanted to hear Della scream. I wanted to know her pain and feel her suffering—not that I needed further motivation. But each day she suffered was partially my fault for not stopping it.

"They are." I smiled thinly, trying to be polite while seething that such atrocities were happening right under my nose. "In fact, each one risks my damaging these fragile pages. Close it for me?"

Lily did. Her eyes swept my table of open grimoires. "Any luck yet?"

"Same as yesterday."

Lily's disappointment was palpable. Eventually, she'd have to realize her quest was futile, but until then, I indulged myself in both that still-fascinating task and my new one.

"Can I ask you something?"

Lily lowered herself onto the chair across from me. "Sure. What's up?"

"Those test subjects—the ones screaming—are they human?" I wanted to know whether Lily trusted me with the truth before I asked the questions I needed. Lies only wasted my time—and Della's.

"Not exactly." Lily looked out my narrow window at the busy workers. "You noticed those plain doors along the perimeter of the lab."

"Of course, but I figured they were closets."

"Given your situation and how much I need you, I think you should know the truth. You and I aren't the only ones looking to solve the vampire problem. Those two men I'd told you about—"

"The ones who are deceased?" I added, fully remembering the grim detail as a glaring warning signal.

"Instead of trying to reverse the curse and allow vampires a second chance at a human life, they were working to develop a serum that would destroy vampires outright—a toxin. Dr. Greg Barrett had used one daughter's blood as the base for what they affectionately called the 'vampire weapon' and the other daughter's blood for the cure."

The doctor sounded just as despicable as my father, using his daughter for personal gain. "Vampires are still around, but they aren't."

"The previous work had been destroyed, and the next interested parties have taken up the reins."

"Pierce?"

Lily nodded. "The daughters are no longer factors, so the new serum will have a different base."

When an enemy was eliminated, the successor usually learned from his predecessor's mistakes. I dreaded what came next. "And a different cure?"

Her gaze shifted away—her tell for guilt or shame—but Lily didn't want vampires dead. What was really going on? She'd shriveled at the elf's touch. She'd avoided the elf as her date. Lily was...secretive...with me. Lily wasn't in charge. Pierce, the new employee, was, and the elf wasn't making a cure this time.

"How does the serum work? It is like an illness? Some kind of block so they can't turn anyone else?"

"Despite what you hear out there, the elf in charge doesn't want them to suffer," Lily said flatly. "The serum, even in small doses, was fatal, like vervain amplified a thousandfold."

My mouth dropped open. I didn't know how far they'd gotten before, but the idea of a handful of humans and a witch single-handedly murdering an entire faction sent fury burning along my whole body. I swallowed back the bacon-flavored bile threatening to purge itself.

Lily smiled sadly. "Now you know why I want that spell."

I wanted vampires free to do what vampires did best, but they couldn't do their job if they were cured, and they certainly couldn't do anything if they were *exterminated*. I looked at the brittle books before me, filled with spells to create love potions or bring about rain. Vampirism was supposed to cause the afflicted humans to attack and kill their own loved ones, and afterward, kill themselves with sunlight from the guilt. Instead of being effective one-off punishments, vampirism spread. Why would witches allow that spell to remain in existence? It made little sense.

I believed they'd burned the spell the moment it was deemed a failure.

"Everything okay?" Lily asked.

I'd promised to help Della by stopping this, but I couldn't ask Lily for guidance on how, since she was only a staff manager. I wasn't a scientist either. If I blindly when thrashing all the glass out there, I could accidentally release the toxin in its current state—it could be unstable, it could affect more than vampires. Not only could I be the single cause of a global pandemic, but I definitely could never return.

I smiled plainly. "The burrito may have been a little too old, but I'm okay. I'm glad you conveyed the immense importance of my work." I slid the counterfeit grimoire aside and picked up a fresh one from the stack.

Lily's lips pulled into a satisfied smile. "I'm heading out for lunch. Don't let me get in your way." Lily closed the door on her way out.

Now was my chance to do the only thing that could make a difference to someone.

13

Breaking a Promise

Indie

Shifty glances, shaky hands, and jerky movements attracted unwanted attention. They were all clear signs a person didn't belong, or that they intended to do something uncomfortable. Confidence, silently announcing a person had familiarity and purpose in where they were going, became a free pass. Confidence had served me well, whether in a crowded market or a busy gas station. Those nearby would turn their cheek, not wanting to confront and inconvenience someone with clear authority.

Unlike my previous successful uses of confidence, I was now recognized. I wore street clothes and read books all day. Although most of the humans ignored me, they knew their jobs and their associates, so I couldn't fake authority. And they'd know I had no business snooping around near the unmarked white doors. So I had to be extra careful.

With Lily gone for lunch and the elf nowhere in sight, I had a small window of opportunity. I ducked down to discover a weak point in my stealthiness by pretending to tie my shoe. No one bothered me or interrupted my innocent task. And down here, I was mostly out of sight. With a quick spinning motion, I barreled inside, shut the door securely, and flipped on the light switch.

I didn't know how much time I'd have, and I couldn't waste it, which, as an immortal, was a strange feeling.

Della squinted at the blinding light showering upon her head and shoulders like divine judgment. Embracing Lily's viewpoint on vampires, I'd already judged Della as innocent, not that it was my place anyhow. But if she'd done terrible things, this torture had more than made up for it.

Disappointment sagged on her pretty but bruised face. "You're back. Since you can't get me out of here, I'm guessing it's bad news."

I approached Della slowly. "I learned they're making a serum called the vampire weapon."

"Again?" Della rolled her eyes. "It's so unbelievable, it's hilarious."

I couldn't find the humor in it. "The source of the serum is different this time, and the formula is incomplete. I can't risk destroying whatever's in process. The results could be catastrophic."

"Or benign."

That was a risk I couldn't take. "I'm sorry."

"So that's it then?" Della's hopes faded away. "I'm stuck in here until they finish the new serum, and then I die a prisoner."

"Not if I can help it."

Della looked up at me, big blue eyes hopeful once again. "What are you going to do?"

My brilliant handmaiden had said to me before she'd perished: *you need to live today and fight tomorrow.* If only I could've saved Birgitte, I would still have my best friend. I wouldn't make that mistake twice, so I was going to do the only thing I could—save one prisoner. "I'm getting you out of here."

Della lifted a skeptical eyebrow. "I like the change of heart, but how?"

Her chains were iron, but I had cloth. Since I was magically human now, and she was hungry, I still had to trust her with her own freedom. "Upon release, will you spare me your hunger?"

After a short beat, Della laughed. "You're getting ahead of yourself, but I promise I'll never bite you or anyone you care about in this generation and all future generations, if you can get me out of here."

That was unnecessary, but the gesture was appreciated. "Can I borrow a little of that?" I pointed at her dirty, worn, patient gown.

"I don't care to count how many people I've flashed. If it helps, I'll go naked."

I lifted the bottom hem of her dirty gown and brought it up to the loop mounted in the wall. My heart pounded. If I'd assumed incorrectly, I could be throwing away the only protection I had—and it was no easy feat to get—and exposing myself to the worst imaginable danger. Della's big blue eyes looked up at my hesitation. Her face was still so bloodied...so young. I couldn't risk my life for a dance, but I could risk it to save her life. With a quick exhale, I used the gown as protection and tapped the iron loop.

"I wish I had a chainsaw too," Della said.

I gazed at her, waiting for the reaction I feared. "Think I could sneak one in?"

Della snorted. My skin didn't hiss. The fabric had been sufficient. I gripped the iron rings and pulled with my entire body weight. All that happened was a few metallic squeaks. I tried again, face heating, arms shaking, but it was as futile as finding that spell. Panting, I released the chains and lowered her gown. My allergy was hidden by the spell, but of course, my strength was too.

"I appreciate the effort."

"Are there keys?" I asked.

"Doubt it. They've never let me loose for anything." Della moved the shackles around, but there were no keyholes at all, as if they'd been welded right over her wrists.

I sat on the floor in front of her. "I'm sorry, Della."

Her light had faded along with her hope, but she lifted her lips in an attempt at a smile as if relieving me of guilt for failing. "Rockwell,"

The name startled me. "Pardon me, but what did you say?"

"You tried to save my life. Might as well know my name, in case the medical records seized by authorities are released, and a gripping monograph is written about all this. I mean, all I can do is dream of what would happen if this place burned down. Look me up. I'll be under Della Rockwell."

A little flame, a tiny spark of hope, flickered to life. "Any relation to Soren Rockwell?"

The light returned to her eyes. "He's my older brother. He's alive?"

My heart pounded as a new plan formed, and I smiled warmly while trying to hide the bubbling excitement. "Owns a bar."

She cackled. "I can't believe you know him. What's my ass of a brother actually doing these days?"

Her laughter was contagious, and I beamed. "I'm serious. He owns Fully Loaded in Marinette. It's a small town about forty-five minutes north of here."

"I know the area. I never would've guessed he had the ambition, let alone the patience, to deal with the public. Soren was always wilder than me, bloodlust insatiable everywhere he went, and yet Oliver despised *my* escapades."

I hated to think of Soren ripping into throats all over, but he was a vampire, and so was Della. Despite Lily's altruistic view of vampires, I paused. "But you have that under control now?"

Della shifted her hands. Chains rattled. "I've been given a shot glass of blood a day for the better part of half a century. I'm talking to you levelly, without trying to tear out your throat under the thrall of the need to feed."

I swallowed thickly. "You do seem lucid."

Della's lips curled in dark amusement. "Blood association torture can do that to a person, but I wouldn't decline indulging. I hear there are blood bags these days. The convenience of a portable drink without the chase, the sweat, and body odor. Can you imagine? I wonder what other tasty advances I've missed out on. You have to tell me about Oli. What's he up to these days?"

"Oliver is married. Currently globetrotting with his bride. I haven't met either of them, though."

Della beamed. "Good for him. I'm glad someone finally liberated that stick from his well-groomed ass."

I laughed. Giving her happy information about her family was rewarding for me, too. "What do you mean by a stick?"

"He turned us, and carried the guilt for it. He hated himself for the longest time, wore suits to hide the monster he believed he was and obsessed over making money to appear...I don't know, like a gentleman or something."

That was deeper than I thought she'd go. This woman suffered so much.

"What about Sadie?" she asked.

But that was where the news ended. "I don't know anything about Sadie. I'm sorry."

"Is Evangeline still here? Or what about Stacey? I haven't heard from them in a while."

"You're the only person I've met behind these white doors."

Della sagged against her chains. "It's been quiet lately. Either the experiments finally killed them or they somehow escaped...and left me behind. I don't blame them."

"Why do you say that?"

"You're the only person I've met who's willing to help me."

"Can I ask how you ended up here?"

"I was being chased—hunted by an elf, really. You've heard of those?" I nodded. "I made a mistake in believing there was only one hunter that night. While I'd dodged the elf, I was caught by a vampire—one of Newt's handful of puppets. At first I thought he was helping me, but by the time I figured it out, I only got a few swings in. After all these years, I guess I should be grateful. If not for imprisonment and torture, I would've been killed by an elf. Make sure that ends up in the monograph."

I softly chuckled. Della was a fighter, who was honest and direct. A strong woman, who had family out there waiting for her to come home. A survivor who, despite decades of captivity and torture, still held onto hope of a life worth living. I admired her tenacity, but I could never be like her.

She deserved more than a few edited sentences in a book. "I'm not giving up on freeing you."

Della eagerly looked at me. "What's the plan this time?"

I climbed to my feet. "I'm bringing help."

Soren

I was beginning to wear the finish off the stool, so I'd returned to the B&B and embraced my bump-on-a-log status. Now I could avoid all the unwanted advances—it really did get old after a while. And man could only take so much of his hope ripped from his chest until he became...a bump currently occupying a leather log. I swirled my drink, which I realize now wasn't mixed nearly strong enough, and tried to focus on the drama in front of me.

My phone rang. I casually lifted it, hoping someone thought I was in the market for an extended warranty. I might manage to argue enough to distract me from the crushing regret consuming my waking thoughts. When I checked the ID, my brows lifted. "Hey, back from the dead?"

"Soren, what is going on back there?" my brother asked, worry in his tone.

I sipped from my drink, making sure he could hear the slurp. "Not much. Custody battle over the baby, you know, the usual."

"Custody...*what*?"

Oliver still had that stick up his ass, despite traveling the world for months with his new bride. "Remember that thing called TV? I'm not sure if you remember what yours looked like, but you won't recognize it now. I upgraded, and now I'm missing the custody arguments."

"I got a credit alert. Did you spend a vast sum of money lately?"

"Yep," I answered and smiled. I was finally enjoying myself, but I didn't think it would last.

"You didn't spend that much on a TV? Please tell me you didn't actually buy hookers and blow." There was that condescending tone I missed so much.

"More blow, less hookers, but you're not far off. Speaking of which, I've got a lady waiting for me, so make this quick before Nicole wakes up. She doesn't like hearing me."

"That's gross, Soren."

I chuckled to myself. My brother, so damned gullible. "I bought a business. You might actually like it."

"A business?" I could hear the shock in his voice. "I hope it wasn't something successful, because now it's going to fold."

I expected that sentiment, but I couldn't help the sting burning through my chest. "It's doing just fine."

"For now. I hope you didn't waste all that money on some fleeting whim."

"You wouldn't notice if I did."

"I did notice, hence my call."

"A credit alert doesn't count. You literally wouldn't have noticed the change in numbers otherwise."

Silence. I liked being right. I smiled smugly to myself and sipped.

"What business did you buy?"

"Do you care?" I shot back.

"Enough to ask."

"Fully Loaded." I hoped owning his favorite bar would give me authority over him in some small way.

"Don't screw it up."

"Thanks for your amazing support, as always," I said dryly. "Not that I mind your absence, but are you planning on showing up someday? I want to make sure all the hookers are gone when you get back, so all the pearl-clutchers can be spared their mock offense."

"Look, I appreciate what you've done for me, and I'm glad you found something of interest. A heads-up would've been nice. I had a card declined."

I snorted. Sucks, didn't it? "I'll keep that in mind."

Oliver hung up, and I shut my phone off and tossed it onto the cushion. My niece was disappointed in me. Indie rejected me, and now Oliver gave me the usual big brother paddling. The vacuum started up again, but I couldn't handle another pep talk. I dipped away for a shower.

14
Lion's Den

Indie

I NEEDED TO FIND Soren, and I was far more nervous than I should've been. As a witch, Lily could defend herself against whatever vampire family members she was trying to save, but I was a defenseless human who could not, under any circumstances, risk a bite. I would be remiss to ignore my changed self-preservation. I broke off a sprig of vervain from Cora's dried bouquet.

With a deep exhale, I replied to Soren's last demanding text, *'I need to speak with you.'* I expected an instant and enthusiastic response, but instead, I waited and waited. Swallowing back my nerves, I dialed the number, but my call went straight to voicemail. That wouldn't do at all.

I turned to my roommate, who was unrolling her curlers in the bathroom mirror with the door open. "Cora, do you know where your boss lives? I need to talk to him, but he's not answering."

Cora grinned at me. "Oh, honey. For you, I wish I did. I hope you're getting some of that ass tonight."

I couldn't stop my cheeks from blushing. "Any ideas who might know?"

Cora dropped each cylinder into a dish as she worked from front to back. "When I met you, Soren mentioned Allison Kincaid, my old coworker. She might know. I have her number."

I had it too, but I didn't share any information unless needed. I had been deliberately ignoring Allison, who I didn't need anymore...until now. Cora scrolled through her cell phone and read off the digits.

"Thanks, Cora."

"Anything to help a woman out. I hope you have a fabulous time."

My unwitting roommate was great, and I smiled before typing out a text to the same number already saved in my contacts. *I'm looking for Soren Rockwell. Do you know where he lives?'*

The reply was quick. *'What's the status on a witch?'*

I should've expected the question. I couldn't tell her I no longer needed her services. That would lead to a string of further questions I wasn't comfortable answering. *'I found one but need to work my way up to it. I'll keep you posted.'*

'Try the bed-and-breakfast on Riverside. You didn't hear it from me.'

'*Thank you.*' Clearly, the two of them weren't friends, but I was grateful for the help.

Wearing a floral sundress and coordinating wedges approved by Cora, I pulled to the curb in front of the address in my beat-up older sedan. I deliberately kept my mouth from dropping open as I took a moment to marvel at the luxuriousness of it—specifically, the thick scrolling columns and the bright balcony overlooking the Menominee River across the street. I bet the place had over half a dozen bedrooms.

Why would a vampire who owned a bar crash at a short-term residence? It was a logical assumption that he owned this establishment, too. Vampires with lifetimes of experience worked smarter, not harder, and that explained why he was rich in the first place. Even his suit had been impressive, although his tailor needed a new measuring tape.

Soren likely had several income-earning properties to bounce between. I couldn't imagine such a lifestyle. I'd never stay in any place long enough to own one, and the necessary low profile meant I couldn't afford the exposure of living out of a hotel. So, car it was. Having a piece of the world waiting to wrap you in warmth, safety, and privacy—reliable and comfortable—that was something I could never have.

My standards were far lower than Soren's, obviously. I'd been raised in a castle, but that had been built for strategic defense, not comfort. The walls were cold stone, the floors musty and hard, and the tapestries hanging from the tall ceilings had been inadequate for warmth. But most of all, the pile of stones felt like a prison. This place, which clearly hadn't been built with a thought of war, felt like what a castle should've been: cozy warmth, comfort, and luxury.

I climbed the concrete steps to the fancy bed-and-breakfast, feeling too far out of my league. From the outside, it didn't look any different from a fancy human's home. But like elves and witches, vampires came from all different backgrounds. Soren had been flirtatious at the bar, in public, with an employee right beside us. But in private, what was Soren really like? I squeezed the sprig of vervain in my dress pocket. I had to do this for Della.

My father would roll over in his grave if he could see me now, walking into a vampire's den to help another vampire. The possibility of spiting him put a spring in my step. I knocked and waited, and I knocked again. This was a bed-and-breakfast, a public venue according to the sign in the front yard, so I tried the doorknob. It wasn't locked. I stepped inside to peals of laughter and the roaring of a vacuum. An elderly woman cleaned the floor while Soren sat on the couch, feet resting on the edge of the coffee table, laughing at the TV screen. It was a ridiculously huge screen, too. I recognized the old woman as Nicole. Why had he wanted a fake date to impress the maid?

The vacuum cut out, and Nicole looked right at me. Not knowing what to expect, I froze as if her sight was based on movement. Slowly, a grin spread across her lips, and I stepped back, pointing at the door over my shoulder in a silent apology for the intrusion.

Soren continued laughing, and the sound was like a sweet harmony to my ears, smooth as silk, tempting as a forbidden sweet, and contagious. Despite my embarrassment, a smile pulled at my lips. He was not at all what I had been expecting.

The old woman gestured for me to come closer. "Stay. Please come in."

At Nicole's invitation, Soren's laughter cut off, and he twisted over the backrest of the couch. My heart leaped into my throat at his intense green gaze.

I waved awkwardly, and Nicole ducked out of the room, rolling the vacuum with a smile on her face.

Soren gripped a T-shirt in his hands and strolled toward me while shrugging into it, giving me a sneak peek of the body beneath. He was broad-shouldered and V-shaped, but there was a soft, cuddle-able layer over those strong muscles, and a dusting of dark hair over his pecs. He wasn't gym-ripped and hard, but I didn't doubt his strength for a moment. Dark jeans hung low on his sculpted hips, and he was barefoot. Floppy, damp hair hung loosely on his shoulders as if he's just gotten out of the shower, and he still wore the bright red ruby ring on his finger. He had looked ravishing in a suit at the party, but he was knee-buckling and heart-pounding while casually half-naked.

This was a vampire, I reminded myself. He was meant to be attractive, to lure his prey. Lily's humanizing spell must be making me susceptible to his magnetic pull. I gripped the sprig of vervain in my pocket as a reminder. I needed his help, not what he kept stored under those jeans. Although right now, I wanted both.

Soren stopped before me, his fresh soapy scent filling my nose. With a husky voice and a looming gaze, he said, "I never thought I'd see you again. But if I had known you were planning a visit, I would've dressed in something more appropriate."

There was nothing wrong with the fabric clinging to his curves. A second-best outfit sprang to mind. "Like what? A suit?"

"Socks." He wriggled his bare toes.

Despite myself, I laughed.

"Can I offer you coffee, tea, or...seltzer water?" Soren motioned toward the bar.

I was flattered he'd remembered my drink order, and I followed his gesture. The bar was crafted from dark lacquered wood, with rows of beverage choices in front of a mirrored wall. A potted fern rested at one end of the bar, a small, decorated trash can at the other, and an antique chandelier hung overhead. Thick, medium-tone wood beams traced around the trim and streaked along the ceiling. It was handcrafted and impressive. The interior of this place was just as fancy as the outside.

"No, thank you."

"A mimosa, then?"

"Isn't it a little early for that?" Of course not. He was the owner of a bar.

"Time is nothing but an arbitrary marker denoting the passing of the sun."

As an immortal, no truer words had ever been spoken. Days ran together, months blew by, and years ticked over like a clock, all of it with no end in sight. And after running for so long, time held no meaning.

"You okay?" Soren asked.

I gave him a smile to disguise what lurked beneath. "I'm fine."

Soren added with a steamy grin, "Are you here to repay the debt you owe?"

For a flash, I pictured his hands on me, swaying to the music, breath in my ear, scent filling my nose. As much as I wanted to test Nicole's boasting of his skills, now wasn't the time. "Maybe another night."

"So you're telling me there's a chance?" He grinned like a hopeful teen, and then I saw it. Della's dark, rumpled hair. Her gently sloping nose. The cupid's bow above her soft lips. She and Soren were siblings, and she was suffering right now. I couldn't be so selfish as to enjoy what Soren had to offer while thinking of her.

Soren's sweet flirting slipped away. His critical gaze swept over me, and his broad shoulders tensed. "Are you okay? Did something happen with Lily? I swear, if a witch hurt you…"

The protectiveness made my heart soar, and now I believed he was strong enough to make a difference. But there was a story there—one possibility relevant before returning to the lab. "What makes you think she hurt me?"

Soren raked a hand through his shaggy dark locks. "I don't like witches."

Something about Lily disturbed him. "Then why did you send me to her?"

"She's the only witch I tolerate, but I still don't fully trust her. She had been swayed to the dark side before."

That was how the elf had described their business in the lab. Had Lily returned to the dark side already, or had she never left? "Lily gave me what I needed, so thank you, and she's also the reason I'm here."

Soren paused, taking in my words, and the tension drifted away as the flirt returned. He closed the distance between us, his chest inches from mine. His lips were within capturing distance. My heart sped up. "Then I should thank her," he said darkly.

He couldn't be aware of what Lily was doing in Green Bay, because if he were, he wouldn't be friendly with her. I had to whisper the words to get them out. "Probably not after you hear this."

The flirting drifted away, and he invited me to join him on the couch. A character named Kyle threw a beer bottle. I didn't want to judge a person by what they watched, but from what I knew of vampires and what I'd seen of Soren, I was so damned confused. Who was this vampire?

15

A Purpose

Soren

I wanted the return of Indie's steamy gaze as she'd watched me put on a shirt. If she would've arrived not twenty minutes ago, she would've found me in a towel instead. And when that gaze returned, I wanted to sweep her off her feet and dance until the sun rose and chased away all the shadows. Then I wanted to spend all day in bed with her until she screamed my name over and over. I tried to keep my hands steady as I shut off the television to listen to her bad news.

I generally had very healthy self-esteem on any given day, but lately, the world seemed to want to crush me like a cockroach, and I couldn't figure out where I belonged or what I was supposed to do. Then, like a neon blinking sign from my favorite bar, the stunning blond returned for help, and whatever danger existed in the shadows, that was my calling.

"What did Lily do this time?" My mind conjured all kinds of stupid things, but I kept my anger in check. If my own family was hurting people, I was going to stop them, even if it was Lily.

Indie pressed her hands between her knees and glanced at the floor. This wasn't the self-assured woman brushing off unwanted advances at the bar. She was scared. She'd told me she was always on the run and great at acting. Perhaps whoever she'd been running from caught up to her, and the idea of anyone hurting her or scaring her made me want to rage.

Please be the elf, please be the elf, I silently pleaded, wanting an excuse to stake that asshole once and for all. "You can talk to me," I pressed. "What happened?"

"The winds change," she whispered and finally met my gaze, her big blue eyes giving nothing away. She appeared much older than her thirty-some years.

"I don't understand." And I wanted to. I clung to every word she spoke like a dying ember in a night-shrouded forest.

"It was something my family used to say whenever events out of our control shifted. We had to pivot and adapt to survive. I'd done it my whole life, but I've never done it like this."

I needed more. "Like what exactly?"

"Putting myself in direct danger."

I stiffened, ready to pounce and maul. I hadn't devoured a fresh meal in a while, and I could tip that statistical balance in my victims for the better. "What's going on?"

"Lily's help came with strings."

"You didn't like what she was after? You don't like something she's doing? Is she holding you hostage?" Sure would be reassuring for Indie to have a valid excuse for not returning to me.

"Slow down. She brought me to this lab in Green Bay—"

My heart leaped into my throat. That was the lab where I'd been under the mind control of a witch, who ordered me to do his dirty work. I wish I could burn the place down. "Don't you dare tell me there's fuckery in that lab again."

Indie's eyes widened. I hope I didn't scare her with my tone. "You know about it?"

"More intimately than I'd like."

She frowned. "Lily said it was our secret. That's what she wants help with."

As if I'd been walloped with a two-by-four, I fell back against the soft couch and pressed a hand to my forehead. Stacey hadn't been bluffing when she'd threatened me and Oliver with it. "We destroyed everything. That lab was supposed to have been shut down—abandoned. You're telling me it's still functioning?"

Indie paled and tilted her head, confused. Her reaction wasn't what I'd hoped for. "You'd destroyed *everything?* Well, the lab is very much still running. It actually looks well-funded, heavily stocked, perhaps a little understaffed, but I didn't think you'd want her research abandoned."

If she knew about the research, she knew my kind existed, and since she never once mentioned it, she didn't want me to know. My statements just told her I didn't want vampires killed by painful serum, which probably horrified her. I wanted to trust her, but experience told me not to underestimate anyone. I dropped my angry tone and smiled as friendly as I could, grateful I had vampire speed over a human's lumbering slow movements. "Of course I do. I was there when Newt died. Pierce helped, oddly enough. You met him that night—he was the blond."

Her confusion grew. "Pierce helped you? How is that possible?"

"Bribes can be very handy." My brother had offered the elf a chance to stake me if he helped rescue Daisy. Didn't take much for that featherbag to get off his lumbering ass. I wished I knew exactly what Lily knew, but it was hard to ask the right things without giving away what I shouldn't. I could compel it all away, but if she was chummy with witches, they may have protected her. Indie had said she needed protection.

Indie straightened her spine, and for a flash I saw pure hatred in her eyes, piquing my interest. "I made a promise to a woman there, but I cannot fulfill it by myself. I need your help to free her."

Indie specified a woman. Did she not know the prisoner was a vampire, or had that lab slid further into even more disgusting and despicable things? Since the two masterminds were killed and all their inventory destroyed, the lab likely beefed-up security. I hardly made it out alive last time, and I had an elf and my brother helping. Right now, I wouldn't ask that elf for a rope if I were drowning, and Oliver was busy traveling the world. Could I risk my bacon for this human?

I gazed into those beautiful blue eyes, and for a moment, I saw something deeper, something more, hidden behind her calm exterior. I wanted to chase away her fears, solve all her easy human problems, and I wanted to see her smile again. Above all else, I wanted her not to run away when she found out what I was. Most of that was a wish list. So, I'd settle for something minor but realistic for such a massive ask. "I'll help you rescue one of their test subjects if you give me that dance you owe me."

Indie blinked. "You'd wager a woman's life on a dance?"

I beamed at her, my flirtiest lopsided grin. "It's not as shallow as you make it sound. I think it's fair, sweetheart."

Indie's face became cold, and she rose and smoothed that sexy little dress of hers. "She was right about you. You're an ass."

My turn to blink. This prisoner knew me well enough to describe me accurately. I rose, blocking her path, stopping inches from her. She didn't back away. "Come again?"

Indie's heart thumped wildly, but she didn't give anything away. "You're using a woman's life as leverage for your own gain. I can't believe this."

I gazed into her eyes, willing—but not compelling—her to understand my side. "I'm asking so little of you in exchange for a massive risk to my life."

Her big blue eyes tried to read me, and her anger softened. "I tried to free her myself, but I couldn't. You're the only one I know around here that I thought I could trust, and when she named you, I had a misplaced confidence. I'll agree to your petty deal, but don't you think for a second I'm happy about it."

I leaned in just a little closer. Not quite whispering in her ear, but the heat pouring off me had to tell her just what I wanted her to know. The tease, the intensity, was only a tiny taste of what was to come if she'd give me that chance. "Having a little time with you is worth it to me, even if I don't make it out of there alive."

Indie's gaze returned, and the thumps were even wilder. Her cheeks blushed. There was something different about her. I couldn't quite put my finger on it, but I wanted to know everything about Indiara Niskatar. This amazing actress could say whatever she wanted, but the insides didn't lie. I couldn't help feeling a pinch of satisfaction in her response to me.

A lock of damp hair fell down over my forehead. Indie lifted her empty hand as if to brush it away, but she stopped herself. Her voice was husky. "Get my friend out of that lab, and I'll give you a dance and full night you'll never forget."

Her hand must've held an invisible stake that caused no pressure or pain. I must've died and gone to the Other Side. Lust clogged my throat...and elsewhere—fully loaded and ready for release.

16

A Sprinkle of Trust

Soren

I WANTED TO BRUSH a tantalizing lock of blond hair away from her beautiful, determined eyes, but she wouldn't appreciate my touch...yet. I'd never wanted someone more, and I'd never been denied so hard before. The lure of Indie was something magnetic—natural, smooth, and irresistible. The crazy surge of lust punching at my cock with Indie's earthy pine scent inches from my face sent me trembling to explode.

"Is something the matter?" Indie asked, focusing on my lips—so close, yet so far away. I reached for her shoulder, but she tilted away from my touch. Her hand slipped into her dress pocket.

I couldn't imagine my monstrous fangs penetrating that delicate skin of hers, or the subsequent paralyzing fear. But I wanted to know what she tasted like. Did a salty B travel through those veins or a far more velvety O-negative?

Perhaps my preference for A, but since I didn't see the spark of love in her eyes, she wouldn't be the best flavor. Not yet. The artery running along the side of her smooth throat called to me, urging me to settle this important debate, cure the curiosity nagging me.

At this moment, I could see the allure of the blood bond. I'd teased Oliver about it for decades, but now I understood the desire to exchange fluids until near-death, so both lovers flowed with the same life force. The urge to make Indie mine forever was almost overwhelming. But I couldn't get this human to allow my touch. She wouldn't accept a permanent, life-altering, immortal commitment to me.

"I need a drink," I said with gravel in my voice.

Because I wanted her trust more than anything, I wouldn't dare drink from her. I swiftly—but not vampire swiftly—moved over to the bar and poured myself a glass of wine. This time I abstained from mixing in a blood bag for obvious reasons.

Indie followed me over, both hands visible and empty. I drank down the glass and set about refilling. Any old bottle would suffice. Oliver wouldn't mind the price tag, and quality was not on my radar. I needed quantity or a high proof.

The edge eased. My mind cleared enough for me to focus, but I shifted my cock in my jeans while behind the bar. Speaking of...I couldn't go roaring into that place full-cocked. I needed to be prepared, so I'd get that full night with Indie.

Indie sat on the stool across from me, watching me refill my glass—third or fourth already.

"We need a plan, because for obvious reasons, I want to get back out of there." I flashed her a steamy gaze, and she blushed. "First, what kind of shape is your friend in? How long has she been there?"

"She guessed about forty years. She's banged up but stable, and I'd say quite lucid considering." Indie visibly startled, as if not wanting this information out. Either this friend of hers was going to join the bridge club with Nicole, or a magical being was locked up. Witch? Unlikely they'd harm their own. Elf? Possibly, and I would love to see it. The more I considered the possibilities, the less I was afraid to head back.

"And you trust her to be free? Experience tells me it's not a great idea." Everyone who'd sprung free from that lab had been...feral. Hell-bent on damage and destruction, and in the case of Evangeline, vengeance.

Indie contemplated for a few moments. "I trust her."

That was good enough for me. I gestured to offer her a drink again, but she waved it away. I had to ask, "Why are you so against having a drink? With me, it's free."

Indie tucked a short lock of blond hair behind her ear in a swooping motion. "The mimosa was good, I'll admit, but the time before—the time when I'd sworn off alcohol entirely—I'd accepted a few too many from a stranger. Since I'm a frequent solo traveler, I had no one to watch my back."

I didn't like where this story was headed already, but I listened, grip tightening on my glass—eh, Oliver's glass.

"The drunk assaulted me."

The empty glass shattered in my hand with a tinkling sound on the lacquered surface. Indie startled.

"I'm sorry. Let me get that." I swept up the shards with my bare hands and dumped them into a small trash can at the end of the bar. This time, I lowered myself onto the stool next to her, wanting to be a shield for her. The minor cuts healed instantly, and I brushed the streaks of blood on my dark jeans. Playfully, I said, "I need to remind Nicole to replace these old glasses before someone gets hurt. Please continue." So I could hunt down the asshole and knock him into next Tuesday, and then drain him dry. I liked my drinks shaken, not stirred.

Or into next Friday. My show aired new episodes on Tuesdays, and I didn't want to miss out and risk spoilers being posted online.

"Well, I broke his nose when I knocked him out. There was blood everywhere. I ran before the police were called. Ambulance came. Witnesses were everywhere. Cell phones recording. Cops asking around. And that's why I'd said I could handle myself."

I laughed. This gorgeous, stunning human woman managed that? "You didn't."

She smiled bashfully. "Out cold, and I had the bruises on my knuckles to prove it." Her smile slid away, and her gaze became distant. "I can't afford to be in that situation again."

Was that why she was afraid and on the run? Legal trouble? The urge to place my hand on hers was powerful, but I resisted. I understood not wanting to be touched without permission, and I could read between the hesitant lines.

"Indie, I would never place a hand on you unless you wanted me to. Please understand, as long as you're in my bar or next to me, no one else will, either. If anyone attempts anything or if you feel uncomfortable for any reason, you can call me, and I'll be there. I promise you're safe with me."

The flush up her throat and cheeks returned, and so did that steamy gaze I so yearned to explore. Her heart stampeded in her chest, and I shoved down my raging lust. I knew she wanted me, but something or someone held her back. That was the key—I had to hunt down and destroy whatever kept us apart. A fire roared through my chest—a strange feeling. It wasn't anger or frustration. It was—purpose.

"You have no idea how much that means to me," she said softly. A woman on the run, a self-declared excellent actress—how could I not understand she wanted to feel safe? Perhaps the previous men in her life were animals. Perhaps she was running from an ex. Indie deserved far better than that.

"If there's someone out there making you run, making you afraid, point me in the direction, and I'll fire."

Indie stared at me, not with lust but…a hint of sadness, maybe. "I think I could use that drink, but I want you to know I appreciate the offer, whether you meant it or not."

I rose and moved around the bar. "Seltzer water?"

Indie beamed, and I'd do anything to see that look on her face again. "Please and thank you. What else do we need to plan?"

I made up the drink for her as quickly as I could. Of course, I meant the offer. She didn't realize just how strong and persuasive I could be. The sooner Indie's friend got her freedom, the sooner my hands found Indie's hips. So, down to business. "Who's in charge in the lab?"

"Does it matter?" she asked, perplexed.

"I need to know who or what we're up against for the highest chance of success." I settled the drink in front of her on a coaster.

Indie eagerly sipped from the straw, and my chest swelled. I was getting through that thick, defensive exterior. "Lily said she's more like the staff manager. I don't know if that means she's in charge, but she said someone else is working behind the scenes to undermine her efforts."

Not surprising, but still interesting. Maybe someone to lean on if the situation called for it. "Any idea who?"

"Lily wasn't sure herself, but my personal opinion is it's the blond guy she was with that night you were…stabbed.

She'd called him the new guy, but he acted like he owned the place."

I bit back several swears. But then I realized my dumb luck. Nicole would be so proud that I had a valid excuse to stake the elf after all. "You're kidding. Tell me you're kidding."

"I'm sure it was Pierce, and I don't trust him."

That was a relief. I wouldn't wish an elf's fate on my worst enemy, who, ironically, was Pierce himself. "Your instincts are spot on. He'll help anyone if it benefits him, but watch your back—he's a conniving sewer rat."

"Because he doesn't mind...stabbing...a person in the back," Indie finished for me with a sarcastic smile.

I caught her pauses around the word 'stab', when the correct term for what had happened to me was 'staked'. Considering she worked in a lab crawling with a witch, an elf, and untold vampires, she had to know the right word. She still didn't want me to know she knew about my kind.

Now I wasn't so sure about her acting skills. What else was she hiding from me? Why didn't she want me to touch her at all? I squinted at Indie, trying to find the answer behind her beautiful eyes. "Since you were looking for a witch, I surmise you aren't one."

"I'm not." Indie's gaze fell as if this was uncomfortable territory, but I was sticking my neck out for her. The least she could do was tell me what she was.

"Anyone with a keen sense of smell would've picked up the scent of what's inside the fridge. You didn't react to my cuts either. But most tellingly, you walked through that door without an invitation. My very-much human niece is on the deed."

Indie squirmed as she chose her words carefully. "I'm not a vampire."

The prisoners were pumped full of vervain to slow the healing process and prevent them from compelling their captors into freeing them. So Indie had to be acting of her own volition, but why? A human *wanting* to free a vampire? Indie had no idea just how dangerous this all was. "What does the woman have over you? How is she making you help her?"

Indie scowled. "I want to help her."

Interesting. "So you know how to defend yourself against a vampire."

She tipped her chin up. "If you're going to interrogate me instead of help, point me in the direction of Sadie, and I'll be on my way." Indie rose from her seat with the same closed-off features as when she'd strutted out of my bar after reluctantly agreeing to my fake date. I was going to lose her soon.

But I couldn't let that name go. "Why are you looking for Sadie?"

Indie crossed her arms over her chest, and I met her, chest to chest, once again so close, but now further than ever. "Sadie was the other name given, but since I knew where to find you, I chose you first. Clearly, this is going nowhere, so tell me where to find Sadie, and maybe she'll help...without deals."

Indie didn't look for my help because she wanted me. Pierce was involved, so this whole ruse could be a trap for me. And yeah, I wouldn't put it past the elf to set Indie on this path, the traitorous, devious featherbag. "Why would you think I know where a 'Sadie' is? Who is this friend of yours? Did Pierce put you up to this?"

Indie tipped her chin up. "Her name is Della Rockwell."

I stared, blinking a few times before the name registered through my thick skull. I stepped back and fell onto the stool I'd just vacated. "You're sure the woman—the test subject—is Della Rockwell?"

Indie didn't budge. "You're wasting time. Please tell me where Sadie is."

I pressed a hand against my forehead. I'd been right there, right on the other side of the door. When Oliver and I raided the vials, I should've stuck my nose deeper into Newt's business. I should've freed all the prisoners before I'd fled—even if they would've been feral, blood-lusting fiends who needed to be staked, anyway. After all these years, I could've had my sister by my side. My sister was *alive*. Well, undead. Same thing, sort of. I couldn't believe the good news.

Or this was all a low-brow, down-dirty, despicable trap, which was entirely in the realm of Pierce Evansson. So if Indie wanted Sadie's help instead, I'd gladly send her. "Fine.

You'll find Sadie a few paces northwest of the hunter's cabin in Peshtigo off Highway 41."

"I'm not that familiar with the area. Do you have an address?"

"I don't think it has one. It's an unmarked cemetery. She's buried between my mother and Oliver, but clearly, his grave is empty."

Indie flinched. "Sadie's gone?"

"Pierce's father killed her forty years ago—you know, that elf lurking around the lab—the sewer rat. That's the one." My tone was knife-sharp. Yeah, I still held a grudge, but at least Oliver had avenged her.

"You're certain she's dead?" Indie asked, horrified.

"I saw her desiccated body myself, and I buried her with my own hands—and a shovel. We *assumed* Della had perished, but yes, I'm certain Sadie is gone."

The coldness and irritation drifted away, and Indie reached out toward my chest with an unusual empathy, a warmth yearning for connection. But she stopped. I fought myself from moving into her touch. I'd made her a promise, and I would respect it.

Indie's hands folded back over her chest as if hugging herself. "I'm sorry. I didn't know. Della doesn't know," she said softly.

Indie was being genuine. The elf hadn't used her as bait to trap me, and I'd do whatever I needed to get my sister out of there. Oh, and the full night with Indie, in addition to the sexy dance—well, my luck was just popping. "Della needs to be freed. I've done this before, and since your choice is between me and me, I'm your best chance at pulling this off. But you have to be my partner in this. We have to work as a team and trust each other. So the question is, can you handle me?" I slathered the innuendo right there on the surface for her to lap up deliciously or spray away with a metaphorical hose.

And I was already wet, waiting for the offer to be licked clean.

Indie gave me a sly smile. "I guess you're better than nothing."

I grinned, mocking offense. "Ouch, seriously. That hurt."

"You'll live."

"Technically..." I trailed off. I wanted to continue this playfulness, but knowing a person was a dangerous predator was far different from accepting it.

"You're already dead," Indie said with a flick of humor.

"You knew," I said breathlessly.

Knowing what I was, yet still wanting my help, and not shrieking and running away. Not terrified. Not horrified. A strange lightness lifted me. She was my partner in rescuing my sister, a vampire most deemed unworthy of living not so long ago, and Indie had made her a friend. A current surged through me, and now, more than ever, I wanted Indie, this kindhearted human, willing to stick out her neck for a vampire. When I said I protect her from some bumbling, handsy drunk, I'd meant it. And when I said she'd be safe with me...well, I'd burn the world to keep her safe. But right now I wanted the touch and feel of her lips, her hands on me. My cock hardened and throbbed.

"Now that the big secret is free between us..." I trailed off, wondering where Indie would take that statement.

"We can make a realistic plan," Indie said.

Right. Yanking on the e-break, I tried to clear the webs of lust clogging my...upper head this time. I focused. First Della, then Indie. I was going scorched earth to save my sister. So I could have Indie in my arms.

17

Too Tempting

Indie

"Now that you know," Soren said with heat still radiating from his gaze, "I'm going to have a vampire-approved drink, if you don't mind."

Soren, with his damp messy locks, clinging T-shirt, and dark jeans hung alluringly low, stood so close to me I could feel unexpected heat rolling off his body. How could a vampire be warm? How could a vampire walk in daylight? Soren broke the known rules, and I hadn't meant to let him discover I knew. I'd been afraid he'd discover his compulsion hadn't worked, and the string of questions would ultimately lead him back onto the dangerous path of discovering what I was.

He didn't even ask how I knew. With my identity once again behind a precarious curtain, heat surged through my body, culminating in a delicious throb down low. That flirty grin only made it worse. And he could indeed hear my racing heart, like now, and my cheeks flushed hot, but...I didn't mind. He might've given up tracking me down, but he still cared enough to help me. And he clearly still wanted me.

Soren and his family had a dark past, but that was none of my business. What mattered was that he was gentle and thoughtful, and even better, so respectful of my body. And when he'd promised to keep me safe—the one thing I wanted most in the world, and as a *vampire* I believed he was capable of giving it—I'd nearly jumped his immortal, blood-drinking bones.

This was torture of another kind. I couldn't trust a touch, a scratch, a kiss, or a bite. If Soren found out what I was... No one could resist the value I posed to my enemy, certainly not a vampire who liked his luxury.

Despite my body screaming for him, he'd have to change his mind on both the luxury he was accustomed to, but also his clear hatred of my kind. He'd have to be more selfless and open-minded than anyone else in history.

More than my family.

And miles more than the rival elf's family.

Experience told me what I hoped for was far rarer than Lily's original vampire-creating spell, lost to the millennia and weathering of time, that she somehow believed I could find and translate, and she could reverse. But I so wanted to believe...

...that his vampire-approved drink wasn't going to shatter my hopes. I gripped the sprig of vervain in my pocket. If I lost my identity, it wasn't only my life on the line. I wouldn't be able to save Della.

Soren hovered close, so close my heart pounded, but his gaze stayed on mine. "I don't know how much you know about my kind, but you don't have to worry about me. I've been around for a long time, and my reputation precedes me. But I can assure you I have full control over my needs—all of them."

The huskiness in his voice, the deep tone of seduction, made my breaths quicken, and the throbbing continued, testing my ability to resist. But those beautiful green eyes of his were just as radiant as a field of fresh-cut lawn.

"When I'd said, as long as you stay by my side, no one will hurt you, I meant it. No one will touch a hair on your head if you don't want it. And when I'd said, I promise you're safe with me, I can assure you I won't ever hurt you, or even touch you, if you don't want it. You are completely safe with me."

I moved my hand out of my pocket, releasing the sprig of vervain.

That devious grin returned. "But no one else is..."

I stared at him, dumbstruck. Soren didn't know the real me, but he vowed to protect me as long as I'd let him. Soren was leaps and bounds above every man I'd ever met—human, vampire, or elf. "I don't mind if you need a special drink. I'd rather you're not hungry."

Soren's crooked grin sent my heart pounding again. He moved around the bar, and the vacuum he left pulled the air from my lungs. I settled myself on a bar stool and exhaled deeply.

Soren ducked low and tore into a blood bag. He mixed it with red wine in a tall glass, and the muscular arms shifting beneath the tight fabric mesmerized me. He asked, "Is the side access door at PDI still locked?"

Dragging my gaze away from the broad-shouldered and barefooted sexy vampire before me, I reluctantly returned to business. I recalled the tour Lily had given me. "It's been bricked over since the last security breach."

"That's got to be a fire code violation or something." Soren chugged down the glass and immediately refilled it. He'd been very hungry since I'd arrived, but still he remained in control of his actions and lucidity—as he'd claimed.

"They torture vampires in holding cells. The only safety they care about is for their research." I gazed upon the floppy dark hair falling over stunning green eyes. This charming vampire adored the person he thought I was. The urge to tell him, to let him in, was powerful.

Soren sighed. "The only rule they follow—keep the supernatural hidden world hidden at all costs. Never knew where the precedent started, but just that lab existing means they take great liberties with it."

I wanted to tell him the heartbreaking story, but like the legend of the rule, I had to remain a mystery. "The side access door is out. Between the front door and the basement, there are several security checkpoints. We'll need tools to get through, but the more we carry, the more we slow down."

Soren finished off his next blood-wine mix. He licked those soft lips. "Don't you have an employee badge?"

"When the lab is empty—after business hours—it shuts off. Guess they don't want people meddling around unsupervised."

Soren tossed the empty blood bag into the trash with a mischievous grin. "I find the art of meddling to be delightful. Bring it with you, but we don't need tools. I can tear doors off hinges."

I raised a skeptical eyebrow. "Even secured doors with air locks?"

Soren tilted his head in amusement. How much was simple fact and how much was boasting? If he was trying to impress me, he didn't need to. My gaze shifted to his mouth. I wanted to kiss his skin. I wanted to feel the tickle of his groomed whiskers against my face. *A mar of the flesh shall break the seal.*

Why couldn't I have had my ring refueled instead? Then I could've done whatever I wanted—to him—without concern.

"I know plenty of people who'd like the chance to stake me. Many of them probably deserve it. So, I keep myself as close to full-strength as I can. With a little fresh topping-off, no doors could keep me out." Soren tore into another blood bag, but this time, he poured it straight. He slammed down most of the glassful and flinched, as if the bag had gone sour.

His expression worried me. "What's wrong?"

He coughed and wiped his lower lip. "I prefer Hot-N-Ready over Banquet."

Translating that out of vampire-speak, I said, "A meal walking and talking instead of prepared and refrigerated?"

"You *have* done your research." Soren sent me a hungry gaze, but it wasn't for food. As he strolled around the bar and closed the distance between us, heat bloomed through my chest. So close once again, and that lopsided grin returned as if he knew how badly he teased me. My mind drifted down low to the throb, pleading to be satisfied. Despite being a gentleman, he probably *wanted* to eat me...at both sensitive ends of my body. I was too hot. I needed a fan or ice—a cold shower. Picturing us in the shower wasn't helping...

I slapped my forehead in frustration, sharply scattering those distracting thoughts. I believed the effort was temporary, if entirely futile, but it brought a much-needed minor relief. My breath released unevenly.

"Don't hurt yourself." Soren chuckled and moved back around the bar. He lowered himself onto a stool next to me.

I froze. Could I mar my own flesh and break the seal by accident? That was a horrifying thought, and now I needed to be even more careful. I swigged down some seltzer water, and the bubbles tickled my nose—a much-needed distraction. "Tearing down the doors will trigger security."

"I'll compel anyone we come across. Unless…" Soren trailed off. "If Pierce is mucking about down there, are the guards human, or did he convince Lily to fill the building with elves?" Soren paused at the thought, and I stiffened—not only worried he'd realized his compulsion hadn't worked on me, but that the idea was a nightmarish possibility. "I assume you're familiar with elves?"

I exhaled. Lily had assured me that the lab was completely safe for me, and she'd only seemed stressed when Pierce had shown up. "I think the guards are human."

"If they don't volunteer their wings and ears, you wouldn't see them. I'll bring along my blade in case any featherbags get the jump on us."

"Featherbags?" I repeated. I couldn't tell whether the term was derogatory or affectionate.

Soren chuckled. "By volume, elves are more feathers than brains." I couldn't refute that. "If you saw one, you'd understand. So that leaves clothing."

As a lifelong avoider of sticky situations, I'd never attempted a heist of a medical research facility before, but the more Soren and I planned, the less afraid I was. In the face of great personal risk, he made me feel…safe. "Are we trying for invisibility—camo or black—or should we aim for incognito, like scrubs or white coats?"

Soren's steamy gaze caressed me from my short hair, down my chest, along my legs, and to my feet and back. I wanted him to use his hands instead. I crossed my legs, trying to ease the throbbing, but it wasn't helping. "Personally, I think you'd look best with nothing."

Another flush of heat rushed through me. For the first time in my life, I enjoyed the company of a vampire.

I never would've guessed.

18
Play Nice

Indie

I was not going naked, no matter how much Soren believed it would 'work for him'. Anxiously, I undressed and redressed, struggling to find something proper—a mix of confidence, authority, and...sexy—but not too far from my normal. The combination would've been much easier had we been crashing a party in a club. A medical lab was far less...tantalizing.

I finally settled on a black sleeveless blouse and black jeans, which would cover suspicious stains while still being comfortable enough to run. I smeared a dollop of texturizer in my palm and worked it through my short blond waves.

"Indie? What's up with you?" Cora asked, startling me.

Soren and I needed enough time, enough quiet, and plenty of darkness to pull off our plan to break Della free. After hours was as good as we were going to get, which meant I had to go to work today like nothing was wrong.

Being on the run, I'd had no issue with disappearing the moment things became thick, but now I was staying and facing it directly—as a human, no less. Walking into that lab today, knowing I planned to upend it, made me tremble with nerves, but at least I could update Della on the plan and reassure her the torture was almost over.

I was committed to freeing Della, and I had a vampire by my side, willing to return to the house of horrors to rescue his sister. His dedication despite the risk earned him the highest esteem in my book. I wished I had a family who loved me for who I was, not what I could do for them. In a twisted way, I was almost jealous of Della.

"What do you mean?" I asked and washed the extra texturizer off my hands.

Cora leaned against the bathroom doorframe, wearing dark slacks and a loud blouse for her shift tonight at the bar. Long black curls were pulled back into a wild bun. "I saw you with a gorgeous man in the back room during the party. Are you going to see him again?"

Her not using his name had me confused. "I saw him last night."

Cora beamed and pressed her hands together. "You did? Ah, ha! I knew it. I knew it was only a matter of time. You can bring him around, honey. Anytime you want more privacy, just let me know, and I'll disappear."

Although I trusted Soren not to drain me dry, losing my human protection was a horrifying thought. "No, please don't disappear on me."

"Tell me about him." Cora grinned.

A sexy, six-foot vampire who loved television shows, word puzzles, and red wine. Who had eyes like glinting emeralds, wavy hair calling my fingers, and thick arms pleading to hoist me into the air and pleasure me. He was a vampire of unknown age and untested strength. And he either surged with courage or was downright suicidal in his loyalty to his sister.

Cora could question my sanity at how preposterous it sounded, but since she had a vervain bouquet on her dresser, I couldn't take the chance. I needed my human shield to stay put. "He's—"

"Tall, blond, and deliciously muscular? Like he could bench-press a car?" Cora interrupted, placing a hand on her curvy hips.

That didn't describe Soren at all. Who did she have in mind here? "Quite the opposite. Dark messy hair, bright green eyes, and a smooth body wrapped with lean muscle."

Cora frowned. "Not my type."

"Then maybe I'll bring him around after all," I said lightly.

My roommate's smile returned. "That's a great idea. I met a delicious hunk of man meat, too. We should do a double date tonight. I think you'd like to meet him."

Despite the inescapable current between us, Soren and I weren't anything beyond a running promise of a good time, and I wasn't interested in meeting my roommate's date. I wanted to leave her life unaffected. Why would I want to further entangle myself? "I already have plans."

"You got a date with Tall, Dark, and Handsome?"

A non-romantic one, unfortunately. "A work thing. I have to stay late."

"On a Friday night? Girl, you got that kind of boss? They better pay you overtime. What a waste of a perfectly good Friday. Such a shame." Cora shook her head.

The way she ignored Soren entirely made me curious. "What about your boss?"

Cora pressed her lips together and stared blankly, as if trying to remember who he was. "What about my boss?"

Someone tampered with her memory. The question was...why? "Nothing. Forget it."

Cora shrugged and strolled away. I peeked into her bedroom. The bouquet of vervain was still there, but she didn't seem to know anything about the hidden supernatural world. She was being used.

By someone other than me.

I'd be out of her life soon enough. Just a quick jail spring, and then it was me, my trusty car, and the sunset on the horizon once again. I looked at myself in the mirror over her dresser. That plan had always served me well. Thinking of the road moving under my wheels had been freeing, relaxing, and somehow, at the same time, exciting—because it meant I was safe. But now, the idea of putting pedal to the metal twisted my insides, as if an invisible force dragged part of me away by the trailer hitch, leaving behind a nothingness inside—a hollow that somehow still weighed so much.

Indie

Lily didn't accompany me today, leaving me with my car to use for the getaway later. I should've unloaded a few of my boxes into Cora's tiny house so I'd have room for Della, but I was so nervous, I hadn't thought of it. She could ride in Soren's car.

Assuming he didn't ride a motorcycle...I should've asked.

Too late now. Time to head inside for a nerve-wracking day. I needed to use my authority posture to be invisible, while still memorizing every nuance on my way to the underground lab. With squared shoulders, I entered the four-story building sweeping with activity. Right away that confidence was difficult to maintain. I avoided eye contact, as if looking at me gave away my traitorous plan.

With shaking hands, I swiped my badge at each stop and scoped out all the obstacles—who stood sentry and where? What kind of access panel locked each door? Which turn down the corridors, left or right? Without pressure, that type of detail wasn't needed or was easily navigated, but when fleeing, preparation made all the difference.

When I reached the lab, I wanted to turn around and repeat the process, but a security guard strolling the hallway nodded at me. Wanting to avoid him and his suspicion, I ducked into the lab. A hand clamped on my shoulder, and I nearly jumped out of my skin. The masculine chuckle in my ear turned my blood cold. I shifted out of his touch and turned to find Pierce with a half-smile, attempting to be friendly.

I stifled a scream, and I trembled harder, fighting the urge to run. I watched him for a beat, waiting to see if he'd inadvertently broken the seal, but he only gazed at me with ordinary, if obnoxious, interest. "Please don't touch me."

The elf raised his hands in surrender. "I didn't mean to scare you, but I get it. This place can be intense. How are things going for you so far?"

The bulky elf wore a short-sleeve band T-shirt that I'd never heard of, and cargo shorts, like an inappropriately dressed visitor and not someone who pulled strings around here. His blond hair was gelled back, and his brown, scrutinizing eyes bored into me. Knowing I was immune to a touch didn't help relieve the itch to get away from him.

"So far, so good," I said generically.

"What does Lily have you do with all those books?" His intense gaze wouldn't leave, but I kept alert for the green of compulsion—in case I needed to act.

I figured a piece of the truth was harmless enough. "I'm helping her find a spell."

Pierce considered, but the pause told me he was suspicious. "That's all?"

"A personal favor to her, yes." I needed to change the subject before that statement delved into territory I wasn't sure he knew about. Lily had said she wanted the specifics kept quiet. Even though Pierce was her friend, with her discomfort I assumed she'd used that word quite loosely. Soren had called him a conniving sewer rat, as if I needed any more reasons to avoid him. So, I changed the subject. "How's the serum coming along?"

Pierce's thick brows rose, and then I realized maybe I wasn't supposed to know. He grinned and said, "Same as you, so far, so good. Maybe we have more careful staff this time around, but we haven't lost a vamp lately. Not sure if that's good news or bad." He chuckled.

That meant their prisoners were surviving the torture, but since Pierce hated the vampires, the bad news had to be that the serum wasn't viable yet. Which meant I wasn't too late. I smiled politely.

Pierce added, "We need more people on our team, working together to speed this along. I'm glad you're here, Indie. Very glad."

A shiver ran down my spine, and I shifted my posture to hide it. "Thank you."

He moved his hand, and I tracked it with alarm. He pressed a palm against the bare wall, displaying broad biceps and...blocking my path. "If it's not too forward of me, I'd like to talk to you more about our plans here, in private."

I didn't want to be anywhere alone with the elf. Ever. "That's not necessary. I'm willing to do my job and not ask questions."

He leaned closer. The trembling returned in full force. "See, that's the thing. I'm a great cook." Not following, I frowned. "I want to fix you dinner at my place, where we can discuss all of my plans for this place. It would be my pleasure. What do you say?"

I'd rather not give the elf any pleasure at all. "Wasn't Lily your date at the Fully Loaded party?"

Pierce didn't react at all, as if she ultimately meant nothing. "Oh, that? We're strictly friends. Completely platonic. You have no worries there."

The only worry I had was for Lily's safety.

"With that settled, what time can I pick you up tonight? I can prepare dinner whenever works for you." Pierce flashed me a grin. But so far, he hadn't attempted to compel me.

"I'm sorry, but I'm busy," I said dismissively.

"If it makes you more comfortable, I can cook and divulge at your place. Cora won't mind the intrusion. I'm sure she'd want to bring her own date and make a party of it," he pressed.

The persistence would be commendable, except a male elf only wanted one thing. I couldn't give Pierce the same excuse I'd given Cora. He could easily confirm with Lily whether I was expected to stay late tonight. And I had a sinking sensation Cora's double date idea hadn't been her own. "I recall there's a phrase regarding dipping pens in company ink. I think it's wise to follow such a proven adage."

The joyous sparkle in his eye told me I'd given him a challenge. Just great. Pierce's arm fell, releasing me. "I get it, but the offer remains open."

With my stomach in knots, I swept past the predator in disguise, ducked around stock boxes, red plastic order containers, and workers zigzagging around. When I reached my office, I rushed inside and pressed my back against the flimsy door, as if the hollow wood were a shield.

Since I had a full workday before our plan began, and I needed to wait until the right opportunity to slip into Della's cell, I pulled out a chair. I picked up a different grimoire, the next in line, and began the arduous skimming process. As my cloth-gloved finger slid along the page, searching for relevant words or phrases in the variety of languages I'd encountered, my focus fell. Every rustle of paper, every clink of glass vials and test tubes, every click of nearby equipment buttons, sent me bracing for the scream.

But it didn't come yet. Della was still alive. She had to be. I couldn't be too late.

I turned the page and found plenty of protection spells against bad spirits, fertility spells for harvest and livestock, and health spells for ailments. My eyes glazed over the irrelevant runes, wanting to focus on what really mattered: an imprisoned woman in peril. A smile lifted my lips when I pictured Soren bursting down the door like a caped crusader. Sure, the woman was his sister, but he'd agreed before he knew who the victim was. He was a courageous soul, willing to risk his own life for others.

I respected that.

If he showed up.

A scream tore through the lab, and my hand jerked, tearing the page. I frowned at the damage and skimmed over what I'd destroyed—a spell to treat diphtheria, which wouldn't work, anyway. Antibiotics were readily available now, and there was no excuse to skip the vaccine. Determining no real harm had been done, I closed the book.

That scream was Della's, and I couldn't wait any longer. I had to see her now.

19
Trapped

Indie

I stuck my head out of my office to check if the path was clear. Workers moved about, heavily focused. They'd probably been compelled to do the work and stay quiet about it. I dug in my pocket and pulled out a bill. Since I had no idea if there was a vending machine at all, it was the perfect cover.

I casually moved across the processing area to the row of plain, unmarked doors. I spun to face the nearest counter and used my peripheral vision to check for witnesses, but no one paid me any attention.

I slipped inside. The room was bright for a change, and a worker, a human male with neatly trimmed hair and bold glasses, stood near Della. He wore an apron, spritzed with blood, over a white lab coat, and he held an enormous syringe filled with dark red blood. The gauge of that needle made me squirm, and Della's condition enraged me.

I tucked the bill away.

Della panted in pain, and as her gaze locked on me, the stuffy worker turned, catching me. I wanted to knock the human against the wall and berate him for lacking such empathy natural to humans. Instead, I froze.

Surprisingly, Stuffy wasn't alarmed at all. "Finally. I have processing to get done." He lifted his supply tray and thrust it into my arms. Impatient eyes swept me up and down. "You look new. When you're done filling all of these, leave them on the counter. Black isn't going to stop the blood from soaking in. There are aprons in the drawer outside the door. I can get you one."

I gave him an appreciative smile. "That won't be necessary. This is a special waterproof polyester. Blood wipes right off."

The worker shrugged and took off his apron as he left. The door closed behind him, and I exhaled.

Della still wore the same torn hospital gown, and her dark hair was still disheveled. I had a feeling the prisoners didn't get to bathe or change clothing often. Or at all.

"Now this is a curveball I should've seen coming." Her voice was gravel from thirst or from what Stuffy had done. I didn't know which, but either was deplorable.

I looked at the tray in my hands with guilt and set it on the floor. "I'm not here to hurt you. How are you holding up?" I asked her gently.

"Same old, same old." Della swung her arms in demonstration, and the chains rattled. "For a second, I thought you had a change of heart."

Since Della's tale of vampires hunting for test subjects, I couldn't know for certain if any vampires were on staff, so I carried a sprig of vervain in my pocket. But I couldn't carry any defenses against Pierce without harming myself. To the best of my ability, my mind, my body, and my choices were always my own, and no one could change that. "You can trust me."

"Yeah?" The question was a challenge. She wanted to quarrel with me, likely a result of what Stuffy had just done.

I sat on the floor in front of her, cross-legged, avoiding the mess left behind by Stuffy's carelessness. "I found out about your family."

That light returned to her eyes. "Are they here?"

"Soren and I have a plan to get you out of here tonight, so I need you to bear this a little longer. Security's tight, and we can't make any careless decisions."

"Okay, all right. I get it. What about Sadie? She wouldn't sit this out. I haven't seen my sister in so long. God, I miss her so much." Della snorted. "At least I know her life's been better than mine."

Would the news fuel her escape or resign her to this fate? I wasn't sure if I should tell her at all, but if things went sideways, she had a right to know. "Sadie passed away. I'm so sorry."

Della's brow furrowed. "Trying to get me out of here?" She rattled the chains at her wrists, trying to break free from the iron hoops on the walls, but it was still useless.

"From what I understand, her passing was a while ago. Decades."

Della stilled against her binds. Revenge seeped into her angry features. "Who killed her? Where is the bastard? I'm going to... Oh, I'm going to tear out his—"

The door opened behind me, and a different worker stopped short with a tray of empty tubes dangling from the crook of her arm. "Oh, I didn't know anyone was in here. Subject six's test tubes haven't been filled for processing yet. Is something wrong?"

I needed more time and less suspicion, so I smiled earnestly at the young woman and said, "I'm sorry. I'm new, but I'll have them done soon. Is that okay?"

The woman lifted a brow, inspected my tray, and looked at my seated position on the floor. She sighed. "Well, hurry up. I'm not staying late tonight." The lab worker walked out, closing the door behind her.

A lump formed in my throat as I refocused on Della. "I really don't want to do this, but unlike them, I'll be gentle. Otherwise, I have to leave before they get suspicious."

"I understand," Della said softly. "Get it over with and make sure those bastards clear out on time."

Torturing the prisoner I'd vowed to free was going to hurt me worse than her.

Soren

I didn't want to draw attention with Oliver's outlandish candy-apple red 1967 Shelby. Even the color's name was ostentatious. In case things went south, I didn't want to soil the interior of my Prius either, so I drove my brother's Mercedes. He wouldn't mind, maybe.

I sped down Highway 41 to the lab in Green Bay, navigated into the parking lot and found the only car left in the fading light. I parked and dropped the vanity mirror to check for any missed blood on my face.

Normally I chose my strategy by my mood, but the ticking clock forced my hand. So, ambush was the appetizer to a series of bitter, but necessary, meals. The fact that Indie knew what I was but still talked to me like a human was so unfamiliarly courteous. Others had to be compelled not to scream, including all my meals today. I tilted my face around the tiny rectangle and smiled. No residual blood anywhere.

To me, this was both a chance to save my sister and a date, so I wanted to look the part without being overdressed. I borrowed a gray and black striped button-down shirt and rolled the sleeves up to my elbows for better flexibility. I patted the front pocket of my black dress pants for the stainless steel blade I always carried. Satisfied I looked like a proper, semi-casual gentleman, I climbed out of the Mercedes and peeked into Indie's passenger window.

Indie gestured for me to climb inside. I did, and her intoxicating scent of pine filled my nose. Being this close to her, my heart thundered in my chest.

She wrinkled her nose. "What's that smell?" she asked, meaning me.

I sniffed my borrowed shirt. "Oliver's leftovers?"

"No," she chuckled for a second. "It smells...industrial."

"Oh, that's gasoline in my car." I must've gotten some on my hands. I was surprised she could smell it, because the only thing I could scent was fresh pine—almost overwhelmingly so. Then I noticed the little tree dangling from her rearview mirror, and a flash of brown caught my eye. The back seat was filled with boxes.

"Going somewhere?" I gestured to the stockpile behind us.

"My temporary place doesn't have enough space for me."

Temporary—she was in the process of moving. She'd told me at the party she was always on the move, staying invisible. I hoped she didn't intend to leave after tonight.

Indie checked my bare hands. "No weapons?"

I grinned. "A special blade in my pocket. Everything else I need is retractable. Never leave home without 'em."

Indie's face was impassive—neither disgusted nor amused. Since I was funny, she must have been nervous.

With an impending break-in and rescue of my sister, I was jazzed, and with a belly full of fresh power, I was itching to get moving. "Are we going to do this?"

Ducking awkwardly around the steering wheel, Indie's hands trembled as she put on her sneakers and laced them tightly. Very nervous.

"Nice kicks. Planning to run?" I asked playfully.

"Prepare for the worst. Hope for the best. Expect something in between." The excitement she'd had while we planned was gone. I couldn't fault her lack of confidence. Considering what we were walking into, she had no real strength. If I were in her shoes, I'd be terrified too, probably. I wanted to reach out and reassure her with a touch, but I respected that boundary. "I won't let anything happen to you. You understand that, right?"

Indie sat upright and looked me in the eye. The evening sunset lit a halo around her blond hair, and she looked like an angel—in the purest, most awe-inspiring sense, and not the multi-faced, hooved variety. "Can I ask you something?"

"Anything." And I meant it. I didn't want to keep any secrets from her.

"You're a vampire."

"Last I checked."

"You're the only one I've met who can walk in the sun. How?"

I liked easy questions. "Long story short, my mother was a witch, and we'd been suffering through a drought. The crop yield looked bleak for our winter survival, so she'd infused a series of rings with a spell of good fortune. After we'd been turned, she realized what the side effect of that spell meant. 'Protection from the sun for those who walk in the dark.'"

"Your ability to daywalk is an accident?" Indie asked, surprised.

"And isolated to a vampire who can befriend a willing witch. My idiot brother calls the rings 'weapons', since technically we're more dangerous with them, but he's always melodramatic."

"What is it to you?"

I looked at the ruby stone inlaid in a silver band, and it glinted in the fading light. I'd stalked my prey during the night, feeding on their fear—and sometimes their love—while moving from one shithole to another. From a cabin to hotels and campgrounds—I'd always been on the move for food and shelter while acting as a puppet for a witch. Whenever I'd compelled a human to invite me inside, I'd always left a mess. I had no other choice but to become the thing people feared—to succeed at something. So, I leaned into it, keeping myself isolated from my brother's disappointment, my niece's, and my long-lost siblings, whose judgment I could still feel.

"My humanity."

Indie gave me a wry lift of her lips. "And you say your brother is the dramatic one."

I didn't want to admit that the dismissive attitude toward a deep revelation stung. I had to explain myself only because I wanted her to understand…to accept. "Contrary to popular belief, there is no magic switch where you can shut off the biggest part of yourself—embrace the darkness without guilt. Even though I knew that, I'd spent decades questioning whether I still had my humanity. A few decades ago, Oliver and I were snacking our way through a sorority in Derry, New Hampshire. We were drunk on alcohol, high on blood, and the pumping music sang through our veins."

Indie listened quietly.

"Then Oliver got a call from our niece, Nicole. Bodies were piling up back home, so he cut our trip short. If I'd known what was to pass, I would've stayed behind and enjoyed more Kappa Deltas." I grinned at the memories of those enthusiastic, beautiful young women.

When my gaze met Indie's, I dropped my smile.

"Sadie had arrived for the homecoming, but Pierce's dad lurked around, hunting Evangeline—or so he'd claimed. Sadie's loss was devastating, and the guilty elf paid the price."

"I'm so sorry. How horrible. Pierce's dad was a hunter?"

"Like father, like son. That's what elves do when they're bored—or when they think their territory is being pissed on—hunt vampires for sport." I studied the sparkly ring again. "Newton Reed was in charge of this lab, using a doctor to craft a serum fatal to vampires. He'd used Evangeline and Stacey, the doctor's own wife, as test subjects. Della, too, but I didn't know. For forty years, I was under a witch's spell, going in and out of that lab, handing him new subjects, and furthering research toward my own demise. On my missions, I'd hunted and killed both vampires and humans. Without my ring, I stalked the night, a predator terrorizing humans. I was what they feared: a monster."

I paused, but I couldn't look her in the eye. I'd wanted someone, anyone, to listen to my story. Did Indie consider me a monster now? Regardless, I had to finish. "I hurt a lot of people. I couldn't even count if I tried."

"Do you remember them?"

"I'm terrible with names and dates, but I remember their faces, their voices as they screamed." I closed my eyes as the onslaught of images returned.

Indie touched my hand, ripping me from those nightmares. That tiny sympathetic touch, when she had been so against the feel of her skin on my hands, meant so much. I fought back tears. When I found my voice, I continued, "For my loyal efforts, they gave me a dose of the known successful recipe. I should've been put down, but when I was moments from death, my brother freed me, and Daisy gave me a second chance at life. I didn't deserve her forgiveness. But to make a long answer even longer, if I'd never got my hands on this ring, I don't know if I would've reverted into the monster I knew. I don't know if my brother would've staked me to wash his hands of me, or if I would've decided Daisy had been wrong and given myself over to the sun. But I do know without a doubt, I wouldn't be here with you."

Indie said softly, "I understand being forced into something you don't agree with, and no one can fault you when you didn't have a choice."

I waited for her story, but it didn't come. Even though Indie wouldn't open up to me yet, she touched me. She wasn't afraid. And that was more than I could've hoped for.

20

Mission Impossible

Indie

Soren had never described how and when he'd been turned, which I imagined would be traumatic for anyone, but his story involving this lab alone was simply heartbreaking. How much suffering could one man handle? His immeasurable strength was baffling, but in moments, we were heading into that same lab.

I understood what we were up against, but Soren could still distract me. He could take me away from everything with a simple look in his eye. That was a magic witches could never beat, and the feeling was simply like nothing else in the world.

Distractions were dangerous.

I blinked and focused on the sun slipping under the horizon. Time to go. "Everyone left the building, including Lily."

"We don't have to worry about the witch. Lily is my sister-in-law's sister."

Enemies coexisting...as family? "That's why you sent me to her."

Soren shrugged. "She might not send me a Christmas card, but she wouldn't hurt me—or you."

These people were so confusing, but the way forward was clear. "I expect we'll come across some friction, so I came up with a cover story." I paused, nervous about saying the words, about the request in its entirety. I shouldn't have been, but I was, and heat rushed up my cheeks. "We should pretend to date again. I mean, not a one-off thing, but as a couple."

Soren's lips parted. "What?"

I met his gaze, my face burning hotter than ever. "I brought my badge, but it's not good enough for all the doors, like I'd said before. So when we're stopped, I can tell them I'm an employee giving my boyfriend a tour. The lie seems harmless enough, but it has to be believable. How are your acting skills?" I sent him a flirtatious smile.

"Can I first say I think that's the best plan ever, and hey, I won't have to compel everyone to let us pass." His lopsided grin returned. "But there's no acting needed on my part." Soren gestured for my hand and paused for permission.

I smiled, and Soren brought my knuckles to his lips. Warmth filled my body at his soft touch, and my heart pounded in my chest. I could hear his heart galloping away just the same. I wanted him to continue kissing me all the way up to my lips, and I wanted to feel his body under my touch, feel those floppy strands of hair tangled in my fingers.

"Ready?" he asked, gaze steamy with heat.

We shouldn't have distracted ourselves so much already, and I wanted to hurry up with this plan so we could explore where those kisses would lead. "Let's do this." I opened my car door and stepped out.

Soren climbed out and stretched, and within seconds, he met my stride as we moved across the parking lot. He was suddenly aloof. I hoped he wasn't getting cold feet about this mission, but Soren strolled inches away, which felt like miles.

"Your acting leaves much to be desired," I said playfully. The cover story was perfect, because it was possible for him to touch me safely, and I wanted his arm around me or his hand in mine.

Soren faced me, warming instantly. "Are we talking about a few weeks of dating here or a few months? Still in the honeymoon period, right?"

"Fully inside the honeymoon period. At the stage of excited to learn about his girlfriend's workplace. Heavily enamored, and some pride would help, too."

"You really thought this through, didn't you?" That sexy grin returned.

"I had a few hours to kill while the parking lot emptied out." Hopefully, he didn't catch the part where I'd been thinking of him for hours. "But can you make your acting last more than a few minutes?" I teased, finding it easy to slide into the role.

Soren laughed at my playful dig. "I wasn't the one who bailed last time. I can make it last as long as you need, sweetheart." He offered his hand, and when I took it, he twirled me into a tight embrace. My heart pounded hard. I wanted this to be real.

Soren whispered in my ear, "I can last all night, all day. Just say the word."

I whispered back seductively, "I could break you in half."

Soren spun me out but kept my hand tightly in his. He tipped his head back, and a mixture of a laugh and a groan passed those beautiful lips of his. "Oh, I want to see you try."

I chuckled. "Keep it up, tough guy."

"You don't have to say that twice."

Heat surged, and for a brief moment, I considered making this act far too real—tossing him in a closet. One thing was certain: no matter how this heist ended, I was giving him the dance—and full night—of his life.

Soren

She really had been a great actress, draping over me at the party like a lover anticipating a steamy night. Since then,

Indie had been cool, distant, or downright ignoring me. But I knew something beneath that hard exterior was real, and now she'd finally allowed my touch—allowed me in. I don't know what changed her mind about me, but I didn't care. I'd never believed a reprieve from my troubles, my guilt, my...self-hatred was possible, but here it was. Because of her. My entire focus shifted. Purpose clarified. Desire activated. As if a tree full of songbirds brought their voices together in a sappy moment to drive the point home, I saw nothing but her. Not even my favorite TV show could compare to my real life right now. Holding hands as we pushed through the front doors of the house of horrors, all I could think about was finding a private couch.

I didn't have to pretend while spinning in place, marveling at the interior of the public-facing side of the company. With my mouth gaped in awe, I marveled at the luxury Oliver would certainly appreciate. The floors looked like marble. The front desk, currently empty, was made of glass and quartz. Pale stones surrounded a glass waterfall that trickled in the silence. Plush pale chairs faced the feature, with large potted plants artfully dotting the area, and the puck lighting had been dimmed. It was almost...romantic, a convincing mask to cover the monster lurking below the surface.

"It's beautiful in here," I said, pulling her close and wrapping my arms around her. "But this view is stunning."

Big blue eyes lit up. How would I treat Indie if we were seriously in love, fully within the enchanting honeymoon phase? I didn't have to think about it, but now that I could touch her—she expected me to—I could show her. If my brother would've told me a human was heading my way to capture my heart, I would've laughed at him, because if I had a dollar for every time I told anyone vampires and humans didn't mix, I'd have...well, enough dollars to buy a real date with a human.

"Smile," she said. "We're on camera."

That sweet, teasing bastard—time—was not on my side. "Then I'm going to knock this out of the park for you."

"How?" she asked, her gorgeous face inches from mine, soft lips begging, pleading...waiting.

I moved my hand slowly, giving her plenty of warning. Going from a touch of her hand to...this...in only a few minutes was a leap. I didn't want to lose what progress we'd made. "Right here. Like this," I whispered and palmed her jaw. The contact sent heat roaring through my body, heading straight below the belt. I caressed that soft skin along her jaw and cheek, and her heart thrummed with excitement—the perfect background music to our devious tryst.

I leaned closer, showing her I intended to take those sweet lips of hers. I needed them, but I wasn't sure I could let go. My heart pounded. Her steamy gaze locked onto me, and her breath became shallow, rapid with need. When her blue eyes shifted to my lips, I closed the distance. With one hand still holding her face, I wrapped the other tightly around her, locking her against me, refusing to release her. I had to have her, all of her, and right now was all I could count on.

She didn't fight me. I slipped my hand up to the back of her head, feeling those short blond locks, memorizing the silky feel of...whatever product she used. The scent wasn't pine, but a heady floral number, transporting me to the garden where those songbirds sang their approval.

Indie found the nape of my neck, keeping me under her touch—a birdcage I never wanted to escape. And I pressed my body against hers, as if a single gap were an endless chasm with no hope of traversing. Our breaths mingled, and her heart continued hammering in her chest. All this while she'd wanted me, and she'd finally succumbed to her undeniable attraction. My cock responded, tightening my pants and pressing against her hip.

Indie groaned, and my knees buckled, but I caught myself.

"Hey!" a male voice shouted from across the lobby.

I slowly pulled back. Indie panted, inches from my lips, silky hair messed from my fingers, eyes wild with desire, and I said the first thing she was thinking, "That's not a gun in my pocket."

"Is it a stake?" she asked, and that playful tone of hers had me stifling my own groan.

I chuckled. "Not in that pocket."

"Hey you!" the male voice shouted again, quickly closing the distance.

I would never harm a cell in her body, but that guy was about to make an unfortunate mess on the floor.

Indie glanced at him, but instead of the disruption returning the cold and aloof, as if the secrets of the world rested on her shoulders, she remained light and carefree. She whispered, "Are you ready for this?"

I adjusted myself. "I am now."

Indie chuckled, and I loved that sound.

A chunky guard with a stain on his beige uniform waddled over from a door near the elevators, pointing at us as if he'd never had to actually do anything on the job before. "I'm talking to you."

And so it began.

Indie took my hand, and we casually strolled toward him, grinning like idiots and laughing, as if we were innocently drunk. I certainly was—but not from a bottle.

"You can't be in here." The guard pointed at the front door as if we couldn't figure out where the exit was.

Indie wrapped a possessive arm around me, like I was her gift she wanted to display. "Chuck, it's my boyfriend's birthday." She placed a hand on my chest, and I seized the opportunity to cover it, pressing her palm against my pounding heart. She couldn't hear it, but now she could feel it. "He's fascinated by medical research. In fact, he's considering medical school. Isn't that right, honey?" Indie slipped her hand from mine and glanced at me with a sparkle in her eye. I was convinced she was actually enjoying this. Indie unclipped her badge and confidently flashed her credentials. It was so damn sexy. "So for a gift, I wanted to show him around a little. As you can see, I'm authorized to be here."

Chuck looked us both over skeptically.

"She's right," I added to sell the story. "I'm fascinated by medical research—the scientific method to unlock secrets hidden deep within ourselves. And someday, I want to change the world—you know, give people hope, because everyone deserves a chance." The words sounded convincing to me. So much so that after her passionate kiss, I had to admit I'd allowed hope to root around in my veins.

Indie looked up at me with adoration, something I'd never seen before in anyone, and something I had no idea could be so addictive.

Chuck cleared his throat. "No visitors after hours. House rules." He pointed again, not so subtly kicking us out.

"I don't think you're understanding me," Indie said firmly. "I work here, and I need to pick something up. My boyfriend is tagging along as a gift. So if you don't mind, I'll be on my way, or you can take it up with my supervisor."

Oh, those bossy words—be still, my heart. Indie moved us by him, but his stern tone stopped us in our tracks. "What's his name? I'll confirm your story."

Indie looked up at me, eyes wild with alarm.

"Now what?" I asked her, amused to learn what her daydream of me concocted for this scenario.

She said through clenched teeth, "You said you can 'make' him go away, right?"

I'd compelled Indie to forget I'd been staked by the elf, so she wouldn't remember that I'd tampered with her memory. But I'd told her I was capable of such tricks. "You know I can. Watch this."

"Enough stalling," Chuck said, irritation growing. "You need to leave, or I'm calling more guards up here to get you out."

I turned to face Chuck and captured his gaze. "You're going to let us do whatever we want, and you won't sound any alarms or call for any backup. You won't remember we were here at all."

He stared blankly, processing all his orders.

"Let's go," I said, turning us away and letting Indie take the lead.

"That's handy, but is it going to work?"

"Only on humans. I've been on the receiving end of orders you can't choose. It's violating, so I hate doing it." But with Chuck's attitude, I wasn't feeling very guilty.

"For hating it, you didn't hesitate." Indie countered, as if deciding whether her conscience could accept my ability...that I'd already used on her.

"I only do it when absolutely necessary to protect people from my world or from their own dreadful memories."

She looked at me thoughtfully, as if sliding that moral quandary into the proper file. We were rolling like a well-oiled machine, and I didn't want her asking for a devastating truth as we crossed the threshold into the dark belly of the torturous beast.

But she said simply, "You're trying to do them a favor."

Huh, I never saw it that way. I smiled warmly at her as she brought us to the first door.

21
Blindsided

Indie

VAMPIRES RELISHED THEIR COMPULSION, abusing their ability to dictate human actions, amusing themselves with crude games, and basking in the power of altering people's memories. It was their best tool for remaining invisible in the human world.

But not this vampire. Witches had stolen Soren's free will, and empathy now guided him. The torture he'd endured made him a better...person.

The torture I'd endured made me...hard.

Afraid of revealing too much, I'd let slip minor details of my devastating past when I'd felt the urge to connect. Soren had never pressed for information to satisfy his own curiosity. He believed I was a lowly human—his food source—but he treated me like an equal. And kissing him was like nothing I'd ever experienced before—not just the permission, the respect. I couldn't get enough of him. If we weren't inside a building, in the middle of a critical mission, I'd take him somewhere private and comfortable, so I could show him what that respect meant.

I could still break him in half—if only metaphorically now.

Born a princess, I was supposed to change our world by brokering a peace between the clans. Had events unfolded the way I wanted them to, my father and brothers would've granted me bodily autonomy. I would've been the leader, or at least a member of the council until I'd reached the proper age. But my family didn't respect me, and now they were gone. Hope might be dangerous, but it was also motivating to fight for justice.

I'd lost hope long, long ago.

But I could restore Della's, and reunite Soren with his family. I could make a difference to someone.

At a plain white door, I pressed my badge against the basic black security lock. It beeped, and I opened the door. Before crossing the threshold, nerves skittered through my stomach. "Once we're through this door, there's no going back."

Soren rested a hand on my shoulder. "If you're having second thoughts, I can find my way around, and you can wait here, relax by the waterfall."

I used to be the best chameleon, able to blend in anywhere and slip off my ring for a little compulsion where things weren't so smooth. But I'd never had to watch out for someone else. Soren could handle himself, I was sure of it, but the lab below was a labyrinth of ways to get caught, and I was effectively helpless. "I'm not worried about me."

"Don't worry about me, sweetheart. I can handle myself, and I'll keep you safe."

With one last worried glance, I stepped through the door. Soren followed me down the plain beige stairs to an underground floor where hallways ran in both directions. Around the corner, a nondescript service elevator waited. On the number pad, I typed in the code Lily had given me to unlock its badge reader. Code accepted. I pressed my badge against the black screen, and the elevator dinged as the doors opened.

"Oh, fancy," Soren said. I told him the digits so that if anything happened, he could unlock the elevator. Vampire strength or not, these doors were inches of steel. "I'm not leaving without you, sweetheart." He sent me a confident grin.

"I don't know if there's another way out. Lily never mentioned stairs, and I didn't think to ask. I haven't been here long enough to snoop around, and during the day, security is much nosier."

"Indie, you and I with Della at my side, are walking out of that lab and riding this elevator."

Brushing aside my nerves, I watched the numbers as we sank lower into the depths of the building, stopping on sublevel three. The doors ejected us straight onto a security station. A guard perked up, likely in his early twenties and thin enough I could use him as a baseball bat. His feet shifted off the desk, and he adjusted his glasses in surprise. "No one's supposed to be down here."

Soren and I approached the thick acrylic barrier between us and the guard's quiet station. Our hands were linked again, and smiles filled our faces, but the excitement from the lobby was getting harder to muster. I showed the guard my identification. "I forgot to get something in my office."

The young man squinted at my badge. "And him?"

I pressed a hand against Soren's thundering chest, filled with either nerves or lust, but down here, I couldn't imagine it was still lust. I gave the suspicious guard my best smile, and I name-dropped for legitimacy. "Chuck's letting me give my boyfriend a quick tour while I take care of some business."

The young guard, Baseball Bat, studied us skeptically. Soren and I exchanged loving glances—as we were two distracted lovers running a quick errand. My heart picked up its pace, freeing me from the danger if only for a second. "Chuck agreed to this?"

"He did. Please unlock the door. We're kind of in a hurry, if you know what I mean." I sent Baseball Bat a sly, flirty smile, but the guard was either married to his job...or a virgin. Baseball Bat's features pinched with dissatisfaction. This guy was a hard nut to crack, so I prompted Soren quietly, knowing his sensitive hearing could pick it up.

Soren grinned. "Hey buddy, of course Chuck approved. How do you think we got down here? He opened the door for us." After drawing the guard's attention, Soren captured his gaze, and the vampire's burned red. "You're not going to sound any alarms. You won't remember us being here at all."

The guard stared blankly at the beige wall.

"Open the door," Soren added.

The guard's hand moved, and a mechanical sound cranked and thumped. Door locks released with a hiss. As the guard continued to obey his orders, Soren and I swept through the checkpoint. I steered him down the next hallway of plain doors. Stopping at the correct one, I used my badge at the black card reader, but as expected, it was declined. "I can't get us through this one."

Soren gripped the handle and effortlessly turned it. Metal rang as it buckled inside the lock. We pushed through once more.

As we entered the next hallway full of doors, Soren said, "The side door would've been a shortcut. You're not getting me lost in here on purpose, are you?" he asked playfully.

"Can you punch through brick?" I raised a brow, actually curious.

"Eh, if I had to, but wandering these boring hallways with you is still fun."

At the door marked Research and Development, I pressed my badge against the reader. It actually worked. "Here it is. Look familiar?"

I swung the door open, and Soren strolled in first, scoping the place out. Only rows of counters, blinking refrigerator lights, and the hums of filtered air flowing through machinery. Everything was dimmed in the after-hours lighting. No overtime for the workers tonight. I'd tortured Della fast enough to get her samples processed on time. That had been awful, and I didn't want to think of it again.

"She's in here." I headed straight for Della's unmarked door, grateful no one ever locked it, and as I reached for the knob, a hand clamped on my shoulder. I startled, genuinely not expecting to be gripped so rigidly, and the hand was too small to be Soren's.

Lily glared at me, unamused. Soren stood just off to her side. Those nerves returned in full force.

"What are you doing here?" I asked, trying to keep the accusation out of my voice. I'd watched everyone leave in their vehicles, and I hadn't seen Lily return. Soren had said she was family and wouldn't hurt us, but if I missed her return, who else had I missed?

"Paperwork. What are you two doing here?" Lily folded her arms across her chest.

"I didn't want to believe this place was still up and running," Soren said lightly. "Not a bad gig, Lily, but I'm surprised you're following daddy dearest's footsteps, after what he did to you and Daisy."

Lily looked at Soren with contempt. "You don't belong here." The witch's gaze settled back on me. I was at fault for bringing him, so I had to get us out of this.

Soren couldn't use compulsion on a witch, so I started with a distraction. I said brightly, "I was giving Soren a short tour, but we'll be going now."

"You know you can't bring anyone down here."

I glanced at Soren with sincere apology and tried to smooth our way out of here. "I know, and I'm sorry. Look, I didn't want to get your hopes up, but earlier I found something in a grimoire, and it was still bugging me, so I came back for another look."

"You're lying to me."

Her dark tone pulled me away from Soren's beautiful face, and I came up with a believable lie. "He can help us. With double the eyes, we can search the books faster. Don't you want that?"

The witch pressed her lips together in thought. Her gaze shifted between us. Playing along, Soren shrugged. "You know what? He can. Indie, head over to your office. We'll meet you there in a minute."

My eyes widened. I didn't expect that to work. If he were capable of the translations, I wondered again how old Soren was.

"Soren, can I have a word...privately?"

Taking the hint, I headed around the lab toward my office while Soren gave me a reassuring smile. Despite the personal nature of their relationship, I listened, curious how a vampire could trust a witch—family member or not.

"With your long history in this place, I never bothered to ask for your assistance, but Indie convinced me you could be a great asset. Right through here," Lily said.

I frowned and stopped. That wasn't personal drama, and there were no grimoires on that side of the lab. I turned to see Soren's confused face as he headed into a darkened room.

The witch slammed the door shut, and my mouth gaped open in horror.

22

Broken Trust

Indie

I'd hoped we wouldn't encounter any elf guards. My luck had to run out—but it was a witch, not an elf, who twisted the metaphorical knife in my back. Lily was supposed to be Soren's ally—family—and fully on our side. She wanted to cure vampires, so why did she lead Soren into one of the plain white doors?

I should've listened to the instincts warning me away. I rushed back around as Lily exited the prison cell and shut the door behind her. "What are you doing? The grimoires are on the opposite side of the lab."

Soren banged on the door to be released, but the witch concentrated, as if holding him inside with a spell.

"Lily?" I pleaded, my guts swirling in knots.

After a beat of Lily not answering, I reached for the doorknob to release him myself.

Lily caught my arm. "Don't."

"Let him go."

Lily didn't budge.

Security guards Chuck and Baseball Bat appeared, armed with tactical semi-autos that appeared modified, but with probably six shots each, these guys didn't even have to aim. Firearms were entirely unnecessary for me, so the witch had no intention of letting Soren out. I pleaded, "Lily, this is madness. Let him go."

Ignoring my presence entirely, as if we'd never met, and I wasn't important, Chuck asked the boss, "Which one?"

"This one," Lily said, pointing to Soren's door. Sweat broke out on her brow.

Soren's banging fists thumped against the door, testing the reinforced hinges, fighting against Lily's magic. His yells were hardly a whisper. Only screams ever penetrated.

The men approached the door, and as they passed by me, I grabbed Baseball Bat's arm and tugged. He shrugged out of my grip effortlessly and continued to ignore me entirely. If I had my emerald bauble, I would've removed it and launched these two across the lab before breaking down that door myself. Instead, I hoped.

The guards discussed their plan while drawing their weapons. I fully expected Soren to launch at them, so I stood off to the side to give him room. Then we'd escape together, and every door between here and the open air of the night would be torn from the hinges. When the door swung in, the men fired muted shots, one after the other after the other. I covered my ears.

Soren fell to the floor with a dull thump, moaning and writhing in pain. More shots were fired, and Soren became still...quiet. Little feathery tags were caught on his skin. I'd thought nothing short of a 50-caliber rifle could stop a vampire—if anyone could actually hit one. These two must've used specially crafted ammunition for a pair of 12-gauges to be effective. With angry vampires in these cages, I suspected vervain was the culprit. I covered my mouth with my hands, absolutely horrified and shocked at what had just happened.

Lily wiped her sleeve across her brow while panting from exertion.

The guards dragged Soren farther into the prison cell, his feet disappearing into the darkness. The flick of a light switch brightened the room, and the metal clank of iron chains shifted. I swallowed back yells of protest, threats of violence I couldn't follow through. Lily knew what I was. If I angered her, she could easily remove me from her hair—and into the hands of Pierce. Then I would be in a worse position than Soren.

The guards nodded at the witch, indicating a job completed, and Lily tipped her chin, responding in the affirmative. A silent, effective, recognized conversation among colleagues familiar with each other's questions and answers. The guards left, taking their weapons.

All could hear was the pounding of my heart in my ears.

Lily said calmly, "Thank you for the unexpected surprise. Next time, spare the begging. The subjects don't really care once they wake up."

Soren had trusted her. Lily was his family, and I was disgusted, but with Soren a prisoner, I couldn't afford to be stripped of my access to the building. If I couldn't convince the witch I'd done this on purpose, there would be no course correction. I composed myself and said calmly, "I did want help with the grimoires."

Lily chuckled. "If you knew him as well as I do, you'd know Soren isn't the type to do anything with a book, except fix a wobbly table, or set a naked woman's ass on it."

I wanted to slap her for that. Instead, I focused on the act. "But you told me you wanted a spell to—" cure them, I was going to say, but I cut off with the sudden change in Lily's posture and expression. I knew that look more than I cared to.

Lily became...chummy and pleasant. "I also told you Pierce is a *friend*, remember?" Her eyes widened as she enunciated the word. "Come with me."

To the next cell? Not a chance. I crossed my arms over my chest. "I'm going to have to decline, so am I free to go?"

Lily's fake smile returned. "Come. With. Me." She enunciated the words slowly, giving me a clear, bold message. Things weren't what they seemed. With an urging gesture of her head, I followed Lily into her office. The witch softly closed the door behind us.

"How could you?" I asked. Nothing else needed to be said.

Lily exhaled and faced me. The fake smile was gone. "There are closed-circuit cameras down here now. We have ears and eyes on the floor, so I couldn't say anything that could compromise my position, and that meant I did what I had to do. You left me no choice."

"Who installed them? Who's watching?" I knew the answer, but I chilled in anticipation of hearing my enemy closing in.

"The elves."

Plural. My stomach twisted, and my chest constricted. I couldn't draw a breath, and I fell into a chair. Maintaining my composure with Pierce lurking about was difficult enough, but being on their—plural—radar around the clock was another entirely. "You said closed-circuit. No one sees anything unless they come down here to review the footage, right?"

"Look," Lily said, "if I didn't lock him up, the elves would be here in minutes. They can fly way too fast for my liking." She paused. "No offense."

"None taken."

"My priority is keeping you and your work safe. I'll do anything to keep the elves placated and their attention elsewhere, so before you ask again, no, I can't release him or Della."

I needed a new plan.

Soren

My throbbing head lolled on my shoulders, and I had the worst crick in my neck. So bad, in fact, fiery pain radiated through my entire body, as if my nerves had been set on fire, and now I smoldered at the perfect marshmallow roasting temperature. I could hardly drag in a breath, and sweat rolled down my back and into my eyes. When I moved a heavy hand to wipe my brow, chains rattled. The hell? Vampire vision was enhanced, not X-ray. I needed a teensy drop of light to make out shapes, but all I could see was inky blackness. So, either my vision had taken a vacation, or I'd been blinded.

My eyesight and this endless, raging...blinding...pain should've been healing. Then I remembered what the hell had happened. Goddamn vervain. The world would be a better place without it.

The moron guards hadn't shot me up enough to kill me, and judging by these chains, that hadn't been the plan. The worst burning was where the vervain darts still bit into my skin. I swung a hand to pull one out, but I couldn't get close enough. They'd already caught me. Couldn't they have taken some of the pain away? In their position, I wouldn't have shown mercy either.

I was trapped in the lab of nightmares, buried deep beneath the house of horrors, where my brain had been scrambled by Newton Reed, evil and, thankfully dead, witch extraordinaire. I had a sinking feeling I wasn't going to be a witch's puppet collecting test subjects this time.

Lily's deviousness was not wholly unexpected. She'd been on the enemy side before, partnering with Pierce Evansson, Jamie Harris, and Allison Kincaid to burn witches at the stake. So original. But afterward, Lily had claimed to switch sides. I snorted. Obviously, that was a lie. I couldn't think of what I'd done lately to deserve this. Sure, I hurt a lot of people over the years, but I'd been clean from nefarious forces for months now, and Lily was a friend and family. A Rockwell. That meant I would've protected Lily forever, because I loved Oliver and respected Daisy. And if Daisy trusted her sister, then that meant I did, too.

But I shouldn't have.

Lily had sent a spy to manipulate me, and Indiara Niskatar was definitely the right bait. Damn. I should've seen it coming. I should've been suspicious that a beautiful human—who, despite all my efforts, had rejected me—magically popped back into my life, fully accepting this wolf in fraudulent clothing, and delivered a heart-rending truth about my sister. Of all the places in the world my sister could be, what a coincidence she'd been down here all along. Della was ash, feeding some grass where the squirrels shit.

The betrayal cut deep.

Despite her incredible acting skills, I should've seen it coming. On our way down here, Indie had been hesitant. Her heart pounded—not with lust, as my stupid heart hoped—but with nerves. Maybe a few regrets had been cracking through, or maybe a sprinkle of confidence had been wavering, slowing her feet. She was terrified of me. She knew I was a raging animal tearing throats out of innocent humans, and she was terrified I'd discover her betrayal before she had me secured. This type of shit was always obvious afterward. Fine. I should've read those warning signs, but I didn't. Why? That damn human stirred something deep inside that I hadn't felt in a long time, and my useless parts—namely my heart—blinded me with hope.

I was right. Always had been. Humans and vampires didn't mix. Full fucking stop.

Duped by a beautiful human with more courage than I'd seen in decades.

Wasn't the first time.

Probably wouldn't be the last.

If I got out of this mess.

Each prisoner was isolated and tortured with pure darkness and silence in between sessions, except for the bustling sounds of the workers during business hours. I supposed that was another form of torture. Help was just outside the door, and they could hear you, but they ignored your pleas for mercy. How long had I been unconscious?

"Hello?" I called.

No response.

I tugged and pulled on the chains with every aching muscle in my body as if my life depended on it. How would I get out of here after? I'd been so weakened by vervain I'd need to chow down on half the lab to regather my strength and tear down the doors. One problem at a time.

I strained. Everything trembled with the force I exerted. Even the chains groaned. But my strength drained rapidly. Goddamned vervain. I slackened the chains and allowed myself to rest against them, panting.

"Can I have a knee pad or something?"

No response.

No help was coming.

23

Enemy Lurking

Indie

To PROTECT MYSELF, I'd tolerated an elf literally breathing down my neck, but now, watching my every move on camera shifted me into full-flight mode. Could I run away and start over? Absolutely. I'd done it hundreds of times, and keeping myself alive by leaving was hardly shameful. I'd always slept with one eye open and never laid down roots anywhere, and that wise lifestyle had kept me alive—safe. Now it was time to heed my roots. I had my magic cloak. Staying to help a witch find an impossible spell, regardless of its benevolence, was pointless.

I almost didn't return to Cora's to collect the few necessities I'd unpacked. But I'd been determined to leave my roommate with as little damage as possible, and I couldn't burden her with unanswered questions and my clutter. Worse, I couldn't have her calling the authorities and starting a police investigation.

From the back corner of Cora's couch, I slid out an empty box. I headed for the bathroom. Cora watched me with interest, but she had just gotten home from whatever date she'd tried to invite me on as a double. Since she wasn't booming with enthusiasm, I assumed it hadn't gone well. She apparently wasn't in the mood to ask what I was doing, but an unfamiliar feeling urged me to tell her, anyway. Except, someone had tampered with her memory. I didn't know how helpful she could be, and I'd already used her enough. Soon, I'd be setting her free.

Because of me, someone else wasn't and never would be again.

I picked up my things slowly, one at a time, and placed them in the box, and I stared at my handful of belongings. So little of me existed. After only a couple of boxes, I'd be gone, never to be seen or heard from again. I could disappear myself, but the damage I'd caused would remain.

Could I start a new life while Soren's life was over?

My roommate popped into the doorframe. After a few short moments, her liveliness returned. "Did you quit?"

I looked at her, hair up and fancy, makeup beautiful, clothing flattering to her shape. She stood out. There was confidence in everything she did. "I think I did. I should go—move out."

"If my boss made me work late on a Friday, I'd quit too, especially since you look all strung out. Screw him. But don't go, Indie. One job isn't the end of the world. Ever bartend before? I can get you a spot at the bar. It's good money, if you can act like you care about random strangers' drama."

There was that word again. "I'm not the bartending type," I said and brushed a line of tears from my lower lid.

I carried my pitiful belongings out to the living room. I dropped onto the couch and set the box on the coffee table in front of me. Only a few feet stood between me and the door. I should just go and tell Cora not to worry. My sweet roommate had just offered to put in a good word for me, but I didn't believe Soren would be returning. There'd be more unanswered questions. Another police investigation.

Cora settled next to me. "Oh, honey, what happened?"

"I tried to do the right thing, but it backfired. And now, because of me, someone is in very serious trouble."

Soren had sacrificed himself to save his sister, but he knew the risks. I'd made them very clear and tried to tell him I'd felt uneasy about right beforehand. Besides, now Della had Soren to keep her company. With their strength and incredible hearing, they could make a plan to break free together. Soren could handle himself. He didn't need me.

"If it's your fault, you have to help," Cora said. "Even if you think you don't have to, that kind of stuff will eat at you."

I couldn't get Della out when I had no suspicious eyes or cameras watching me, and I was fresh out of ideas. "Believe me, it's not that easy."

"Honey, if you need help solving a puzzle, you've got to spill for me. I can't rearrange the pieces if I can't see the picture. Help a girl help you out."

Trust was the most valuable thing someone could have. It was also the most fragile. One slip, one wrong turn, and it was gone. Irreparable. Soren had trusted me, and look where it got him. Could I trust Cora? Probably, but I didn't know if I was talking to Cora.

Eyeing my box, I rose. I still wore my running shoes, and my gas tank was full. "I'm going to go. Don't worry about me, and I think your boss is going on vacation for a very long time. I've caused enough trouble as it is, and I'm sorry for impeding on your life."

Cora rose and stood between me and the door. "You can't leave. You know how hard it is to find someone who keeps the kitchen clean and does their end of the chores? No, thank you. So save me from that awful stress and stay."

As tempting as that flattery was, it wasn't enough. I lifted the box in my arms, but now it was heavier. "I'm sorry for the inconvenience."

"Is this about that dark, messy-haired, bright-green-eyed hunk wrapped with lean muscle?" Cora raised a suggestive brow.

So now she remembered Soren? Hesitantly, I said, "It is."

"Hang on. I got just the thing." Cora slipped out her phone, tapped away at the screen, and tucked it away. She beamed. "Help will be here in five. How about some coffee while you wait?"

Cora headed for the kitchen.

"Who did you text?" I didn't know anyone who'd help with Soren's imprisonment, but I was willing to entertain the possibility that a solution existed, as long as it didn't involve any feathers. Of course, I couldn't think of a single reason why anyone with feathers would help a vampire. "Coffee sounds great."

"One of my friends. She asked me to contact her if you were upset." Cora dropped down mugs from an upper cabinet.

She? Probably not Lily...I set the box down again and poured myself a mug of coffee as a knock came from the door. When I'd met Soren, Cora had mentioned a previous employee...

I gripped the near-boiling liquid firmly as I answered the door. The one I'd been ignoring out of guilt stood in the doorway with a friendly smile.

"Hey," Allison said with a dainty wave. Her sun-kissed hair was curled along her face and shoulders. Dark-framed glasses outlined her round eyes, and she carried a canvas tote in the crook of her arm. "Heard you could use some help, and I always respond to nine-one-one."

I wouldn't turn down a witch's help. I opened the door, inviting her inside. "Care for some coffee?"

"I won't be here that long." Allison walked the couple of feet into the dinky living room, stopped, and turned to face me. "I heard what happened in the lab."

I stiffened. Coffee sloshed over the brim, and I grimaced at the burn on my hand. Trying to string together the twisting relationships in this small town was confusing. "How did you hear exactly?"

"We have friends in common. So, you have a vampire trapped in a lab, and you need help to get him out. Am I right?"

With wide eyes, I assessed Cora, but she didn't seem to have heard any of that as stared at her phone while nursing a steamy coffee.

"Don't worry about her. She can't hear anything about the supernatural world. The words just bounce off her hair and drift away like drunk moths."

Allison had been the one tampering with Cora's head. Allison, the renowned, powerful witch, had directed me to the bar where this human worked and told me to find a safe place to stay for a while. I didn't appreciate Allison manipulating her, but since I had been guilty of it too, and the witch had only been protecting me while I worked on renewing my own protection, I was willing to hear her out.

"You have the problem right, but I already broke our deal. I'm not in a position to make another one."

"I don't mind. That was a very hard spell, and I'm glad to skip it," Allison said. "I'm not here to make another deal. The slate's clean."

I never knew a witch to be altruistic, but I couldn't put a finger on her motivation. "Don't get me wrong, I appreciate your visit, but why are you offering to help?"

"Because my protégé, Ms. Barrett, can't stand up to the elves—the males, anyway." She sent me a knowing smile, which I did not appreciate. "She's simply not strong enough, but I'm on your side—both of you. Getting the chance to frustrate the elves sends a rush of excitement up my spine." Allison wriggled to demonstrate.

I glanced at Cora again, but she sipped with a smile, watching her phone.

"If you know about the incident in the lab, then you caught the news of the lab's new cameras. Elves are watching. So, what did you have in mind?"

"Are you still able to get in?"

I did have my badge, but I figured I was no longer welcome, to say the least. But Lily, the boss, wanted the original vampire spell more than anything. If I went back, pretended all was normal, I could keep searching. And if I found it, she could cure them—problem solved. But if not, I had time to figure out a new plan—one that included a powerful witch on my side. A rare flush of excitement tore through me—not urging my flight, but a renewed focus. Hope. "I should be able to. I...I have to go back to the lab."

Maybe I could sneak visits with them both. Ease their fears, plot something with all four of us.

Allison grinned. "That's excellent. I'll let you know when I'm ready. Until then, be my eyes and ears in the lab."

Now returned that word I dreaded: act. I had to face everyone after what I'd done. Most of the workers probably wouldn't know anything, but I had to play nice while Soren and Della screamed in torture. Move carefully in front of cameras controlled by my ultimate enemy.

On top of that, would Della forgive me for not showing up? I hoped she'd be easy enough to sway. But Soren...what that vampire thought of me right now soured my stomach. How was I ever going to make that up to him? How would he ever trust me again? The most valuable and most fragile thing...I had it and I lost it. Regardless of what they thought of me, I was going to save them both.

I emptied the box.

24

Crown or Curse

Soren

I HAD TO FOCUS on all the ways I'd been utterly boned. Otherwise, I would try for the hundredth time to break these chains, which did nothing but drain my strength and drive my hunger. Since my captors deigned to offer me a television to pass the time, the smarter tactic was to figure out what had been flying invisibly by me—if for no other reasons than to show my captors I wasn't at fault for being boned, and to prove to them I was the sharper tack in the box.

I rewound events to catch that invisible whatever the hell it was—the point at which all the blinking, waving red flags I'd missed had begun their march, firing off colorful, deafening explosives. Newt's mind control had made me a vile puppet. That sucked. Then, Pierce had killed the witch, and when I thought I was free, I was still dying. After Daisy cured me, life was pretty...mellow for a while. No red flags there.

Next came the barbecue where I'd saved my brother's ass twice—still nothing unusual yet. But that evening had turned out to be more exciting than I'd expected. I'd killed a witch twice—the same one—and that had been fairly novel. Jamie Harris was still dead, so not the cause of my current predicament. The climax had to be my assassination of the elf clan leader, Logon Larsen, whom I staked with his own weapon while he kneeled but refused to beg for his life. Ignoring the atrocities of war itself, that had been pretty badass. I'd heard Pierce even cried over it. That was probably the highlight of my month, which I promptly spent celebrating on Oliver's couch, enjoying his personal bar and the newly installed TV. No red flags here.

Nicole didn't like my style of celebrating a personal achievement, and as things had settled, she started pushing harder for me to find a woman, so I bought a bar. I'd thought it was a fair trade. According to the paperwork, business had been continuing at a predictable, even pace. Then I threw the party, but the whole idea for it was inspired by...negotiating for a date, because *she* walked into my bar. Oh, that was the first little red flag—negotiating a date.

Who did shit like that? Because I never had to.

And yet it happened, because Indiara Niskatar—seriously, what kind of name was that? Probably fake—came looking for a witch and didn't want anything to do with me. I almost could retract that first flag. The woman had claimed to be always moving around, trying to be invisible, so she'd been on the run—from what? That likely wasn't a factor. Of all places, she'd stopped in Marinette, Wisconsin, to find a witch. Protection was a reasonable assumption. Fair enough. But I was right there when she'd negotiated a favor in exchange for the witch's help. *Boom!* Flag number two.

Indie wasn't an innocent human uncontrollably turned on by this handsome shit that was me. Oh, no. She was a terrified mouse, using herself as bait to catch the cat on behalf of the witch. I was the damn cat, and I fell for her act, hook, line, and sinker. *Act...*

How could I have been so stupid?

That led me to my first major defense for this boning, and I think it could work in numerous situations. The male body had precisely one brain, anatomically speaking, but following that mythical second brain allowed for idiotic things to happen. Admittedly, the primary male brain wasn't very evolved as it was, so that left the mythical one completely moronic. Thank you, cock, for delivering me into enemy hands, courtesy of a tall, blond pixie as beautiful as the first sunrise after sliding on my sun ring.

That led me to my next point. The witch in charge—dead. The genius creator—freed from witch mind control. Oliver and I had emptied out every vial in this lab, dragged the boxes to Dr. Greg Barrett to identify the cure, and when none were it, I'd destroyed the entire supply. Then the source of the serum and its cure had changed their blood, so the recipe the doctor had created was simply...gone. Not long after, the doctor had been killed—good riddance. With no one running the lab, and no scientist doing his mastermind work, no supply to reverse engineer, no supply to start over, the lab had been effectively shut down—kneecapped.

So what the hell was I doing here?

Indie's ridiculous story drove me down here in desperation to rescue my sister, but Della wasn't here. Oliver and I would've heard her all the times we'd reluctantly come down. Red flag number three. If I would've thought how far-fetched the story was in the first place, I wouldn't be down here. That was on me. And right before opening the door where my supposed sister had been locked away for forty years, Lily shoved me into this black hellhole. Her goons loaded me with vervain and chained me up.

Lily and Indie conspired to lock me in here. For what? I couldn't tell time in the black, mostly silent prison cell, but I was sure the answer would be flaunted in my face, eventually. Witches always loved a good gloat.

I figured out what led me here, but aside from somehow breaking these chains, I didn't have a plan to escape. The vervain burning me alive dend melting my brain wasn't helping. So, needing a distraction from the pain of torture and the boredom of nothing to do, I wanted to know why I was here. None of my red flags revealed that. The door to my prison cell opened, shining a blinding light into my retinas that silhouetted a stocky man. The stretching shadow reaching the top of the doorframe settled like a rock in my gut.

Of course, Lily wouldn't be working alone.

"Your manners, although expected, are disappointing. Got anything to eat around here, elf?" I asked.

Pierce Evansson flipped the light switch on, and I was even more blinded. Elves didn't have our sharp night vision, and they thought they were the superior species. My ass.

"I stream a lot of TV shows—"

"No spoilers," I interrupted.

He ignored me but grinned broadly in a way I hadn't seen before. "But watching the security footage in this lab was the most exciting thing I'd ever seen."

I scowled at the visual. "I don't want to hear about your private time watching me. That's disgusting," I said, wondering if that were the reason I was here. The elf wanted a sex slave. I guess it could be worse, but then my comment probably made it worse. *Open mouth, insert foot.* To change the subject, I said, "I'm flattered you came for a visit, but don't you have a day job healing humans?"

Pierce smirked at me. No quick comeback about anything I'd said. He just stared as if marveling at me. "If you want me to strip, I should get a shower first."

Still no reaction.

"If you only want to watch—I mean, I get it, and I'm not judging—but I need more reach. Slacken the chains?"

Maybe he liked the teasing and my squirming. Gross. I sighed. "I'm all about putting on a show, but there are innocent eyes out there, and they don't need to be traumatized. Can you at least close the door?"

Pierce shook his head, grin firmly still in place. He finally stepped into the claustrophobic room and closed the door behind him. At least his pointy ears were working. As he shifted, I noticed a fat syringe nestled between his fingers like a cigar. Withhold judgment here, please. I did on occasion read stuff, and while Milton was too optimistic for my tastes, I had to appreciate his lines about dark clouds revealing their silver linings, because I found one. The elf intended to inject me with some unknown substance that was likely to cause much pain and suffering, but the good news—he just wasn't that into me.

"I can't believe this. I just can't," Pierce said, still amused by my presence.

"I can," I mumbled.

Pierce stepped closer, giving me a perfect view of his shiny boots—leather, well-worn, and most importantly, steel-toe. I tipped my head up to meet his gleeful gaze. "Would you ever take a witch at her word?" The question had to be rhetorical because he didn't give me a second to answer. "You could be a mirage, artfully detailed by my witch to buy herself time to finish the job. They are crafty. I have to see for myself."

"I'm pretty sure your eyesight is working," I mumbled.

Pierce reeled back and punched me in the right eye. My head snapped back, and my vision sparkled. My ears rang. The tank could hit like a train when he wanted to. There was definitely an effort there. Pierce shook his injured hand, but he still grinned like a loon.

"Feel better?" I asked.

"You look good, Soren." The elf chuckled as if he amused himself—more feathers than brains. "I can't believe my luck, and your stupidity."

I'd already determined where my blame landed in this predicament. "You had your fun. Now, are you going to let me go?"

"You murdered my grandfather. What do you think?"

"He died with honor in battle. Not dragged out in pointless torture behind closed doors where I'm defenseless. And you staked me at my own party. As far as I'm aware, we're even."

Pierce gave a chuckle-snort of disbelief. "You think your tiny, healed puncture is comparable to taking a life?"

Not that I wanted to compliment the elf, but the wound hadn't been tiny. "Two dozen of your people tried to murder us, and you came armed. Our part was self-defense."

"You can be the judge, fanger, but I'm the jury and executioner."

Great. I warily eyed that syringe. "Not that I want to encourage you, but I thought your vengeance would've lasted longer."

Pierce followed my gaze. "Oh, this? Today is not your judgment day. Hold still." Pierce leaned close enough I could smell the acrid stink of gym rat, and he pushed my head to the side. He stabbed my neck with the needle, and pressure built as he emptied it into my delicate flesh. I grunted with discomfort, but I was sure he enjoyed it.

I coughed. "I thought paramedics could hit a vein. Isn't that a beginner skill?"

Pierce took a few steps back. "Save your breath. You might want to use it for something more useful than your endless babbling."

Nicole had wanted me to stake his ass a while back. I refrained only to avoid another war—that I wasn't confident we'd win based on numbers. But if I had free hands and a stake right now? I'd take my damn chances.

The pain hit.

"Vervain?" I croaked. "I'm already chained up. That's low." A searing, blindingly fiery flame ignited me from the inside out, spreading from my neck up to my head and working its way to my extremities. With my muscles rigid with the burning swell of the allergen, I was fully incapacitated.

Pierce reached down and ripped the sun ring off my finger. "You won't be needing this any longer." He rose and dropped it into his pocket with a smug smile.

Feeling like I was going to combust, I said through gritted teeth, "You must not be too confident in your ability to keep me here."

Pierce frowned, actually considering the optics, and dug back into his pocket. He threw my ring into the corner of the room, and it bounced and tumbled with metallic rings way too far away. "Feel free to add more excellent ideas when I see you tomorrow."

The elf left, enclosing me in the darkness again. With the vervain in my system, the swelling in my new black eye wouldn't recede anytime soon, but I didn't need my vision to stare at more darkness. I needed to heal, and the hunger gnawed at me, growing by the minute. If only I could reach that knife in my pocket, I could pry something loose and get the hell out of here. No matter how much I tried, I just couldn't reach it.

I was truly trapped.

A prisoner in need of rescue, but this time was physical instead of mental. However, both were embarrassing and awkwardly emasculating. Pierce was going to drag this out for a while, so I had time to concoct the perfect vengeance on them all. I visualized the corner where my ring rested. The elf wanted me to fight for it, to yearn for that freedom, to be tortured by all that power so close but yet so far. I'd already had those.

I'd told Indie there was no switch to flip to turn it off, but that wasn't entirely true. What my ring meant was something I could easily do without. No longer the crown I wore proudly, that ring was a curse. That ring was my switch.

25
Driven

Indie

By nature and necessity, I was flighty, and I wasn't ashamed, but I was incapable of fixing the problem I'd caused. Without words of encouragement from Allison, I would've been a few states away by now, learning how to manage the guilt. Instead, Allison needed a spy, and Lily needed me to find a spell that would thwart the elves. The cameras had terrified me, but I had been enjoying the research, and I now had witches on my side. Allison had grounded me, giving me the courage to stay for Soren's sake...and Della's.

Somehow, the witches and the vampires and I were going to take down the elves entirely. That started with me.

Knowing the power on my side and my overwhelmingly exciting goal, I found pretending to belong easier than I'd anticipated. I strolled into the building with my head held high, and rather than full indifference, Chuck and Baseball

Bat nodded in appreciation at me. All they remembered was I'd lured in a vampire—a not-so-easy feat for anyone, let alone a human. Even with the cameras lurking overhead, I had a spring in my step and a secretive smile on my lips.

Business was usual down here, and I wove my way to my office. I settled in, but this time, I chose the seat in front of my narrow window. The grimoire's binding crackled as I split it open with care. Page after page, I skimmed the ancient script, but like the grimoire, my attention was split. On a notepad, I recorded the staff's movements—times, tasks, interactions—and to keep the secret, my handwriting was purposefully sloppy. While I watched the staff, my gaze moved to the plain white door. Who entered and when? What did they carry? Was it more or less than when they'd entered? Nerves skittered through my stomach.

Despite the new prisoner taking up residence, nothing out of the ordinary happened, except I hadn't noticed any screams. With the lunch hour reducing the staff, I could finally do something I'd never done before. Those sticky situations I always avoided meant I never needed to fix anything—just pack up and go. But I had no chance of fixing the problem I'd caused if the siblings wouldn't trust my plan, and by extension, me.

I tucked the data I'd collected under the grimoire, rested my glove over it, and lifted my decoy mug. My hands already trembled, so I didn't need more caffeine, just an excuse. I set out across the lab, dancing around workers and avoiding boxes of supplies piled all over. This lab truly needed more staff if only to catch up on proper stocking.

I reached Soren's door, and I turned away from it, as I had done before, to appear busy and purposeful. I checked for any suspicious gazes, but no one cared about what I was doing—no one that I could see. With the overhead cameras, there remained a risk, but I had to. When I felt confident, I pretended to collect something off the counter, and I moved through Soren's unlocked door. If a vampire escaped their chains, a simple locking doorknob was like crushing a stick of warm butter to them—as Soren had already demonstrated.

Heart pounding wildly, I closed the door behind me and flicked on the light. My heart crumpled at the sight of Soren kneeling on the floor, hanging limply by the chains around his raw wrists. Blood streaked his clinging, wet dress shirt and speckled his pants and the floor, but the pattern was different from Della's. Soren hadn't been subjected to sample collection.

Head bowed low, Soren mumbled, "I've got nothing to give. Go away."

I wanted to rush up to him and tear the chains off. I wanted to hold him as he collapsed into my arms and smiled with gratitude. This was my fault, but all I had for him was an apology. Maybe some hope. Even that I figured would be a long way off. I stepped forward, bracing myself for the heart-breaking coldness I deserved.

I called gently, "Soren?"

At my voice, Soren lifted his head with slow, jerky movements. His bruised and swollen face, streaked with crusted blood and matted hair, wasn't healing. But peeking at me through one twinkling eye, an electric smile lifted his lips unevenly. I covered my mouth with my hand, and tears filled my eyelids. He'd been suffering, while I'd been worried all weekend about how he hated me, and how I was going to regain his trust. If only I'd known he would've been thrilled to see me, I could have been spared. But my torment—to even consider it—was selfish. Someone took personal liberties in torturing Soren. The immense guilt was heavier than I had imagined.

I didn't rush to his side. This could be a hungry, manipulative predator as much as the vampire I'd wronged.

"Indie!" Soren coughed, voice raspy like Della's. "You came! I expected a few decades of poking and prodding, like always. But not this time, because you can save me."

"How?" If he had a plan, I was ready to throw everything aside to break him and Della free.

"Are you willing to do it?"

I kneeled in front of him, meeting his gaze. "Anything. Tell me what to do."

His puffy, twinkling gaze studied me. "My knife." A dirty finger pointed down. "It's in my right pocket. The stupid elf never thought to frisk me."

I wasn't following, and his dress pants were heavily soiled and strained from his kneeling. I'd have to bring my arm very close and struggle to get it out. "What good is a knife with these chains?"

Soren made a noise resembling a snort, and the twinkle in his eye blinked out. "When you stab me in the back this time, aim between the ribs. If you can't hit my heart this time, at least pop an artery while you're at it." As Soren held his fake smile.

I gasped and covered my mouth. The tears returned. Holding back the choking pain, I said, "I'm not here to hurt you."

"Too late."

The silence was suffocating, like thick smoke, unable to see, unable to breathe. "Soren, I—"

"I thought you were special for one reason, but now I know you're special for a different one. The only thing I haven't figured out—and it's a tough balance, one I have lots of time to continue pondering—is whether to be disgusted or...impressed. The jury's still out, but I have this feeling the jurors are flipping their votes, one at a time, becoming pretty unanimous. Want to guess the verdict?"

I needed air, and I swiped away tears. Instinct was telling me to run, but I couldn't. For Soren, I couldn't give up that easily. "Please allow me to explain."

Chains rattled as he shifted position, and he grunted with discomfort. "I see you feel guilty. I didn't expect that. But if you can't literally stab me, and I get it—there's a certain chutzpah required—there's something else you can do."

"What is it?" I asked calmly, suspecting another terrible idea.

"Twofold, really. God, I'm so hungry. First, give me a nice, deep meal, and then when I'm satisfied, I'll turn you. Part two—a baby vampire can break my chains. You know, I've always said we didn't have enough vampires around here. So, that solves..." Soren shifted his fingers as if counting. "Four...problems? Hunger...healing...extra vampires...freedom. Yeah, that about covers it. One last thing, though, for the sake of full disclosure, I'm not a babysitter. When you free me, have a nice life, and I mean that...probably."

The more he spoke, the more heartbreaking things he said, and I was terrified that there was no end to the depths of his darkness. This had to be the Soren he'd hated—the man without his humanity. I'd broken him. I'd destroyed him. But as I'd suspected, I couldn't do anything. I wasn't capable of taking the change, so there was no point in considering the insane idea from a vampire I'd driven to insanity.

Before I could decline again, Soren snorted. "Oh, there it is. I can feel it."

"What?" I asked reluctantly.

"I think it stings. No, more like crushes. Yeah, that's a nice, even squeeze. I've been dishing this out left and right, but now I know what disappointment feels like. I gotta say I'm not a fan."

I couldn't rescue anyone in this condition, so I had to bring him back. Since he couldn't run away, he had to listen. "While waiting for you, I sat in the parking lot for hours, watching everyone leave, including Lily. I daydreamed about us, picturing what it would be like to have you in my arms—what it would feel like not to fear your touch."

"And the terrified human award goes to..."

"I never saw Lily return, or I would've—" What would I have done? Delayed Della's rescue for another Friday night?

"Changed your mind?" Soren snorted.

I looked at him evenly. "No. If I'd seen Lily, I would've asked for her help." At that point, I hadn't known about the cameras.

"That's the best cover story you can come up with? I thought I was worth more effort than that."

"It's not exciting because it's the truth. I didn't set you up. I've told you the truth."

Soren's battered face curled with anger. "You tossed me to my enemies like last week's garbage. Congratulations on doing what the elves couldn't—what Pierce ultimately didn't have the guts to do. When they're bored with their vengeance, they'll stake me, so that's why the only thing you can do is rob them of the pleasure. Get your pokey-pokey done, and I hope it doesn't bother your weak constitution."

"I'm sorry that our plan failed, but I'm not giving up on you."

"Actions speak louder than words, my little starlet, but humor me with one bit of truth."

"Everything I told you is the truth."

"Is my sister trapped in this evil facility or did you use the hope I carried for her as the vilest carrot imaginable?"

Without hesitating, I said, "She's here. I swear to you. How do you think I knew about your family?"

Soren studied me, mouth snarled with disgust. "Even if—now humor me for a little bit, because I'm a tad short on entertainment, and I'm missing my favorite show—but even if you think you're telling me the truth, I can't trust a word passing your lips. Witches are powerful. Elves love to diddle around in your mind, and I never felt any vervain protection on you, so obviously you wouldn't have any black nightshade either. For all I know, you're a puppet." Soren laughed, a crackly, hoarse-cough mixture. "While I'd delivered plenty myself, you, little puppet, were tasked with bringing in one test subject. Kudos, really, for your success in bagging the best, but using *humans*? Oh, that's low."

The door opened behind me, and I sucked in a breath as a lab tech entered. It was Stuffy, the human with short, trimmed hair and bold glasses. "Oh, Indie. I wasn't expecting you. Someone must've messed up the schedule this week. Since you're in here, could you draw the sample? I've got a backlog, and the boss is breathing down my neck."

The tech shoved his tray into my hands. "You know where they go when you're done." He left before I could refuse.

Soren snorted and repeated, "Actions speak louder than words."

"Okay, at the risk of getting caught, I had to draw a sample from Della, so I'm telling the truth—she's here. I don't want to hurt either of you, but I'm determined to get you both out of here."

"I'm tired," he said dismissively.

I shifted the tray in my hands. If I didn't do this, the watching elves would become suspicious, and I could lose any chance of returning to these rooms. Anyone else taking my place wouldn't be as gentle. "I know you don't understand, but I must do this." I withdrew a tube, an enormous needle, and a disposable tourniquet. There were no alcohol wipes—not that I expected any regard for the prisoners' health.

Soren snorted in disbelief and shook his head. "Sometimes, just once in a blue-ass moon, it sucks to be right."

Since he'd invited me to stab him in the heart, I didn't think he'd fight me, but I approached cautiously. He dangled there in irons, battered and bruised, defeated, and spitting vitriol I'd never heard before. My stomach clenched. He was in so much pain, and all of it was my fault. I'd come to ease some of it. Instead, I had to make it worse.

He wasn't healing, like Della. He had to be loaded with vervain, and so very hungry. I kneeled in front of him, close enough his fingertips could brush my cheek, and I tried to capture his gaze, but he refused. The blood streaking down his dress shirt hurt me more than I thought possible. I raged with the desire to heal him. To free him. But he had the same iron chains as Della.

I palmed his scruffy jaw and raised his face to meet my gaze. His beautiful green eyes bored into me, and I wanted to embrace him. To hold him and weep with endless apologizes at the immense pain I'd caused. Because the only thing that mattered to me was his forgiveness. My heart pounded hard, and what I felt for him wasn't fake. "I know you can hear me. I'm not afraid of you. That's not fear."

His eyes softened for only a flash, and he repeated, "Actions and words, little starlet."

"I have to play along, so I can return. Anyone else doing this won't be so kind. I'm sorry." I shifted his arm to find a vein, but he didn't fight. His skin was excessively hot and clammy with a layer of sticky sweat mixed with the aged blood, and I was worried. He was starving, fighting off the toxin, and weakening by the minute. Under the thrall of hunger and with his insatiable hatred of me, he could take what he needed, but he didn't. Not even when I slipped the awful needle under his flesh or attached the collection tube, spraying red blood into it. "Does it hurt?"

"Not how you do it." His voice was calm, softer than it had been, and he allowed me to fill tube after tube. When the tray was full, I had nothing to bandage the wound I'd caused. A trickle of blood ran down his arm and dripped to the floor.

Soren shifted and smeared the site with his ruined shirt. "The leaking blood tickles."

I pressed a thumb against the wound to ease his discomfort. "I'm sorry. I really am, but I'll be back as soon as I can."

"Take your time, really."

The stubborn vampire wasn't through with me yet.

26

The Hunt

Indie

Soren wasn't in a position to listen, but I heard him, and he told me what would begin the process of earning his trust back: action, and specifically, his hunger. Capturing vampires wasn't easy, so I couldn't imagine the lab would be so careless as to lose one before schedule. The witches and elves must store bags of blood around here somewhere.

I swiftly moved to the oversized glass-door refrigerators and skimmed the rows. I found arrays of test tubes, all coded for their present stage in the process of making what Lily had called the vampire weapon. No bags of blood here. I dipped low, checking the bottom shelves, but still found nothing. I turned and flagged down the first lab worker to brush by—careful not to startle her with a box full of vials.

She scrutinized me as if I were a complete stranger. "Can I help you?"

"I'm looking for the bags of blood." The worker tilted her head in confusion, so I added, "The rations."

"You must be new," she said slowly as if trying to recognize me.

I faked a smile for her. "You caught me. I have so many questions the training didn't cover, so if you could point me in the right direction, I'd appreciate it."

"We don't have bags of blood."

That couldn't be right. "Then how do you feed them?"

The lab worker's eyes glazed over as if trying to find information that should be there but wasn't. The classic sign of compulsion. She shifted the weight of the box in her arms. "I don't know. Sorry. Maybe ask Lily." She shrugged and walked away.

"Ask Lily what?" The male voice behind me chilled my blood. I turned to find the elf with a flirtatious half-grin. His fiery gaze swept my body, and I hid my shiver. "You look good, Indie."

I dragged the fake smile back onto my face. "Pierce, how are things with you?"

"I've been waiting for you to accept my offer." He moved closer. "An amazing feast and lots of information."

A persistent elf—how novel. "I'm not in a place to date right now."

Pierce raised his palms once more in defense. "You said it, not me. I only wanted to feed you and talk to you about our operations down here, you know, give you some training."

He'd heard me. He'd been watching. My heart pounded.

"But if you insist on blindly helping, I can respect that. Me and a few others are going to the bar tonight, and I'd like for you to join me."

I'd turned down a date request only to be met with another. He just didn't listen. "I'm not into the bar scene, really."

"I can make it worth your while." Pierce grinned, attempting to flirt, I thought, but he failed miserably. I hadn't met an elf this dense in a long time. No wonder our species was dying out. Not fast enough, though.

"I'm sure. Thanks for the offer, but no, thank you." I faced the fridge and gripped the handle again, waiting for him to get the hint.

"This area is for the techs. What's our bookworm doing over here, anyway?" he asked, referring to me in the third person.

I bristled, and the urge to fling him across the lab made my hands tremble. I exhaled deeply and reminded myself that he was still a very dangerous threat—far more than he even realized. So, I dragged that fake smile back onto my face and turned. "I'm getting something."

"I can see that. But what?"

"Why do you ask?" He had to suspect something, and I wondered if Lily had told him exactly how Soren got here—or if he'd watched.

"Why are you deflecting?"

I needed to be invisible, not intriguing. A human woman on the receiving end of unwanted advances and intrusion would have somewhat of a backbone. "Not everything that happens around the lab is your business. Now, if you'll excuse me..."

Pierce leaned in closer with a smug smile. "Lily manages this lab, but since her dad's life was inside these walls, she has a misplaced sense of ownership over it. Obviously she still has value, but let me be clear, she's not in charge. I'm here to make sure the clan's orders are followed, and we don't like when people disobey. Now, where do you prefer to stand?"

Way over there. "I'm only doing what I was hired to do."

Pierce leaned closer and pressed a hand against the glass refrigerator as if telling me it was off-limits. Satisfaction spread across his face. "That's the spirit. I'll see you tonight." Pierce walked away.

My heart pounded even harder, and the familiar urge to flee tensed every muscle in my body. I exhaled a few deep breaths and calmed my instincts. The bar tonight wasn't an invitation, but there was no way in hell, under the threat of fire from a thousand suns melting my retinas for all eternity, I would go on a date with him. I had no qualms about his disappointment.

Pierce was watching, and the lab tech said there weren't any bags. Despite the elf's thinly veiled threat, I wasn't giving up. I headed into Lily's office, catching her while she was on the phone. I waited impatiently, and when she hung up, I asked, "If your test subjects are so important, you have to be feeding them. Where are the blood bags?"

Lily invited me to sit with a gesture, but I couldn't. "Pierce removed them."

I made fists at my sides and kept my language neutral to the underlying mission. "But if there's an emergency, how do you save a subject?"

Lily leaned back in her seat. "The workers are on a rotation schedule, but as you said, that's only for dire emergencies. Is this about Soren?"

I'd never known so much anger. "Torture and starvation—how do you think he's doing? This is cruel."

"I know. That's why I wanted your help in finding the spell. It's the only way to stop all this."

I didn't believe that spell existed, so it couldn't be the only solution. But I was powerless, so I had to know that if something happened, Lily had my back—to choose me over Pierce. "Do you have a problem with my visiting the vampires?"

"I don't, but there are cameras, so if he gets suspicious, you have to back off."

She'd only support me as long as she kept her nose clean. I may have been too late. "I can't say for certain, but either Pierce doesn't like my extra involvement, or he doesn't like my rejections."

Lily leaned forward. She glanced through her door and then looked up at me. Her volume lowered. "When he sets his sights on a woman, he never gives up until the option is off the table entirely or someone new piques his interest. Pierce didn't give up on my sister—no matter how much she loved Oliver—until she became a vampire. And he wouldn't leave me alone until you showed up. But don't worry. He doesn't know what you are. His persistence is normal. So while I know what you're going through, I couldn't really imagine it. If I had a choice..." Lily trailed off, and I suspected there was almost as much disgust there as I had.

"I appreciate what you've done for me, but can I ask for a favor? Where can I find blood bags?"

"The Menominee Blood Donation Center, but it's not exactly a grocery store where you can walk in and order what you want. Try asking Nicole. She's kept them fed for years." Lily smiled softly.

I thanked her and left. I had no time to waste, and I cursed not having access to my wings during the long drive back to town.

Indie

I pulled into the long driveway at the bed-and-breakfast in Marinette, and I knocked on the door this time. I still felt terrible for walking in unannounced the last time.

Nicole answered the door without a vacuum in her hands. "Hello, my dear, please do come inside."

I did, and the woman closed the door behind us and faced me. "Can I offer you a drink?"

Rather than argue with her kind hospitality, I gave her an easy option. "Seltzer water, please."

Nicole nodded and headed to the bar with a limp—one I wished I could heal. She reached for a glass, and a sparkle in her eye appeared as she asked, "You've got me so curious, Indie. After your date, Soren's been moping around like a lost puppy, and I was excited he finally found someone who affected him so, but his moping meant you didn't feel the same way."

Nicole was wrong, but I had to figure things out for myself. "It's been...complicated."

"With him, it always is. Well, you're here now, but I haven't seen Soren around. That's not a coincidence, is it?" Nicole settled the bubbly glass on a coaster.

A flash of guilt tore through me. "Soren's in trouble."

Nicole exhaled. "What did he do this time?"

"He was helping me, but he got caught."

Nicole leaned toward me, resting on her elbows. "My idiot neph—" The old woman paused and gave me a warm smile. "I bet you know he's not my nephew. He's my great-great-great grand uncle, but I leave that out. He doesn't need to be reminded of how great he is, especially when he gets his ass caught in the snare."

I yearned to hear more about this family side of the vampire. "It's happened before?"

"I think I'll need a drink too, something with a bit more kick." Nicole poured straight vodka into a glass and downed it in a swallow.

She knew a lot and cared deeply for Soren. "Can I ask why he treats you as the maid?"

Nicole smiled warmly. "I've been looking over this place my whole life, and I'd be lost without it. Soren's laziness has nothing to do with my work ethic. Now, where was I? The story of Soren Rockwell. It begins with the Peshtigo Fire of 1871. That was the night the Rockwell children fled the fire with their mother. Their only place of sanctuary—a cave—happened to be occupied by a vampire who was escaping the witch hunt. He turned Oliver as a diversion, and my boy, lost to the bloodlust, attacked his family. You can imagine what happened next, and Soren never forgave his brother."

I couldn't compare my unwanted situation with Soren's, but I had a small idea of what it felt like. "It's terrifying, exhausting, frustrating to adapt to becoming something different."

"He was definitely afraid. I think the trauma of the change affected him for a long time, and being forced into the shadows didn't help his psyche any. Soren's fear of exposure led him to develop a rule—humans and vampires don't mix—and when his own brother risked that very exposure,

Soren acted swiftly. I don't believe Oliver ever forgave him for Evangeline, but he still holds that silly rule close to his impenetrable heart." Nicole's sadness was clear on her lined features. "Imagine my surprise when you were his date."

Perhaps that rule wasn't so fixed after all.

"My family had its legends of the vampire brothers, told as fairy tales during reunions. No one believed the stories, but I did. I wanted to be one more than anything. When I was a teenager, Oliver appeared, explained who he was, and asked me to be a caretaker of this place. I jumped at the opportunity to please him and earn the right to the change. Well, it's been a successful business for decades, but both boys always declined my request. While age wore me down, our family tree was pruned by time, accidents, and other forces of nature until there was just me. Years passed when I never heard from either brother, and I'd thought they'd been returned to the natural order of things—ashes floating on the breeze. So, I used to sit on the patio overlooking the dark rolling river, and talk to them. I'd tell them what they became didn't define them, and I'd wish them peace and happiness."

Nicole poured herself another drink. "A long time ago, Oliver finally appeared and gave me a way to contact him. When bodies with throat punctures appeared, I made that call. That was when I learned the legend of the vampires wasn't all the darkness hid. We had witches and elves too, all struggling to find a balance—a peace. Just as quickly as the bodies stopped, Oliver had left once more. I waited all these years, never losing hope that the only two family members I had left would stay. Be careful what you wish for." Nicole smiled and swallowed down the glass with a cough.

"Not too long ago, Soren had finally returned. He was in terrible shape, so much so that I couldn't recognize him. He tore off my vervain and made a mess of everything. The witches had turned him into a hunter of his own kind, and when Oliver and Daisy pulled him from the brink, Soren was...lost. I think he stayed here to keep himself away from everyone else for their own safety."

I was enthralled by the heartbreaking tale. "He made himself a prisoner."

"No matter how much I explained what he did wasn't his fault, he still hates himself. He needs to let someone in, and that special someone has to show him he's not the monster he thinks he is."

While Soren was in pain on the inside, he was beautiful on the outside. I couldn't imagine how he'd gone this long without finding someone. "He's never brought around anyone? Not one person he seemed interested in?"

"He's brought women here on occasion, but only for a painfully obvious reason, because he still holds tight to his rule. He's also jaded about witches, so he doesn't go near them if he can help it. And he doesn't go for elves at all." My mouth dried up. I sipped from the water while Nicole refilled her glass. "I hate that he's lonely. It just kills me, but with you, dear, he felt different, and I had a glimmer of hope he was breaking through that stupid rule."

The barrier against humans was understandable, and his hatred of witches justifiable, but the last one had my chest constricting. "Why...why not elves? Has he said?"

The battle I'd finally accepted and had been fighting was as futile as the company of human warriors with their black nightshade-dipped weapons at our gates. On his principle, Soren would refuse me, and since I believed he had feelings for me, revealing the truth would devastate him. Nicole had feared he'd been ashes on the breeze, and he'd already begged me to end his life over his imprisonment. Another betrayal would make her fears come true. All those years ago I'd fled that battle and saved my life. This time I couldn't leave—not until I repaired the damage I'd caused. But I feared for my heart.

Nicole's crooked smile had me gripping every word of why this battle was doomed. "Within the safety of these walls, Soren is a laid-back kind of guy. The sort of fellow who'd watch trash TV with you and bring you some popcorn or an extra beer just because he got up. I only want him to be happy, so I've pushed, sometimes too hard, but he's a stubborn mule. A few slaps when he's braying back help move his feet. In my need for him to be happy, I asked. Let's just say that regardless of the opportunities the exterior brings him, he's not that laid back."

"I'm missing something."

Nicole patted me on the wrist. "There's an imbalance in the hidden world that causes a lot of trouble—much of it right here at this doorstep. I don't know the details, but somewhere a while ago, a great battle devastated the elf community, and as a result, they'd lost the last of their females."

It was weird to hear my history told to me. I sipped the water, and a trickle of relief flowed into my chest. "Soren doesn't desire men or males."

"You got it. So, who caught Soren this time? Don't tell me it was that damn elf again. I swear, if he doesn't stake the bastard, I'm going to do it myself."

I didn't want to worry the woman who cared so deeply for him, or risk trying anything, and I didn't want her to hate me. "I'm working on getting him out, and I was told you have a supply of blood."

"I always keep the refrigerator stocked. How many bags do you need?"

I didn't know the volume required to quench a vampire's thirst—especially one who'd been tortured and starved. But Pierce wouldn't allow me to carry a full box into the prison cells. Discretion was necessary. I considered my bra size and the snugness of my waistband and said, "Four?"

"Coming right up." She reached down, opening what sounded like a small refrigerator, and dropped four on the bar. "The emergency stash is kept with the booze, but don't worry about taking more than you think you need. I have a full supply downstairs. Indie, I'm not in a position to help them squeeze out of their hijinks anymore, so I'm grateful you can step in. It's scary out there. Do you have protection? I have spare black nightshade. I don't suppose you need vervain, but I have that too."

I smiled warmly and swallowed back the clog in my throat. I wished I could be part of this family...to actually have a family who cared. "Thank you, but I'm well-protected." As long as I didn't get scratched...

"I wish I could help more. Soren needs you more than he knows. Good luck, Indie." She patted my wrist once more with a sparkle in her eyes. This time, they were tears.

I was the only one willing and able to get him out, and I was going to do anything to get him back to his lovely woman.

27

Vengeful Featherbag

Soren

I WANTED TO BELIEVE what Indie had said about her innocence, but I couldn't trust her words. Of all the devastating things she had done to me, a literal knife in the back should've been easy. But I wasn't surprised she'd declined to show me mercy. The elf wouldn't allow his puppet to damage the goods. He saved that for himself.

I'd been dragged through mud before, but I had to hand it to the elf. I didn't think he was capable of starving me and delivering a daily dose of torture. Even with my stomach gnawing with stabbing pains and my head throbbing, and my body on fire from the inside out, none of it compared to the pain Indiara Niskatar had delivered on a beautiful, sensual platter.

A tiny droplet of hope had me believing that somehow I could break that grip on her mind, and maybe—just maybe—if the skies cleared and the stars aligned, if the road to her gated heart creaked open, she might consider freeing me. Indie's lifespan was depressingly short compared to mine and the elf's.

And since Pierce became obsessed with his fixations, nothing short of a change of heart from the entire staff or a bulldozer was getting past him. I was going to die in here. Not today. Not tomorrow, but someday, if the elf were capable of boredom.

The door to my dark prison opened, blinding me once again. Even though I knew the truth as clearly as a glass full of sweet, numbing vodka, I still frowned with disappointment. It still wasn't her. The smug elf strolled in and glanced around as if he were a friendly visitor in my home.

"When I tossed that over there, I'd forgotten you can't see it." He looked at my sun ring, resting where he'd left it. "Oh, well. I'm not leaving your light on."

My body still burned from his last visit. "Don't you have a punching bag at home to get these needs of yours out?"

Pierce approached and leaned down. One hand held the same stogie syringe filled with a lavender solution from hell. "I enjoy your company more. Take it as a compliment."

"I'll try to keep that in mind while you're kicking a defenseless, chained guy suffering from starvation. Elves taste like shit, no offense, but I'd make an exception for you."

"I'm flattered, really. But I'm here for your next dose. My little vampire needs to keep up with his meds."

Pierce uncapped the syringe and jabbed it into my throat. I gritted my teeth as fire burned from the site throughout my body as if a tiny dragon crawled inside me, blowing flames and cooking my flesh as he moved. The visual was cute. The pain—not so much. Through the pain, I tried to brace myself against the next step in the proper administration of my medicine, as he'd called it. I clenched my abs the best I could, being short on the healing juice lately.

The wallop to my jaw was unexpected. Lights flashed across my vision as my head snapped to the side. I ran my tongue around my mouth, checking for loose teeth. Not finding any, I spat the blood onto his stupid leather shoe. I should've kept it for my strength, but I had to show the elf who was boss here.

"If you don't have the cash to reimburse me for that, I'll have to take it out on your eye," Pierce said. "Actually, that might not be a good enough motivator. I mean, you do have two of the things."

He had two of something else he didn't need. "Workplace hazard, featherbag. Being on the payroll, don't you have reimbursable expenses? If not, sounds like shitty management. But since you're not feeding me anymore, you can afford those cute blue booties. Get some hairnets while you're at it. Complete the look."

Pierce reeled back his fist, and this time I expected the wallop to my face. I couldn't brace against it, though, and it stung like hell. I knew what he wanted, but I'd take all this punishment, so he didn't have the satisfaction of my tears and begging.

"A stain on my shoe will eventually rub out until it's nothing, nonexistent, and forgotten. Just like you."

"Ouch." I frowned. "This pointless feud between our kind has been going on for so long, no one knows why it started anymore. Don't you think it's a little...unhealthy for you to take this so personally?"

"And that's part of why you're here—to understand. My grandfather was personal, and no, I'm not over it."

Great. "Oliver is going to stake your ass if you kill me." Not a compelling argument, but all I had.

"I can manipulate Daisy into having that fanger leave me alone again. The other part of why you're here is very interesting. You've been exposed to the original serum, so you know how much it hurts. Our new recipe will hurt tenfold, and the poisoning process will be much slower, so much so that it's transmissible in your bite." Pierce leaned forward, shoving his face in mine, and his glamoured long, pointy ears and folded feathery wings made him look like an overstuffed giant chicken. "I would be thrilled if I could journal your feelings during the process."

Stab my ears out with a fork. "You've finished your day's game, so how about you leave me alone?"

Pierce straightened, attempting to intimidate me with his broad chest and obsession with leg day. "If alone is what you want, so be it. Isolation is an effective torture for humans. How long until you crack?"

"If you think I've never been tortured before, you're in for a long, boring wait."

"Good." Pierce turned and headed for the door, but he paused with his hand on the switch. He glanced at my ring on the floor in the corner. "Vampires don't need sleep, right?" He walked out, leaving the light on.

He actually did have some idea of how to torture effectively. This sucked. But now I could work on my daydreaming skills. And all I'd dream about was rescue by a certain tall, blond pixie who owed me.

She owed me so much more than a dance.

And she owed me so much more than however she'd defined a full night I'd never forget.

So I could daydream with my definition.

28

Earning Trust

Indie

I rested my hand on the knob, closed my eyes, and inhaled deeply, preparing myself for the grim scene. Inside was bright, and in a flash of panic, I looked around for the lab tech, but I didn't find one.

Instead, Soren's sun ring sat in the corner, discarded. He'd told me the ring stood for his humanity. Since there were no skylights, he'd given up on me. I hadn't returned quickly enough. I pocketed the ring so no opportunistic lab tech could take it.

Soren hung limply from his chains. I kneeled next to him and set down my incognito tray. My chest squeezed as I searched for signs of life—his version of it. Rivulets of blood had dried along his bruised forearms. His face was swollen in a different place, as if he'd been punched again. More blood streaked his pants and chest. His hair was tangled and now matted.

I whispered, "Soren?"

He didn't move. He didn't respond. No murmurs or groans passed his lips. Without thinking, I cupped his jaw with both hands and tilted his face up to meet mine. "Soren?" I repeated, louder.

Still nothing.

I gripped his shoulders and shook him. The chains rattled, and his head bobbed. He was by definition, undead, but now he looked simply dead. I fought back tears.

"Don't tell me I'm too late. Don't you dare." I pulled a bag of blood free from my waistband, tore into it, and pushed it between his lips. I squeezed. Blood ran down his chin and dripped onto the blood-streaked white floor. I forced his head up to keep the blood in his mouth, and it drained to the back of his throat.

He still didn't respond.

I sucked in my lips and bit down, fighting back the sobs of desperation breaking free. "I told you I'd be back. Why couldn't you wait for me? Damn it, Soren. Don't do this to me. I promised you I'd be back, and I promised I'd get you and your sister out of here. Don't make me break my word." I squeezed the bag harder.

Eyes still closed, Soren coughed.

I gasped in sudden relief, but I shoved down the hope trying to bloom in my chest. "You can do this. Drink, damn it. Drink."

Soren's instincts kicked in, and he gulped hungrily and finished off the bag with urgency. He lurched forward for more, and his eyelids fluttered open. "Indie?"

I smiled gently. "I'm here."

"Thanks for the drink."

"Don't thank me. I got you into this mess, and I promised I would get you and your sister out."

"I'm going to need more to fight my way out of here."

I slipped a bag free from my bra and punctured it for him. I brought it to his lips. "This is all I have for you today. The rest is for your sister."

"Lukewarm A-positive. Almost yummy. You snuck in contraband for me?" Soren gripped the port with his lips and slurped it down hungrily. "Any chance you grabbed a crowbar?"

"I would've been back sooner, but Pierce had ordered the supply of bags to be discarded. I had to get these from Nicole. Lily tells me there's a rotation schedule for the humans to feed you."

Soren finished the bag with a satisfied sigh. "That's news to me."

"I figured."

"So, what's the plan?" Soren asked, warm and friendly—closer to his old self than I expected. Part of me had braced for a nasty insult, but for some reason, I believed I'd finally won him over. He believed me because I'd broken the rules for him.

With a resigned tone, I said, "My plan was to give you the blood. You'd regain your strength and break free."

"That's not a plan. These chains were designed with their prisoners in mind, and that was before the daily vervain doses. At least I can heal the broken bones before Pierce comes to snap them again. I think he gets off on that cracking sound. Get on with your draw and get out."

Tears sprang to my eyes. The blood wasn't enough. Why would it be? How could one meal make up for all I'd done? My chest burned, and as if all the air had been vacuumed out of this prison cell. I couldn't breathe. I needed air.

I remembered when I'd last felt this way. I'd stolen my mother's armor and sword, intending to infiltrate the line at the gate, to defend our weakened kind against the invading humans, but I had been caught. My brother Reku, on the orders of our father, had brought me down to the castle dungeon for my disobedience. Rather than chain me, he'd taught me a few simple moves with my mother's sword. I'd believed he would help me learn what I needed to fight for our clan and see my desires as plainly as I wore them.

He hadn't.

When Reku had sealed me behind those iron bars and clattered the lock in place and walked away without a glance, that was the same heart rend I'd just performed on Soren. I'd given him the sword, lifted his hopes in the face of adversity, and I closed the gate. My family was despicable. I would not do them the honor of following in their footsteps. I glared at the disappointed vampire with determination. "No."

"No, what?" Soren asked with the same dismissive tone.

"I'm not drawing a sample, and I'm going to get you out of here."

Soren lifted his healing face to me. "If you refuse, you're fired, and you'll lose access to the lab."

That was a valid possibility, but one I could bargain my way out of. I needed something else more—something far more valuable than meekly blending in offered. "If I complete this draw, you'll continue believing I'm—what had you called me—a puppet?" I rose to my feet and picked up the tray. Soren's eyes followed me with a rising glimmer. "No one compels me. No one. I don't know how to free you, but I swear to you I will. All I need from you is one thing."

No smarmy grins, no dead eyes, no dismissive expressions. He was listening. He cared enough to listen. I hadn't lost him yet—the real him. "Your options are limited, but I'll try my best."

"I need you to trust me. You're not going to die in here."

The corners of his lips lifted just slightly. "I think I'm starting to believe you."

⤞⤞⤞ ⬳⬳⬳

Indie

A start was enough for me. One more vampire to win over. With trembling hands, fully aware of the spies overhead, I slipped through Della's door and quickly closed it behind me, as if inside the prison cell were safer than out there. I flicked on the light.

Della squinted, and when her sensitive eyes adjusted, she scowled at the prepared tray in my arm. "I was wondering what was taking you so long. I shouldn't be surprised they got to you."

"It's not like that," I said, approaching with my prop tray.

"I don't even know what to think. You came in here acting like a friend, giving me hope, and promising me freedom. Here's a tip for next time, blood bag, don't waste your breath."

I set the tray on the floor and pulled a bag from my bra. "Were you referring to this?"

Her hungry eyes glowed red at the bag, and she licked her parched lips. "Nope. Not what I meant, but if you're offering..."

I popped the port and brought the bag to her. Della cocked her body to get enough chain to grab the bag from me, and she bit into it like a feral animal—not using the port as a straw. While she sucked it down and looked at me with slowly draining suspicion, I'd realized she could've grabbed my arm instead.

But she didn't.

I pulled the last bag free from my waistband, and her eyes twinkled with delight. When that bag finished, I gave her the second. She drained that one surprisingly quickly, and like her brother, she exhaled a satisfied sigh. "Is it Thanksgiving, 'cause it feels like it?"

"We tried to get you out. Things didn't go according to plan, and now Soren is next door."

Della snorted. "I haven't seen a book in a while, but the hunter has become the prey. Is that considered irony?"

"I don't know."

"My brother was controlled by witches, and I could hear him being ordered in and out of this lab for years. I used to dream that if I ever got free, I would rip his throat out myself for leaving me to rot. But now the game has changed. Interesting."

I had a feeling Della wanted vengeance on her brother, so maybe I could ease that animosity, so that when—not if—I got them out, they wouldn't kill each other before we passed the first doorway. "Pierce is torturing Soren, and it's awful, completely inhumane. Soren said something about vengeance."

Della's eyes hardened. "An elf is harming my brother?"

Her anger made me back up a step. "I'm going to get you out of here, both of you. I need you to understand this is a great risk for me, and I don't want to bother if you're going to kill him as soon as you're free. Can you promise me you'll save grudges for after everyone is clean, warm, fed, and level-headed?"

Della exhaled. "Yeah, sure. That's assuming you can even do it."

I had to figure out something.

29

Cranky Witch

Soren

At some point between brutal beatings, burning injections, and stabbing blood draws from the robotic, heartless staff, my ring had disappeared. Even to those who could never imagine its true worth, the ruby and silver had tangible value to humans, so color me shocked that someone had taken the opportunity.

The door of my prison opened. Subjected to endless light—the elf's idea of sleep deprivation torture—my internal clock was broken. The anticipation of a fresh wave of pain made his visits come far too frequently, but the sheer isolation in-between left me begging for a face, a voice, any of their puppets to even look at me. Before, I could bury that need to connect with the TV, pretending Kyle was my buddy and Makayla was a mutual friend I helped him navigate. But not here. Not stuck in my own head. I was exhausted, not that being propped up in the air allowed for a pillow-soft rest, anyway. The footsteps came before the snarky comments, so I looked up to find a blood-filled shot glass in front of my face. I would've chosen something more enticing than a pitifully small serving of blood—no more than a sip—for a hallucination. The award for effective torture belonged to...the elf.

I followed the glass up to the face, and it was Lily. Since the amount—although desperately needed—would be so unsatisfying, I couldn't trust what she might've added to it. "Is that supposed to be a peace offering? Because I can think of so many other options that would serve you better."

Lily set the minuscule shot glass on the floor in front of me—just out of reach, naturally—and squatted down to meet my gaze. "You're awfully chipper considering the circumstances."

"I've had worse." Although technically true, I wouldn't admit the elf was getting to me.

Lily rolled her eyes. "Look, Indie asked permission to visit you, so I know she cares or at least feels really guilty. I can't empathize, but I wasn't going to rat her out regardless, because I don't agree with the elf's mission."

"Could've fooled me. Seriously, bravo. I guess that means you and Allison are constructing an even bigger bonfire? A tip—since clearly you're here for my help—instead of beer, bribe us with willing co-eds. I run on a tight schedule these days, but I think I can pencil you in this weekend. And if you want a fair fight—" I paused, considered the past events, and said, "—a *longer* fight, you might want to let me go now, so I can fuel up. Because that isn't nearly enough." I pointed at the shot glass, but Lily didn't look up at my fingers.

"I'm not like Jamie or Allison," Lily said calmly. Getting comfortable, she kneeled on the floor and sat on her heels. A little company—no matter how irritating—was at least a little welcome.

"Really? I thought you were there, but my memory's a little fuzzy. Were you the one conjuring the ring of fire, or were you crushing us to the ground so we'd bake alive while slowly dying from battle wounds? Come to think of it, I can't see how the elves are cordial with you. In your futile attempt to repeat history, they'd suffered more losses than us."

"We've all done things we regret, hypocrite. So if you're done ripping apart my mistakes, I came here...well, for a peace offering."

I managed the energy needed for a smug smile. "You recognize another mistake, and you're here for my forgiveness? Wow, what did you do this time, I wonder? Maybe, just maybe, you'll actually realize your mistake before you make it next time. Third time's the charm, as they say," I said dryly. "Or is it 'our little girl is growing up'?"

Lily exhaled as if trying to maintain her deadpan composure. "You are such an asshole."

"When the situation calls for it," I said and glared at her.

"Now that you've got all that out of your system, can you listen?"

Actually, I did feel a little better, so I said nothing.

Taking my non-answer in the affirmative, Lily said, "When Daisy was scrambling for a solution to her magic, she'd been searching for the spell that originally created vampires, expecting to use it to reverse the curse, so she and Oliver could be together. I helped as a favor and to satiate my desire to learn and to explore grimoires. Once she'd become one of you—against her will—the hope that had driven her became my own."

I chuckled. "And how's that going for you?"

"I still have a team out there collecting grimoires from all over to build the library down here—both as a repository for witch knowledge, but also in hopes of finding that golden ticket inside one of the ancient and delicate tomes. Allison had warned Daisy how impossible the task was, and I didn't want to face the truth that Indie had tried to explain. Only under extraordinary conditions was it even possible for the spell to have survived the centuries."

Witches spouted lots of confusing woo-woo talk, but that made no sense. "How would Indie know that?"

Ignoring my question, Lily continued, "You freed yourself from this place once, and I never intended for you to return, but once you stepped foot inside this lab, I no longer had a choice."

"Is that supposed to be an apology? Because it sucks."

Lily pressed her lips thinly. "Daisy argued with me a lot that fiery night, and I spent a lot of time thinking about her words. My dad never expected me to become a research scientist because I didn't need to be pushed. He loved me just the way I was. My sister was the black sheep of the family, and that explains why she saw something in you. But I can't. Like at all."

"Thanks," I said dryly.

"My dad wanted to save people with treatments and cures, and to the detriment of my family, he'd fought back when Newt forced him to make the serum fatal. I believed he hoped to design the serum so you wouldn't be able to bite anymore or humans would taste terrible or sting you when bitten—something less...immediate and messy. As I said, I'm not a scientist. I can only use the skills I have, and those led me to the hunt for the spell—for the same result. Vampires would no longer pose a threat to humans. Since my plan is growing dimmer by the day, you're left with Pierce's. It's still not what I wanted, but the finished product will be closer to what my dad had imagined than Newt. The only way you're getting out of here is through that redeveloped serum."

"A body bag doesn't count as 'getting out' just for the record."

"The final recipe won't be a single fatal dose." Now I was listening. "It's an infection, transmissible by bite, that's terribly painful to drive your need to feed and spread it. It lasts a long time in the system—a few months—to maximize its effect, and in the end, it cures."

A few months of suffering in exchange for a viable cure? A few months was…nothing. I'd vaguely entertained the idea here and there, but since it wasn't possible, I'd never taken it seriously. Becoming human meant I would no longer be on the wrong side of this hidden world as a feared creature of the night, avoiding discovery and pitchforks. No more bloody clothing. And be real, no more having to expend the effort of planning an ambush or a happy meal strategy for every single snack. It was exhausting.

Above all, no more being a…monster. The appeal was there and growing.

With a cure, I could be with Indie all the time as a normal human couple for a normal human lifespan. I hadn't had food in so long, I'd forgotten what it tasted like. We could grocery shop, and I could learn to cook. I'd love to make something with my own two hands that would bring her pleasure. Even better, I could take her to bed and bring that pleasure without accidentally hurting her, and I wouldn't have to hold back in my own pleasure. We could even…have a family. I could get a job.

Eh, that was a bit far. I might not be wealthy—certainly nowhere near my brother's level—but I wouldn't need a job, not for a short human lifespan.

And when the day arrived Indie was called from this world, I could join her, rather than stalk the earth alone in pain and suffering for centuries to come. There was a certain appeal in a fantasy like that. But in taking it, I wouldn't be able to keep her safe from whoever she was running from. Accepting the cure for myself meant I'd lose the best and most useful parts of me just to spare myself the parts I hated.

I couldn't put my happiness above hers.

And I couldn't put my happiness above her safety. After I fixed whatever Indie was afraid of, then I'd entertain the cure...because being a human wasn't appealing enough without her.

Lily added, "It's cute that you're considering it, but now that I have your hopes up nice and high, I suspect you'll change your mind. I didn't agree with Pierce's plan simply because while the serum allows you to die as a human, you don't get to resume a human lifespan. You've already had more than nature intended, so after the serum has sufficiently had time to spread, you just...perish as if you were staked in the heart—a body for the young, ashes for the old. Is there somewhere special you'd like me to spread your ashes?"

I exhaled. Lily had dangled a daydream that I'd always known could never happen. Having that glimpse wasn't as upsetting as discovering this new, drawn-out fatal serum would be forced on me. But since their plan had an oversight, I had a reason to believe their serum would also fail. "You've got one glaring issue in your benevolent extermination plan."

Lily stared at me expectantly and waited.

I snorted in disbelief. "You expect me to volunteer the big, fat piece of your plan that won't work?"

Lily tapped on the inadequate glass. "Tell me what the elf missed, and this is yours."

So generous. "You were going to give me that anyway. Otherwise, you wouldn't have brought it."

Lily pulled it closer to herself.

I frowned, but it was probably better if I refrained from such a teasing amount. Besides, I didn't get the chance to gloat very often, and I didn't think the elf was capable of correcting the basic glaring issue at this point in the process. "Vampires don't bite vampires."

"Genius. Really. We should've consulted with you during the initial planning," Lily said, deadpan. "The serum introduced into your system transmits from your bite into a human, where it sits harmlessly until the next vampire comes around and bites him."

Their starvation tactic would ensure I couldn't resist a bite of infected fresh-tap. "Let me guess. You already drew up a rotation schedule for your human test subjects. But your idol was gung-ho about saving people. How do you know the serum is harmless to humans?"

"We've been testing the serum in their systems to spot any anomalies and make corrections. The whole process is moot if they can't survive it. When we know how much an average adult human can handle, then you are the final phase. As patient zero, you'll be the first to bite the human test subjects during timed trials. Obviously, we'll start with the shortest time possible. We know you'll be very hungry, but we don't want to overshoot on the first try. Eventually, we'll find the minimum effective level of transmission during a normal feed."

I didn't want to be special for once. "Newt had me out there delivering vampires for testing—as many as I could find and he could hold. If just one bite could cure me, you'd need others down here to finish the process, so why am I patient zero?"

Still dry and unaffected, Lily said, "You've been exposed to the original version of the serum. We're curious about how your body reacts because we don't want unforeseen side-effects. And Pierce chose you for personal reasons."

I had to admit I was impressed with the depth and thoroughness of their depravity. With each piece of information, the fantasy of the cure slipped further and further away, while my frustration—my disgust—grew. Pardon me for not trusting genetically engineered food. "If you're testing those people out there with your experimental serum, you couldn't account for their long-term exposure. How you do know it'll maintain its effectiveness with continued transmission instead of mutating away like the common cold? How do you know it won't simply stop working as the human body filters it out? Or how do you know it won't accumulate in their systems with each subsequent bite introducing a little more and still kill them?"

Lily's lips lifted just a little. "Maybe we should've included you in the planning sessions. Oh, well. If your conscience is nagging you, we can easily pivot to animal trials. I don't know how much of a delay that would cause, but I can pitch it to Pierce. Do you like the taste of rat blood?"

Elves hunted us because we tainted their breeding stock—their description, not mine—so I could, in theory, sort of understand their motivation. But I never liked witches, for obvious reasons, but also for obvious reasons, I did like humans. None of this was good news for me or my kind, but the careless disregard for human lives all in the name of committing mass genocide was so far away from Dr. Greg Barrett's vision. Even Newt's had been more humane.

"Who's the hypocrite now?" Anger joined the roaring fire in my veins. "Even if your serum granted us a real cure with a real human lifespan, what right do you people think you have to make that choice for us? You know we take what we need and leave as little trace as possible. We're not flaming...monsters." The word popped out and deflated my rant for a beat. In the end, the term was relative—a point of view based on actions, not by simply existing.

The witch folded her arms across her chest, and a smirk formed on her lips. She didn't like Pierce. He couldn't have compelled her. I had to appeal to the side of her that wanted her family back—that teary Lily who'd begged for forgiveness after the fire.

"Lily, we're family. Can you seriously look me in the eye and watch me suffer for *months*?" Eh, not a great way to start. "Can you pull the trigger on Kevin Fontaine? When you and your friends tried to kill us, Kevin saved your sister and Oliver. Is that how you'd repay him? Turn him to ash? What about Oliver, your sister's love? He'd protected her from the elf's manipulation—from an elf's dreaded fate. Would you tear away your sister's happiness? And your mother...Stacey happens to adore being a vampire. She's free. She's happy." Lily squirmed. I fought back the disgust in my tone, trying to find that empathy for others she sorely lacked for me. "Could you watch everyone you love—even your own sister—suffer and die? Could you bury all of them? Would you prefer to be alone than to have your family, the way they are, who love you just the way you are?"

Lily blinked a few times and looked away. Maybe she still had some humanity buried under all those layers of manipulation, misinformation, and misdirected pain. I was finally getting through to her.

"You helped protect your sister against an elf's fate—the same one that you refused for yourself. You're strong, Lily." I needed to negotiate, to give her a plan of action while she was still hearing me and not the elf. "Free me and Della and let Indie off the hook."

After a pause to gather herself, Lily frowned. "What does Indie have to do with this?"

"You have a family who loves you, but I have people too. Please restore Indie's free will and release her from your deal with her memory intact. You can trust her not to say anything about what happened down here."

"Indie volunteered to help me. I've never tampered with her memory or free will, and neither did Pierce. I protected her from it." Lily crossed her arms over her chest, distorting her white lab coat. "She wants to visit, and you beg for her safety. The two of you are...interesting."

That was such a relief that I almost forgot the burning fire in my veins. But in my pleas for Indie, I'd inadvertently shifted the witch's focus where I didn't want it. To keep Indie safe—to stop her from being used as a pawn against me—I hit hard. "You can stop all this, Lily. Unchain me and my sister. Free those workers out there. They don't deserve to be sacrificed. They have families too. People they love. People who wait for them to come home each night. Take a stand against Pierce instead of following along like a lapdog."

The anger returned. Lily rose and slapped me across the face. I was already a mess—beaten, bruised, and bloody—courtesy of the elf once again, and with the burn of vervain in my system, I couldn't feel it. "You have no idea what goes on around here."

"What part did I get wrong?"

Lily flung the shot glass, shattering the pitifully small tease, and splashing the blood against the wall like an oversized mosquito on a windshield. I licked my dry lips with my parched tongue. Lily pointed at me in accusation, anger rolling off her in waves, but she kept her voice low. "As long as I run this lab the way *they* want, motivate and control the staff, and monitor and assist with the process, *they've* granted immunity to my family. But you can thank Pierce, the new clan leader, for your situation. He'd insisted that the deal didn't include you. Maybe now you regret killing Logon Larsen?"

This wasn't Lily versus the elf. This was Lily versus the whole clan. There was nothing I could say that would change her mind about me now. "The only regret I have is not targeting Pierce while trapped inside your ring of fire."

"Enjoy your next visit with your favorite person." The witch left, leaving me bathed in the light once again.

Lily confirmed what Indie had claimed, and what I'd wanted to believe—Indie hadn't been under any control. I believed Indie hadn't intended for me to be captured, and I believed she felt guilty, and she was determined to get me out of here. That human, who once seemed so terrified unless putting on an act, deliberately defied the very elf whose torture she could see. While Lily claimed she'd protected her, my questioning could've shone a spotlight on Indie's attempts to save me. And if caught, that heartless witch would hand her over. Then Pierce would compel her into becoming what Daisy and Lily had rejected—a life far worse than what I suffered now. I couldn't live with myself if something bad happened to her.

The moment I was free, I would keep her safe from the elf forever, even if I had to follow her in that crappy pine-scented car she lived in. I would be her immortal protector until she took her last breath—because no matter how brave and daring she was, Indie was still human. Vulnerable. Delicate.

Rather than an impromptu picnic on my prison floor, I wanted a fine—although mixed—dining experience, followed by dancing and seltzer water, and a cozy trip to my bedroom. I wanted to lick every inch of her body. Feel the warmth inside her. Taste her—but only a little. Because that alluring and sweet human had been trapped in this war of witches and elves. I couldn't ask her to commit to taking the change for me. So whatever she offered would be temporary, and I'd enthusiastically take a few decades of happiness over nothing at all.

My dignity might be in tatters, but I still had my pride. When that door reopened, and Pierce flung his tired insults around, I retreated to a special place in my mind where there was no pain and no worries. Only Indie. Because every inch of her—from her cute hair to those gorgeous eyes and that sexy sway when she'd walk away to that beautiful spirit—had been captured in my memory, the elf could never fully break me.

Whichever opportunist had stolen my ring needed it more than I, because it no longer defined me.

30
Breaking

Indie

I'd never been more nervous than today, because no matter what happened, I was getting Soren and Della away from that torture. So I was relieved when I'd slipped by security with my billowy blouse hiding another hidden stash. I hadn't brought enough, but it was all I could fit. My strength alone wasn't enough either, so I brought along the leverage that Soren had suggested. The crowbar up my spine was awkward to walk with and frigid against my spine. Now all I needed was the right moment.

And some healed vampire muscle. And for once, Soren's bragging had better be accurate.

With a gloved hand, I turned pages in today's chosen grimoire, trying not to tear the pages from the bouncing of my leg. At the same time, I followed along with my notes on staff movements—the lab's comings and goings—awaiting the arrival of the daily delivery driver. I needed to wait for the peak chaotic time to minimize getting caught and maximize my window. But waiting had never been so awful, so after plenty of consideration, I'd decided to free Soren first. He had been tortured and starved far less so he'd be stronger, and the moment he stepped foot outside that prison, the real race began. I'd need his strength to free Della. Then the three of us would be in her prison with guards armed with semi-automatic vervain dart rifles barreling down on us. This time, Soren would know what to expect, so he could dodge the fire.

I hoped.

But Della would be in a worse condition than her brother. I had to save a little more blood for her. And she'd still need help to use her atrophied legs to escape. Was there a security protocol to lock down all the doors in the event of a breach? I had to assume my badge wouldn't work. I wasn't strong enough to rip through doors. Soren would have to, assuming he was strong enough.

There were so many variables, so many pieces that had to fit just right...for a chance at pulling this off.

So, nerves? None here. I chuckled softly to myself.

Focusing on the pages before me was a monumental ask, but this grimoire was clearly older than I, which helped. The pages were exactly what they should be for this age—tanned vellum. The runic inscribing was nearly indecipherable, even to me, but there was something off about this grimoire. Something that literally felt authentic and not made to appear so. Therefore, the spell would've been the right age. It was also in the right language for the time. I copied what I could into my notebook, logically filled in the missing strokes, and recognized some symbols. The easiest runes to translate were beast, spirits, night, and...*punishment*. Despite my doubts about the whole endeavor, my heart sped up.

"There you are." Pierce appeared in my doorway, startling me.

Since I'd been fighting against my own fidgeting, the page was spared, but my heart kept pounding for a different reason. I dragged a smile across my face. "Here I am. In my office."

"You look good, Indie." Pierce strolled in and browsed my shelves, as if pretending to care about books. I'd gotten the impression he didn't know how to hold one correctly.

"Thanks," I said dryly and returned my attention to my fascinating discovery, hoping he'd get the hint.

"You didn't come to the bar the other night." He stopped in front of my table, ignoring the work in front of me and the fact that I was busy.

I frowned. "I told you I wasn't a drinker."

"I wish you would've come out. I think you'd like the real me if you'd give me a chance."

I couldn't stand to look at the filth before me, but the delivery guy was coming soon, and I needed Pierce to leave—tough, and to do so without suspicion—tougher.

Like most males, Pierce was inevitably driven by one thing, and he wouldn't be able to refuse. "You know what? How about you pick a place tonight, just you and me?"

The elf's brown eyes sparkled with excitement. "I knew you'd come around. How about Schooner's Landing? They recently remodeled."

I smiled plainly and used his expensive choice to craft a sense of urgency. "I know the place. You need reservations, and by now you're probably too late. If that's the case, I don't know what night works for me."

Pierce grinned. "I know a guy. I'll get us a table."

"I'm not getting stood up in a cold parking lot, alone in the dark. Confirm a time, and I'll show, but those reservations fill up fast. How well do you trust this guy of yours?" I asked, trying to lead him away and wishing he'd get the hint.

"I don't want to leave this to chance either, so I'm on it. I got your digits from Lily, so I'll let you know for sure and pick you up half an hour prior."

I didn't want the elf anywhere near Cora, and I didn't like him having my number, but if he was too quick to confirm, I also didn't want him coming right back. "Text me the reservation information. I'd feel more comfortable if I met you there."

"I can do that because I'm a flexible kind of guy. We're going to have a great time, Indie." The elf finally left.

I exhaled in relief and glanced at the ancient page before me and reviewed my notes. It was just a little too...right. A loud crash lifted my head. The delivery driver had arrived and knocked over a delicate-sounding package. Pierce had left. Lunch was around the corner. The clock was ticking. I had to do this now. Nerves skittered along my stomach.

I tore out my notes and tucked them between the pages. Closing the book, I straightened. Now or never. I exhaled a sharp breath. Keeping a close eye around me, I maneuvered through the lab, toward the prison doors, and turned as usual toward the countertop. I gathered a tray essential for a series of draws and ducked into Soren's bright and bloody prison.

Indie

He was a mess. They clearly never mopped. He still didn't look like he'd showered, bathed, or simply changed clothes. Soren was even bloodier than before, as if every drop I'd fed him had been forcibly battered out of him. My heart broke for him, but this was the last time he'd endure the torture, and I had to focus on getting his strength up enough for the plan to work. I kneeled in front of Soren's limp, hanging body and settled the decoy tray next to me.

"Soren," I called gently so he wouldn't startle.

The beaten vampire didn't stir. He was in even worse condition than I expected. I definitely didn't have enough blood, but I couldn't physically carry down enough to get by security and counteract the damage they were doing every day. It had to be enough. I dug into my waistband and slipped a bag up when the door behind me opened. I straightened and turned.

Stuffy assessed me. "Do you have this one?"

I gave him a warm smile. "I certainly do."

He lifted an eyebrow. "You're a little too happy to do this. No wonder management likes you. Well, have fun." Stuffy left, and I sagged in relief.

Who exactly in management liked me? It didn't matter. Those workers were hardly human out there with how much their minds were tampered with. I freed the bag in my waistband and popped the port. He wasn't in a condition to bite into the bag either, so poked the seal and brought it to his lips like a straw. I squeezed, forcing the nourishing liquid where he needed it, but much of it dribbled out.

I'd seen more battles than I cared to. I'd seen the most gruesome deaths and the most miserable wounds. Compared to that, Soren's condition was almost nothing, but having to stand by in my cozy office while it happened was my own form of torture. Almost as much to me as it was for him, I said, "This ends today. Drink it down, Soren. You need your strength, because as much as I'd be willing, I can't carry you."

I noticed the blood rivulets drizzling down his arm. He wasn't stirring despite the tickles. His forehead was hot and beaded with sweat. His skin was clammy. His shirt was perpetually damp with blood and sweat. Even if I could wave away his pain, he would still be miserable. Soren needed to get out of here now. This minute.

But how?

With one hand, I lifted his chin. Gravity to the rescue. The other hand squeezed the bag, spraying it into his mouth and risking it slipping and spraying the walls. If that happened, no one would notice. "Soren, you have to swallow. Drink fast, heal faster. We don't have much time."

His throat bobbed with a swallow, and finally his eyelids fluttered open, revealing the ruby red irises of hunger—starvation. Soren slurped the bag dry in a few long pulls. I grabbed another.

He groaned with a small taste of satiation or the pain relief as he healed—I didn't know, but he took control of his own head, so that was a step in the right direction.

"I can almost look forward to Pierce's therapy sessions. Means I get to see you afterward," he said, licking his soft lips but keeping a sharp watch on my hands freeing another bag.

"Welcome back."

"Lily told me you got your protection, and she knows what you're hunting for is a waste of time. They want something else from you, Indie. You must've figured that out, but you're not compelled, so why not say 'to hell with it' and make a run for it?"

"Nothing has changed except I'm getting you out of here today. Less talk, more drink."

Soren shook his head, the irons gently tinkling. "I appreciate it. I do, but I don't want you at risk."

"The more you drink, the better chance we have of pulling this off, so if you're that worried, drink."

Soren must've realized he couldn't argue me away to safety, so he polished off a little more than half the bags I'd brought. "Your bra is like a clown car. But instead of creepy dudes, I get an endless supply of the second-best stuff I could get."

I couldn't help but smile warmly. "I know it's not Hot 'N Ready, but beggars can't be choosers, so you'll have to file your complaint with Nicole."

Soren chuckled. "Nah, your body heat made it close enough to fresh. These were O-negative. Not bad, but not as fruity as A-positive. Thank you, Indie. You are the highlight of my day."

"Your bar is so very, very low."

He laughed again. There was nowhere to put the empties, and I didn't want the plastic scratching me while focusing on our escape, so I kicked them into the corner behind the door.

"That's much better." Soren smiled with satiation, wounds healing before my eyes. "There's no greater feeling than a full belly and almost maximum strength. I could kiss you for that, and I mean it." Even with his eyes closed in elation, I believed him.

Remembering the press of his body, the touch of his hands, the exploration of his mouth. It was never fake to me, and I wanted that again. I wanted that forever, and I wanted it to be real. But we still had many hurdles to clear, including the least likely. "Here's the plan. You ready?"

"Never been more ready than now." Soren straightened his spine, no longer weakened with exhaustion. No longer sagging with defeat. He was ready, as was I.

"When we begin, break the chains. I brought extra bags for you this time, so it shouldn't be a problem. We're going to head to the left, into Della's cell. I don't know how much time we'll have once we're spotted, but I'm going to feed her as best I can while you break her chains. Then I'll pull the fire alarm to cause chaos, and if any doors are locked, hopefully they'll open in the emergency. Then the three of us move. I'll help her walk, and you clear the way—tearing doors off hinges as needed...or were you bluffing?" I playfully grinned.

"I never bluff and I never exaggerate...because I don't have to." His steamy gaze and undertones were fully read, loud and clear.

"I owe you a dance and a full night you'll never forget," I said sincerely.

"And that's enough plan. Let's do this." Soren shifted his weight, gearing up for the effort. And after a beat, he exhaled a few sharp breaths and forcefully pulled, grunting with the effort, face burning red once more. The chains squeaked as a few links shifted position. He gritted his teeth, and his extended arms shimmied on the taut chains.

And then he released and panted. He couldn't do it. I covered my mouth with my hand. But again and again he pulled, slammed, and forced the chains from the iron hoops, but they remained unfazed. Soren climbed to his feet and pressed a leg backward against the wall. Arms pulled tight, he shoved with his foot, and the strain continued. The iron hoops wouldn't budge. Exhausted again, Soren shook his head, defeat drawing his shoulders. "A half dozen bags still weren't enough to fend off the vervain. It was a nice try."

"Soren—" I started and freed the crowbar from the back of my pants. "He didn't frisk me either. See if you can snap a link?"

Soren's eyes lit up. I handed him the bar, and he reached over his head and inserted the bar through the hoop for leverage, but the angle was a struggle. With the bar through the hoop, it kept sliding as he tried to engage the metal. Finally, he got a purchase and grunted as he pulled. The metal didn't budge or bend. The fixture didn't shift in the concrete. Soren untwisted and sagged. He carefully dropped the bar silently into his lap.

"On the bright side, at least I feel better." Soren shifted his arms, and the wounds inflicted by Pierce healed before my eyes. "Until tomorrow."

The lab workers, the elves, and Lily too, would continue to starve and take from him until they perfected their new vampire weapon. They would not stop until they were ready to release it into the wild to destroy all the vampires—and by destroy, some perverted version of a cure. Their existence helped me—just the way they were. I needed vampires. I needed Soren. And I couldn't sit down here day after day watching him be turned into a pulverized punching bag, drained dry and pumped full of toxin and hope that this was the day they hadn't gone too far. Every day that I came in here was another day closer to them catching what I was doing.

I was already risking my safety—my life—by helping him, and I would not walk out of his cell alone. So, it was time to make a trade. One I'd never done before, and never imagined ever considering. This wasn't just facing my fear by staying, because I had protection that worked. Now I was exposing it.

But then I wouldn't be as defenseless. Time to find out how far the 'mar' definition went.

"I can't fit more bags. The couple I have left are for Della, and I don't think more of the bagged stuff will work."

"Don't bother pulling one of the puppets. The next step is to infect them with the serum, and that's not a chance I'm willing to take until I'm forced."

"I'm not infected, and I'm curious about what you think of my flavor," I said with a melancholy smile. I'd already made up my mind about breaking the spell, and I could give him the strength he needed, but both of those meant he'd see the real me.

Considering his hatred of elves, I didn't expect to get that dance at all. His freedom was more important. I moved my blouse clear of my throat and tilted my head. I leaned close enough so he wouldn't have to strain.

"Indie…" Soren trailed off, sadness pulling at voice. "Not like this. You need your strength to get out of here, too."

"Bite me," I ordered. "There's no time to waste." I pulled my blouse farther down my shoulder and leaned up to his mouth. Warm breath tickled me, sending sensitive prickles along my body. This wasn't what I'd meant when I'd wanted his mouth on me. I imagined something less concrete and iron, more plush and warm.

Now it would have to remain in my imagination.

"Do it," I demanded in a whisper.

"I'd promised I would never bite you." Soren's warm breath shifted away. "I'd rather take Pierce's licks than hurt you."

The stubborn ass. He didn't realize the gravity and strength of what I was offering him, but I couldn't outright tell him or he certainly wouldn't do it. "You're being stubborn. This right here is your answer. You have to take it. I understand what you'd promised, but this situation is different. Refusing is stupid, and you know it is."

The lopsided grin returned. "I come from a long line of stupid. You should meet my brother."

"You can't stay in here like this. He's going to kill you."

"Cure, and then I turn to ash, so I'll take my chances with seeing you every day."

I growled. An actual animalistic growl. I took a scalpel out of the collection tray. Even if I cut my own flesh, he could still refuse to swallow, and I couldn't force him. What else could I do?

"A mar of the flesh shall break the seal," I repeated the spell's warning softly. He wouldn't take my strength, so I had to use it myself.

"What does that mean? What are you talking about?" Soren asked, voice rising in concern.

With one last glance—the last look Soren would give me in that way—I dragged the blade along the top of my wrist, choosing a harmless place that wouldn't interfere with my grip.

"Indie, wait—" Soren said with genuine worry on his brow.

A thin line of blood seeped up and dripped to the floor. I stared at Soren expectantly, waiting for that change within him—the change that would answer his questions—and then...I'd lose him.

"Why did you do that?" he asked, aghast.

I frowned and inspected the scalpel more closely. It was disposable with a ceramic blade. The mar had to include something harmful—to me. I kneeled in front of Soren and dug in his pockets for that knife.

"What are you doing? Talk to me. You're worrying me."

I unfolded the stainless steel—an iron alloy. I made another line on top of my wrist, parallel to the other. Blood seeped up. No hisses and shouts of panic.

Soren only frowned, clearly disapproving of my methods. A touch hadn't marred my flesh. A paper cut—whether ceramic or stainless steel didn't either. To choose between the humanity I'd accepted and the life I'd wanted to leave behind entirely in the only way possible, the witches must've meant something very serious. A choice that couldn't be made lightly—or accidentally. I had to prove I wanted to return to the old me in the only way that mattered—sacrifice. Count me in the column of not liking witches.

I rose and lifted my blouse, ignoring the extra bags of blood still tucked around me. I looked at my skin, so human and normal. Now I knew the force required to break the spell. No one would accidentally discover what I was, and I could live without fear. I could live the life I'd always wanted—invisible, safe...protected.

Soren gazed up at me with worry twisting his features. But what kind of life could I have without someone to spend it with? If I chose my human life, he would remain here until they'd tortured him enough to kill him as a vampire or with their fatal cure. If I chose to save him, he'd figure out quickly I was the thing he hated most, and I'd lose his trust forever.

And in doing so, I'd open myself up to my worst nightmare, but I could make this choice knowingly. There was never any winning, because life wasn't a game and it would never be fair. Right here, I chose to make a trade he wasn't even aware existed. I aimed the blade at my abdomen.

"What are you doing? Indie, don't. We can figure this out. Don't do this." A look of horror stretched across his beautiful face.

All I had to do was muster the courage to do it, which was surprisingly not easy. "There is no other way. I will not leave you in here again."

"Not like this! What are you thinking? Indie, they won't release me to hide me from EMS. They'll carry you out long before that's an option. And the doors being unlocked for EMS won't help me any. Indie, hurting yourself doesn't help me."

I smiled softly at him. "In my ignorant youth, I was Indiara Niskatar, fighter and warrior, but when I'd lost that battle, I'd lost that person—my identity—and I've been on the run ever since, constantly in hiding, and yes, living in my car. I've been acting my whole life as a survival mechanism. That's why I could so confidently when you'd asked. But surviving isn't living, and I'm done being a coward. Now I am ready to face the battle Indiara Niskatar has always been meant to fight."

"I don't understand what you're saying. Indie, please..." Soren pleaded.

Tears welled in my eyes. "Make me a promise."

"Anything, just don't do this."

"No matter what happens next, understand that none of this is your fault. This is my choice, and I'm making it willfully. Promise me you won't succumb to guilt."

I brushed away the tears of goodbye, and I swung my arm, stabbing myself in the abdomen. Fire started burning in my palm and sizzling out loud as if I'd pressed a hand against an electric stovetop on high. It spread through all the tissue exposed to the allergen, and like a rolling fog, it enveloped me until I couldn't sense anything but the singularity of falling completely blind into a black hole of pain.

I fell to my knees. I couldn't breathe, and I couldn't move. As I was about to crash onto my face, I used my hands to cushion the blow, but my burned skin was fused to the blade, and it pulled out with the instinctual movement. Blood pooled.

Soren didn't make a noise, but all I could hear was the sizzle of my hand.

I turned my face to meet his gaze and said in perfect Soren-speak, "That hurt. Give me a minute."

He didn't laugh, only stared, lips parted and eyes wide.

The pain receded enough to move, and I grunted with the effort to pull one sizzling hand free with the other. The blade clattered on the floor. I pushed up toward a seated position, panting with the effort. My hand supporting my lift slipped in my blood. I didn't have time to worry about that.

He was in shock. I couldn't blame him. I didn't tell him exactly what was going to happen. But all that mattered now was getting him on his feet and out the door. With a painful grunt, I climbed to my own feet, and I shuffled carefully to reach him.

"It's still me. The plan's changed, but I'm still getting you out of here."

Soren blinked.

I knew to expect this, but it still stung. When I'd searched for his blade, I hadn't found his keys, so I dug into my pants pocket, found my car keys and pushed them into his hand. "Soren? Soren, can you hear me?"

The gape of his lips closed, and he finally met my gaze.

"Listen to me. Get out of the building. Go to my car, and wait five minutes—no more, no less—and leave, whether Della gets out of here or not. You hear me?"

Soren's lips moved to speak, but no sound emerged.

"Soren, wait in my car for your sister. When she finds you, get out of here immediately. Are you hearing me?"

He still didn't come back to me, but he held the keys. So, that was something. I limped over, trying to ignore the pain in my gut, and gripped the shackle around his wrist. My flesh hissed as if a hot poker fresh from the flames pressed against my skin, but I gritted my teeth against it. With the effort of ripping a cardboard box, I snapped his restraint. Soren tipped sideways.

"Quickly, give me your other wrist." I didn't want to return to the floor and try to get back up again.

Soren slowly shifted and rose to his feet. He met me eye to eye, and that light I adored in his beautiful green eyes had gone out. Tears welled once more. I knew I'd lose him, but I hoped it waited until after he and his sister were safe and free.

Without a word, he lifted his wrist, and I tore apart the iron with an angry metallic groan. I dropped the hissing metal onto the floor with a clatter. I couldn't trust my voice to stay steady, but I didn't care. His life was more important to me than my dignity. "Soren, remember the plan. Go to my car, wait only five minutes for Della, and leave."

He only stared, but my keys remained in his hand.

Tears spilled over. I fished in my pocket for one last thing that I'd almost forgotten. I pinched it between two trembling, raw fingers, and Soren looked at the ring, eyes widening even further in shock as if that were possible. "You're free."

Soren slipped it onto his finger and used his hyperspeed to reach the door in a blink. With one last ashen glance over his shoulder, he disappeared out the door.

Ignoring my stab wound, I shuffled to the nearest fire alarm and pulled. Heads turned. A few people shouted orders to exit calmly. As the alarms blared, I dragged myself toward Della's room. Chairs were tucked under the messy countertop overflowing the supplies to be organized. Draped over a few of them were white lab coats. That would do.

I wasn't leaving until I was done.

31
Trade

Indie

The blaring alarm and strobe light overwhelmed my senses. The burning in my abdomen was spreading. Blood was trickling. I should've been healing—granted, iron slowed the process—but this didn't feel right. Almost as if I were human. But Soren could see me. I had my strength—and sensitive hearing—completely returned. I stretched my glamoured wings as if to take flight, and they were there. Had the spell not fully broken? Did I retain so weakness?

Perhaps witches truly meant sacrifice—completing the process.

With time and my strength fading, I limped into Della's prison cell and switched on the lights. I set the coat on the floor, where it was somewhat clean. As the captive vampire blinked away the brightness burning her retinas, she said, "Finally—"

But then she blinked and really looked at me. Her mouth gaped, and she just...froze. While the vampires' reactions were wholly expected, the timing couldn't have been worse.

"I know what you see, and I don't know what to say." Freeing myself of the harsh, chafing plastic, I removed the last bags of blood in my waistband and bra, gave each a small squeeze to check for leaks. There weren't any. I was afraid to kneel in front of her, because the effort required to climb back to my feet sped up the bleeding. So, I leaned to push the first bag into her chained hand. "Drink up."

As if no longer trusting me, she squeezed the bag herself to check for tampering. Then she bit into it like a starving vampire would, and her eyes glowed red like Soren's had. She dropped the empty and opened her palm wide. I gave her the next and next, and she swallowed them down faster than I thought possible. Then again, if the bag collapsed, the blood could still be sucked up easily.

Not so much with a vein.

After she finished off the last of them, she exhaled and grinned with satisfaction on her bloody lip. Her cuts and punctures healed, and her focus returned to me. "Let me guess—the alarms are for you, and the whole guard is coming? Great timing."

"That's your share. Soren was supposed to help me break you out, but plans changed. I can free you myself, and I couldn't risk his life anymore than needed."

"I can see the change. I have so many questions I can't even pick one."

"I'm sure you do, but you have about three minutes before Soren leaves and your ride is gone. Give me your wrist."

"You can still get me out of here, right?"

I glanced down at the blood soaking through my shirt, the trickle on my pants, and the drips on my shoe. "I don't know. Soren has my car. I couldn't find his keys. When I get you free, cover up with that lab coat. You're a little exposed, and wearing it will help hide you. Meet him in the parking lot. With the alarms going, the doors should be unlocked, and those that weren't, Soren should have broken through."

"There's a lot of unknowns there."

"The list was a lot longer a few minutes ago." I tried to give her a reassuring smile. "Look, I said I'd get you out of here, and now I am. All we can do is plan for the worst, hope for the best, and expect something in between. The longer you wait for the further into 'worst' territory we slide. The elves have cameras all over this lab. They would've seen Soren leaving. They would've seen me, however briefly I was on camera. It's not just the human guards with vervain-loaded semi-automatic rifles you have to worry about."

She didn't lift her wrist. Suspicion arched her brow.

"As you noticed, I've been in hiding. This isn't a trick. I'm not on their side. I'm on yours." With my best pleading eyes, I gestured towards her wrist.

Della reached up, and I gripped the first iron cuff with a hiss. Gritting my teeth against the burn, I tore through the first with a little more effort than Soren's, and then the second with more than I'd hoped. I panted from the pain, the exertion, the...blood loss.

Unable to get the coat for her, I pointed at it. "You need that cover, or you're going to get way more attention than you want."

Della rose to her wobbly feet and looked down at her dirty, bloody, sweaty body draped loosely with a patient's gown that had been tattered with age and wear. Her nest of hair was so matted with blood and sweat, it didn't even move. She had been on her knees for decades, and I'd planned to help her walk out with Soren as our guard. "Can you bear your weight?"

Della took a few cautious steps toward the gown. With care, she bent and lifted the lab coat. While shrugging into it, she carefully strolled around the tight prison cell as a test. "I'll be okay," she said with shock in her voice.

"You are out of time. Find Soren in the parking lot, but if he's gone, don't wait around. Just go."

Della gave me a nod of gratitude and understanding. She wasn't free yet, and I didn't expect to see her again, but the respect in her eyes was enough for me.

She vanished with that envious vampire hyperspeed. Exhaling a sigh of relief, I shuffled to the door and looked around. Everyone had evacuated, but the cameras were still there. If I'd managed to slip by the voyeur, and if Soren and Della's speed hadn't been caught, the elves could still be watching. But even they needed a bathroom break. I smoothed and straightened myself as best I could, but there was no hiding the alarming blood all over my clothes. Since my way out appeared clear, like Della, I didn't want to draw extra attention, so I stole another lab coat and shrugged into it. I buttoned it loosely to reduce the chance I soaked through.

With my mission complete, I held my head high with the confidence I'd earned, and I focused all my effort on the exit. But each step stung my gut. My knees weakened, but I caught my weight on the countertop. I couldn't give up now. I had to know if the siblings were truly free. One foot in front of the other, I forced myself to move. I needed to know.

My chest was on fire, and every pant of exertion drew flames into my lungs. My wound still burned as if a torch were branding me, and from the blood loss, I was chilled. The shackle burns on my hands weren't healing.

The rapid footsteps of boots approached down the hallway. The guards' voices weren't yelling in panic. They weren't firing, but they still kept coming...for me. If the elves thought they'd traded two prisoners for one, they were going to be disappointed. I looked up at the camera and smirked.

My knees buckled again, but this time, my searing palms made the countertop feel like the stovetop on high. I gritted my teeth but jerked away from the pain, and I landed on the hard, cold floor. My shirt was wet, adding to the chill.

My gaze settled on the white-speckled ceiling tiles lit by bright fluorescent lights. It was always daytime in the window-free lab, but was it daytime out there? Della didn't have sun protection, so if she didn't catch Soren on time, she'd either die or be recaptured. I had a feeling she wouldn't choose to return.

I wouldn't.

I had no strength left. I couldn't even move my head. Soon my sacrifice would be complete, but all of this may have been for nothing. As my vision faded to black, I tried to find a clock.

Soren

All the twists, turns, and stairs were a blur, but I made it out intact, if not a little worse for the wear from being inside. Sounding the fire alarm was a brilliant idea. Not one of the doors was locked, and the guards were busy ushering people out the door.

I reached the parking lot, where workers from all levels filtered out and socialized in small groups. Some held their coffees, which in an emergency, I totally understood. The mingling mix wore business clothes, lab coats, and there were a few suits who appeared less than pleased. For most of them, it was a routine drill and a nice break from the grind. But if they saw my clothes—very different from theirs—that would change quickly. I continued exerting myself at hyperspeed until I gained enough distance between them and...

Oliver's Mercedes—still in mint-condition. Well, except for the pungent gasoline containers in the trunk seeping their aroma into the deepest layers of carpeting. I bet he had a fancy place on speed dial that could detail it like new, so I didn't feel guilty about it. There were no key marks or any parking tickets, as if I'd gone inside a few hours ago and now headed out like normal. I truly had no idea how long I'd been down there.

Right next to his car, where she'd left it, was Indie's beat-up old sedan. No parking tickets for her either, but I couldn't tell by the paint's condition if anyone had keyed it. The back seat was still filled with boxes—her entire life on the run. Just a few minutes ago, I had so many questions about what Indie was afraid of—or who, specifically. I'd promised to keep her safe, but at the time, I couldn't comprehend the gravity of that promise. Her softening gratefulness now made more sense. She wasn't a human with a vengeful drunk ex who needed a good scaring.

After I'd gotten drunk myself on bags and bags of semi-pleasantly warmed O-negative, I'd thought I'd overdone it. Somehow the daily dose of vervain had infiltrated my tissues so deeply that even the nourishing blood couldn't quite repair me. That I'd been truly delirious with horror when I watched my beautiful, determined human stab herself. I had been so out of it, I'd thought the special place in my mind, where I retreated for my own safety, had been twisted, morphed somehow, by the vervain. Knowing the elf's experiments, I wouldn't put it past the elf to play with the vervain too, as if an allergen by itself didn't cause enough suffering.

But it was all real. The beautiful blond woman of my daydreams had dug deep for a level of courage I'd never seen before, defying supernatural beings who could turn her into their own mindless puppet with a few words and glowing eyes—or a few words and wrist movements. But the risk was so much more than that, so much more than I could've ever imagined because she was...

...the last female elf.

Details I'd caught but didn't process finally fit, like Lily needing Indie's ability to read old grimoires, and the fighter and warrior part of her speech. Her ability to act, to blend in, wasn't for fun but survival. And when she'd said she understood being forced into something she didn't agree with, my blood boiled. She'd always been on the move—in hiding, in fear—but for how long? Well, since the tales passed down had claimed the last female elf perished.

She was older than I.

And when she'd appeared at my bar, she'd needed a witch far more than I'd understood. How could I? She'd been relegated to stories, myth, embellished over the...centuries. I exhaled and dragged a sticky hand through my disgusting hair. Indie's own life—successfully defended for hundreds of years—had been depending on a spell, the protection spell.

And she'd thrown it away for me.

I dropped my weight against Oliver's Mercedes, denting the fender. Guilt for the car? Nope. Indie had made me promise not to harbor guilt over what she'd done. Yeah, not happening.

The alarms squeaked out, and I was sure five minutes had passed, but still no Della. I wanted to believe Indie. Actually, I did. I believed Della was in there, but the glaring sun in my eyes would be a problem for her. I unlocked Indie's driver-side door and stuffed her keys up above the visor. She'd find them.

The elf—I was going to need a different descriptor for that flaming shitbag now. Pierce—I'd work on it—hadn't frisked me at all. Knife, keys, and wallet were intact, but my knife had been left behind. That was okay. It was woefully inadequate for the damage I intended to inflict. I grabbed the keys out of my back pocket. They weren't too messy. I unlocked Oliver's door and dropped into the driver's seat. I pressed the ignition button.

My eyes watered from the fumes.

While people started moving back into the building, I drove around to the front door, waiting with bated breath that Indie and Della would come out together. I had nothing on me to cover my sister. Turning the shifter knob into park, I pressed the trunk release. I dug through Oliver's neat trunk and found nothing. This wasn't the car he'd choose for a getaway, so he didn't have a blanket or other light-blocking material I could use.

With a frown, I closed the trunk and returned to the seat. I shifted into drive. While idling, I checked the dashboard clock. Five and a half minutes. My foot held the brake, but every inch of my still-undernourished and heavily over-tenderized body screamed at me to...pick a meal from the cattle shuffling inside. Indie had told me to go no matter what, but I couldn't. I could not make myself flee while that woman and my sister were still in there.

I drummed on the steering wheel, and my sun ring glinted in the light. In the days when I hadn't known this ring existed, I'd blamed many of my deplorable choices on being incapable of acting human. How could I pretend to have a conscience when I spent all my time lurking in the dark, hunting the very thing I was supposed to be? I couldn't pretend to be prey. I couldn't be weak like them. Even when I'd dressed in Oliver's fine clothes, I became nothing more than a wolf hiding in sheep's clothing—clothing that did at least command some level of respect among humans, but I digress.

When I'd gotten the fabled ring, I'd always used it as a crutch, thinking myself incapable of that humanity if I were to lose it. It alone permitted a life beyond merely surviving into one of living. I believed it could only thinly veil the real me—a monster—and not change me. And it was the only thing keeping me on this side of the light. During my darkest moments, in the depths of Pierce's torture while believing the only person I cared about most in the world had betrayed me in the worst way possible, while raging with hatred and hurt, Indie, the human, had brought my humanity back from the brink. She'd done it without the gem at all, and she'd done it while I said terrible things to her. Because of her, I no longer needed the ring to ground me, and I'd no longer need the crutch, but I damn well needed it so i didn't fry in the sun. I kissed the stone in appreciation.

I drummed on the steering wheel more, itching to do something. Should I do the smart thing and leave? Or should I continue to be a sitting duck? Something must've gone wrong. Should I go back inside and help? If I were captured once more, everything Indie had sacrificed for me would be thrown in her face. I couldn't do that to her, not even if I hadn't known the depths of her sacrifice.

Finally deciding not to do the stupid thing for once, I shifted into drive. A blur approached using hyperspeed, and the passenger door swung open. A woman, hunched inside a white-ish lab coat that stretched awkwardly over her head, yelped and sizzled as she dropped in next to me and slammed the door shut. She scrambled to protect her bare flesh the best she could. Her naked legs were damaged from the sun, but beyond that, they were filthy with blood, sweat, oils, and everything else that collected without a shower for a long time. The nest of hair was...well, a nest, and she smelled like something had died.

The woman shifted the fabric, interspersed with more yelps, to peek an eye out at me. She had Oliver's blue eye that I'd recognize anywhere. "Della? Is that you?"

"Of course it's me, you idiot. Get us out of here." The blue eye of my sister blinked. "You somehow look so much nicer than I remember, but yet, you look like shit. And what's that smell?"

"I missed you, too." With a smile, I released the brake and moved us away. More yelps as new patches of skin were exposed to the sun lifted my lips further. But one last glance in the rearview mirror clenched my stomach. Indie didn't make it out.

I squeezed the steering wheel as I navigated us onto the highway. "We have an hour before we get home, but there's something I need to know before I let you out of this car."

The blue eye squinted. "Like what?"

"Are you able to control your bloodlust?"

32

Breaking a Promise

Indie

Light returned to my vision, and slowly shapes began to form and sharpen. I'd awoken free of pain, which could only be explained by my having crossed the veil to the Other Side, an alternative dimension where supernatural beings resided before moving on—a ghost purgatory, so described by elves several millennia before humans understood the concept and stole it from us. The most notable differences were that our location wasn't in the sky and it wasn't lore. For my consciousness to be here meant I had unfinished business, but I couldn't imagine what. I hadn't had *business* in centuries.

While I had eternity to solve the puzzle and move on, my *business* might not. I rose, only frustrated that I'd been delivered to the Other Side in my bloodstained, filthy clothing, even though no one on the earthly plane could see or hear me. That meant I missed out on a conversation with my Angel of Death. From the stories I'd been told as a young female, I never expected to be brought across the veil and left to figure out this puzzle on my own.

The first piece—I failed to recognize anything about this place, so it wasn't Cora's home and most definitely wasn't Soren's either. I never got the chance to see the vampire's bed, which was a terribly morose thought by itself, but I couldn't believe his bed would be so ordinary and lumpy. The plain beige walls with nothing hanging on them weren't the bed-and-breakfast's style at all. And likewise, there was none of the beautiful woodwork. Soft music flowed around the house, but I couldn't pinpoint from where.

I picked up the gurgling of a coffeepot, drifting the promises of caffeine my way. But a tantalizing scent made my stomach growl before I could pinpoint it. Eggs and bacon were sizzling nearby, and the scrape of a spatula on a skillet followed along. On the Other Side, sustenance wasn't needed and couldn't be consumed, so how could my consciousness...growl?

Unless Soren had rescued me, delivered me to an ordinary, safe place inside the bed-and-breakfast, and now Nicole was making herself a meal. I'd already told myself this wasn't Soren's home, and yet I kept trying to make it so. Confused, I lifted off the bed and frowned at my clothing. Even if only for myself, I couldn't wear this. I moved to the dresser, but all that rested on its surface was a jewelry box with a ribbon. I opened it quietly, but it was empty. Strange. I opened the top drawer only to find ordinary men's undergarments. With a sigh, I closed the drawer, knowing I'd have to face Soren like this.

He'd understand.

I didn't recognize the living room carpet. The furniture was basic and sparse, as if the owner didn't care what image he projected onto his guests, and that didn't fit Soren at all. At the entry point to the kitchen, I stopped short and gasped. I wasn't on the Other Side, and I wasn't in a unique area of the B&B. I desperately wanted to believe one of those was correct. Otherwise that meant—

Pierce, wearing a white apron, flipped eggs and whistled along to the soft music. And now, like Soren when he'd first seen the real me, I was frozen, mouth gaped. I needed to run. I needed to get as far from here as possible, vanish, disappear, and seek out a new witch for help.

But my clothes were nothing short of a crime scene, so I'd immediately draw attention. But I hadn't been tied up. I wore no iron shackles, and no chains dragged behind me. For the first time in a very long time, I was no longer a weak, helpless human, and I was hungry. Calming my heart rate and relaxing the trembling of my limbs, I watched the enemy I feared with suspicion.

Pierce turned and smiled. "Indie, welcome. You must be starving. Have a seat." He gestured with the spatula toward one of the stools tucked under the kitchen island.

My heart punched into my throat. Reluctantly, I lowered myself onto a stool—the farthest from his reach. "Why aren't I in chains?"

Pierce smiled. "I've made many mistakes over the years, but I'm going to do this right for once. 'Kill them with kindness' is my new motto."

I didn't know what 'this' was, but I cared less about it than about planning my escape. "Where am I?"

He looked around as if assessing his own decorating skills—or lack thereof. "My house. I know it's not much, but I'm not big on entertaining."

"Do I have to ask why you brought me here?"

Pierce poured coffee into a mug. He handed me the steamy brew and pointed out the sugar and creamer in front of me. "I'd offered you dinner at my place and background information. Since you declined, I thought now you might be willing, although it's not exactly the same, but now nothing is really the same. Is it?" He didn't wait for me to answer that. "Besides, waking up here is far more comfortable than anywhere in the lab. And I didn't want to compel all the workers to forget...well, all of it. Does anything hurt?"

I lifted my arms and twisted my waist, feeling the muscles in my abdomen. I discreetly lifted the front of my blouse and felt for the raw, burning edges, but all that remained of my stab wound was sticky blood. "No."

Pierce displayed a self-satisfied smile. "You're welcome."

I scowled. "I didn't ask you to heal me."

Pierce slid bacon onto a plate and made a defensive gesture. "It's okay. I'm not asking for anything in exchange."

Oh, but he did. Otherwise, he would've healed me and allowed me to go moments after the event, and then there was the missing detail of why I'd taken so long to rouse. "I don't believe you."

Pierce added eggs and set the steaming plate in front of me. "On the contrary, I have a gift for you."

I eyed him warily, ignoring the growl once again. "What kind of gift?"

Pierce grinned while removing his apron. "Something you've wanted for a long time."

I was intrigued. I was starved. But I wasn't relaxed or hopeful.

Soren

Della's footsteps thundered down the stairs. Her hair was wrapped in a towel, and one of Oliver's dress shirts draped over most of her body. She looked much closer to what I remembered, and my disbelief in her being here was stronger than ever. But so was the guilt. If I'd known—if I'd looked—I could've freed her myself a while ago. Instead, I'd gotten caught trying to save her, and then Indie had—

One mind-melting thing at a time.

I didn't know if Della hated me for leaving her behind when Oliver and I had broken into the lab and raided it, but the extremely long hot shower seemed to have lifted her spirits. So did nearly emptying Nicole's stash of blood bags, which my niece promptly refilled this morning.

I had to admit I was grateful to be clean and back in my own clothes—T-shirt and jeans. Nicole had drilled me about everything, and the story had begun with a vodka and continued through several refills...for me. She rested on the stool, sipping her coffee. Nicole had been fully captivated by the tale, but my sister interrupted before I finished.

"I don't know half the products Oliver has up there, but man, am I grateful for that stick up his ass." Della paused and assessed us. Her gaze landed on my half-filled shot glass. "Oh, I'll take one of those."

"Oliver has a nice selection here. Take your pick," I said, happy to delay the rest of the story. Why? Because I knew Nicole was going to be...disappointed. And Della's jury was still out. I might need to defend Nicole against Della. I might need to defend myself against Nicole.

Women.

"Anything, whatever. I don't care. Just give me a drink. God, make it a double." Della freed her damp, dark locks and squeezed fistfuls of it with the towel.

I poured her a stiff shot of vodka. She deserved it, but I needed it. I finished mine and re-poured. I'd lost count by now, but since I wasn't buzzing and the bottle wasn't empty, I had a long way to go.

Della drank hers down without a flinch, and she slid the glass back to me, excited for another. She had no residual darkness that I could find. Not once had she looked at Nicole sideways. Della had cleared through much of Nicole's stash herself, and she hadn't begged for more. She hadn't even made a mess. She hadn't slipped out during the night for a stronger, better-tasting fix. Perhaps, as my sister had claimed during the ride home and my niece had told me during Della's shower, years in captivity with rations of blood allowed her to develop control. I couldn't believe decades of torture had *improved* her. Then again, in between Pierce's visits I'd had revelations of my own. Was I a better person now because of it?

There was something not right about that.

Della finished off her second before settling down in the seat next to Nicole. "That's more like it. I'm cleaned, fed, warmed, and now free. I haven't felt this good in a long, long, long time, and I owe someone." This time, she gave me a squint. "You really did get yourself captured?"

Her tone, a mixture of gentle ribbing and disbelief, had me shifting into the defensive. "Lily tricked me, but as soon as I figured it out, I was vervained. The guards unloaded two rifles' worth into me. It's not like I didn't fight back."

"Why would you trust a witch?" Della asked.

"Lily's family, but I think you missed the invite." My turn for ribbing. Della frowned, and I gave her a smug smile. "Oliver married her sister."

Della's eyes widened, and she blinked several times. "I missed way too much. But I have lots of gratitude bubbling over here, so I need to shower Indie with it before I explode. Where is she?" Della glanced over both of her shoulders as if expecting her to appear on cue.

"Why would she be here?" Nicole asked her, but gave me a familiar look, one that meant expectations...or hope...was growing.

"Well, I mean, why wouldn't she fly over? I thought the two of you..." Della trailed off, sensing something between Nicole and me. "Or not, but if I were on the run, I'd go toward the grateful people, not the angry ones."

"What do you mean by 'fly'?" Nicole said, lifting a hand to pause Della's confusion.

I rubbed at the nape of my neck. "Yeah, about that. Indie's not human."

"At first, she was," Della countered. "And that was weird enough, because why would a human help vampires? But then...she wasn't. I like her. She freed me, and she pissed off a lot of elves," Della said, waving her empty for a refill.

I filled her glass and braced myself.

"Are you sure Indie's an elf? I thought they didn't exist?" Nicole asked, and those old gears of hers started turning.

"I saw her fully feathered and sparkly," Della said, beaming over her new friend. Nicole looked to me for confirmation, and I nodded.

"So the last female elf, believed to have passed away centuries go, whose loss had caused the entire elf-vampire conflict in the first place, randomly appears here, infiltrates an elf lab created to destroy vampires, and frees two of their test subjects. And you left her behind. Am I missing anything?" Her voice rose in incredulity.

I rubbed the nape of my neck again. "She made me promise to go so her sacrifice wouldn't be for nothing. I'm upholding my word to her."

"Oh, me too," Della added.

"She made you promise to leave her?" I asked.

"Nope. She made me promise not to tear your throat out. Refill, please."

I poured her another shot glass and hoped Della didn't mention the grave, self-inflicted wound. Indie was the most valuable elf in existence. With the cameras overhead, the clan would've descended on that lab like a pack of dogs, and they would've healed her. They wouldn't give her the chance not to be.

She was so valuable, they wouldn't let her leave.

"Imagine you've been in hiding for centuries, and now the very people you've run from have you. Don't you think Indie would be terrified of her worst nightmare coming true? Wouldn't she want you to save her from that?"

The night of the party, the elf had staked me. Indie helped pull the damn thing from my back, but when I'd compelled her to forget, it never worked. It couldn't. All this time she knew an elf was sniffing close. She'd volunteered in the lab all right—to help a witch in a trade—but she'd stayed to help Della, and she'd sacrificed herself for me. All the while she'd known that her safety, her protection, her freedom could vanish at any moment, but for me she threw it all away.

And now that the elves had her, the clan leader would be in charge. Since I killed the level-headed one, that meant...Pierce Evansson and his meaty mitts. That...that...flaming shitbag had her.

Lily had been wrong. I didn't regret killing Logon Larsen, but I did regret not targeting Evansson in the first place.

I set down the nearly empty bottle of vodka. "I wasn't willing to risk a war for the convenience of ridding myself of a known pest." Nicole grinned, already feeling my hero hair being strapped and locked. "I need black nightshade. Lots of it."

Della and Nicole exchanged excited glances. If I could've blushed, I would've.

"Pardon me, I have a promise to break."

I looked down at my ring—the ring she'd returned to me, the ring I couldn't do this without. This feeling—the opposite of disappointment—felt pretty damn good. I was going to risk war to give her back the freedom she'd lost.

And maybe I could have her in my arms.

33

Secrets Revealed

Indie

ANY MEAL WAS GREAT when you were starving, but I forced the food down while my stomach protested the sight across from me. Since I had to appease him—chains or not—the longer I lingered over it, the longer I was subject to it, I'd cleaned my plate in only a few short minutes. Pierce kept pace with me, as if the meal were a race and finishing behind a female would be a blow to his elfy masculinity.

As human society changed so rapidly, I'd adapted out of necessity, and while I'd stayed in hiding, shifting my pillow against the passenger side door, wishing to stretch out and curl up in warmth, I'd dreamed of what life could've been. To maintain their own independence, elf clans would've read and listened and later watched the human news, making any changes as needed for their own society to co-exist peacefully if not invisibly.

Women fought and won the freedom to be independent, to have their voices heard, their votes counted, their wages...almost equal, and to have respect as a person, not just for what their bodies could do for men. Had the elves viewed these changes for women as something elfkin should emulate for their females? Had they seen the women capable of leadership—and not just to be seen at the male's side, just behind his shoulder?

Well, I'd watched, read, listened, and watched the news, and I'd shed tears in celebration at their victories. Even with a witch's protection, where I could pretend to be one of them, I couldn't risk making my voice heard, trust that I'd have respect or autonomy, and...I couldn't legally vote. I might've appeared human, but I'd never be able to be one, so I wished instead for elves to treat their females like women. Then maybe I'd come out of hiding.

I didn't have to break into a clan, raise a bullhorn and rally a crowd into action to find out whether they'd cheer or confine me. Subtlety was more my style, and with only a quiet and quick meal at an ordinary table, in a plain house, I'd discovered elf males had never changed. I was disappointed, but I could see why. With happy human women, the men they chose would become happy. For elves, the happiness of a female didn't matter. The males always got what they wanted. So, what I'd feared—why I fled—was still very much alive, and I was right to still be on the run.

I hadn't been wasting my nights alone in my car or with my horse all those years, but the vindication was far more bitter than sweet.

When we'd both finished, he collected our dishes and loaded his dishwasher. While his back was turned, I considered fleeing, but I'd have only one chance. When I'd fled before, my captors were busy in battle. This time I'd have to race for my life with an elf nipping at my heels. That lowered my chances of success before considering whether a spell had been placed on this house. Lily might not be friends with Pierce, but she saw merit in his being in her life. Otherwise, she was powerful enough to keep him away. Since I wasn't in chains in a dungeon, this elf was confident in the confinement he'd created, reinforcing my assumption. If I broke that confidence, he'd have to try harder to contain the value in his possession. I wasn't at the clan's residence. This elf, this rogue hunter elf, was likely going to sell me to the clan or use me for some other gain. And I didn't know how old he was to judge my chances of winning a struggle.

In principle, I couldn't stay—not optional, not up for debate. I would not subject myself to what I'd spent my life running from. Since I didn't expect to be able to dart off on a whim, I had to figure out how to manipulate the elf into giving me freedom. My whole life had always been a series of survival situations with no ties to anyone, anywhere, or anything. Then I met Soren. He made me feel wanted, respected....safe. With him, I wasn't a ghost flitting through time. He made me feel alive, and I wanted that back. I had to find him, make sure he was no longer in shock, and make sure the elves or the witches weren't hunting him down to chain him back up—a nightmare so terrible I couldn't think about it. After the shock I'd given him, I didn't know where he stood—where *we* stood. I wanted to be in his arms once more, to sway to the music, to make our own rhythm in the sheets. I wanted him to fight for me, but what could one vampire do against an elf clan? That was a question I never wanted answered.

I startled at Pierce's face so close to mine with a glint of excitement in his eye. "Ready?"

Right, the gift that I didn't ask for and didn't want. Since I was a mess, this was my first opportunity. "I look and feel like a corpse who crawled up and out of the dirt. Am I free to go home and clean up?"

Pierce's gaze swept up and down my body. I couldn't tell what he was thinking, but the slight lift of his lips was unsettling. "Not yet, time for answers."

Since I'd avoided the clans, I was mildly curious about the tales still handed down, but I hadn't been yearning for any answers. For him to presume I wanted answers made me despise that overblown confidence, and that he'd believed the answers so lofty that they deserved the status of a gift, meant he believed I'd subjugate myself for the privilege of receiving them. I could not be manipulated so easily.

I followed Pierce, who lowered himself onto the couch, and a beat-up cardboard box rested on the coffee table in front of him. For my first clue, I glanced at the bottom edge of the cardboard, looking for soaked blood. If I found any sign in the box that Soren had been hurt, I was going to discover just how well this elf could fight with bare hands.

Preparing myself for the surge of rage and the fight of my life, I approached with tension pulling at my movements. Pierce eagerly gestured for me to sit next to him, where he'd placed a clean towel so my mess wouldn't soil his fabric. I gritted my teeth.

"I'm not going to bite, Indie." Pierce chuckled as if not being a vampire was amusing. "Have a seat. This won't take too long."

Keeping a few inches of space between us, I did. The elf reached into the box, and I held my breath. My hands curled into fists, and I trembled. Pierce held out the gift, and I needed a moment to see what it was and not what I expected. With my lips parting, I accepted the small painting, no bigger than the size of a grimoire. For the first time in centuries, I gazed at the faces of my mother, my father, and my brothers Reku and Kalevi. I was but a child then, in front and center of my family. I touched the brush marks composing my mother's face. Her beautiful, stoic features had faded from memory, and I'd only been able to remember her pained face the day she'd been slain.

The trembling didn't ease. Breaking the spell that hid me from discovery was my own choice, but my value to this elf was higher than I'd realized. Rummaging around in my chest of acting skills, I dragged forward an even voice. "You know who I am."

Pierce shifted his position just slightly, so he could face me more comfortably. "As I'm sure you're aware, females were known to be lost long ago. Our kind moved on, adapted to the new world left to us. You can understand that, right?"

I eased only a little. "I can."

"So when I saw you, I was completely shocked."

Yes, completely shocked as he wrapped a meaty arm around Lily's shoulders.

"I thought that face of yours was vaguely familiar, so I pulled out these old heirlooms."

Just as I couldn't remember my mother's face, no one could remember mine, but if he'd recognized me when we'd met...my heart pounded and my head throbbed at the vast implications. So many things I could've done differently.

He'd staked Soren because the vampire was my date, and this elf was staking a public claim on me. Pierce wasn't a man. He hadn't stabbed Soren, and yes, there was irony in a healthcare worker saving lives while taking lives. But Soren believed he'd erased that from my memory to protect me from the hidden world. He'd never known what I was. His shock had been genuine.

But the elf had already known. Lily had said my bauble failed briefly, allowing her to see the truth, too. So I'd toiled for her in exchange for a spell that not only didn't protect me, but it made me weaker. She didn't like the elf, but they clearly had some accord to lock away my strength and manipulate me into believing I had been safe all along. Under those conditions, I never would've agreed to that weakness. I could've freed Della sooner, and Soren never would've been captured.

With every visit to the lab, Pierce had always tried to earn favor with me. He'd planned and maneuvered—manipulated—to bring me to this moment. I'd stayed for Della and Soren. Had I not agreed to that weakness, the ties that bound me would've been released and I would've been gone.

I had been a prisoner without realizing it, and I'd grossly underestimated this rogue hunter elf. I dreaded the deal he'd made. "Whose heirlooms are these?"

"I owed you the respect of your station, Princess, but had I done so, you would've discovered I knew. I didn't want you to fear me, and I didn't want you to flee. Forgive me."

The title made my insides curdle, and once more my fists turned to stone. He owed me respect regardless of my station, and keeping his true intentions hidden as an excuse was insulting, and if he planned to hand me over like property, he was a patronizing liar. I slowly exhaled, trying to slow the trembling of rage burning through me. "I didn't realize a price had been placed on my head. What is the clan offering?"

I'd buy my freedom, but I imagined I couldn't afford to double their offer—and that wasn't to inflate my own ego. My value, my very highly prized value, had nothing to do with my heart and soul or my exterior looks.

The elf's lips lifted into a smug smile. "Princess, allow me to introduce myself." Sure, why not? Then, I could identify the body I'd leave at the clan's doors in my warning note. "Pierce Evansson, at your service, my lady." The elf held out his hand in offer of mine.

Propriety dictated I had to accept the gesture, but I'd fought against propriety my whole life. Into that open palm, I placed the painting. "I don't want anyone at my service."

That patronizing hand moved away as Pierce set the painting on the table. The hunter elf—thief, stealing me from the life I had for his own personal gain—tilted his head. "Don't you recognize my name?"

That ego was infuriating, but I didn't like this elf knowing more than I. The naming conventions of our clans stated this elf, Pierce Evansson, was the son of an Evan, which was meaningless by itself. "Your father's name was Evan. Was he a thief too?"

Pierce tilted his head in confusion, but smugness never left. "Evan Logonson."

My stomach clenched, twisted, and I wanted to vomit at the name I hadn't heard in centuries. A smug hunter elf—yes—but he wasn't a thief at all. This Pierce Evansson was a delivery boy. I couldn't stop the trembling, and I fought to smooth my voice, to maintain the mirage of detachment. "When are you going to relinquish me to your father?"

"My grandfather, Logon Larsen, and your father, Niko Niskanen, came to an agreement that formed a pact of peace between our clans and an obligation to join forces against the humans."

"Your clan betrayed our hospitality and conquered us. The agreement was coercion, and you know that."

Pierce shrugged. "I wasn't there personally, but I was told it had been a mercy. Either way, when we were ready to collect on our agreement, imagine our surprise and anger that the princess had vanished."

My family had been slaughtered by humans, but I suspected from his tone that if there had been survivors, the Larsen clan would've finished them off out of spite. Pierce's rebuttals weren't winning any favor with me, and since he thought he knew everything, and I'd already been caught, defending myself was pointless.

Pierce frowned. "All we had were questions, but one in particular no one could agree on. Even if you didn't like the elders' decision, why would you not protect your home—your people—your family? It all rested on you."

I hadn't then and still didn't believe in self-sacrifice for the greater good, or in my case, being involuntarily sacrificed.

As a confused youth, I'd fought my way into politics to be treated as an equal, but I'd learned I was only a pawn—the lowest of the players on the board, the first to be tossed aside. Being a princess wasn't a station of honor. It was a degrading title, equivalent to walking around with 'pawn' inscribed on my forehead. Opinions clearly had never changed.

But with hardly a thought at all, I'd sacrificed myself—and I would've died—to save Soren. He'd never understand the true depths of that action. While Pierce badgered me with questions of saving my people, he likely figured out exactly what I'd done for the vampire—thus the reason for the continuous fire of insults, condescension, and attempts at guilt. No matter how much Soren believed I'd betrayed him, he'd never treat me like this. I had to get away from here. Coldly, I said, "Only a male would ask that question."

Pierce chuckled. He actually laughed, and I wanted to tear every feather off his wings and shove them down his throat. "You really are a spitfire." He pressed a fist against his chest as if my words had punched him, and he was amused by the effort. The trembles—and my fists—were becoming a true test of my restraint. He should be very impressed. "Wow, just wow! Talking to you is like interviewing the most famous and reclusive celebrity while unlocking the secrets of a tomb of wonders. I'm...I'm just blown away. Not that you need or care about my opinion, but you did the right thing."

I frowned at this sudden change. "Come again?"

"If you had dutifully remained in that cell, you would've married my father and become queen of the Larsen clan," Pierce said simply with a sparkle in his eye once more.

"I knew exactly what I was fleeing," I said, not picking up on the hilarity of the situation. The son was an annoying...featherbag, I amused myself with Soren's fitting descriptor. And at this point, the father couldn't be worse. "So when am I going to meet him?"

"Not for a long time, if I had it my way. A very long time."

"You're not handing me over to the elves?" An unexpected lightness filled me. My fists unclenched, and the trembling eased. No one—no fate—was worse than being a prisoner in the elf clan. "Then who wants me?"

"Wants isn't fair here," he said slowly, watching me intently.

He was being obtuse on purpose, amused with these word games. My brow darkened at this obnoxious thief...*bounty* hunter. "Then who paid?"

Pierce shook his head and bit back laughter. I was willing to go anywhere to get away from this featherbag. Absolutely anywhere, and the sooner, the better. "Then what? Who? Just tell me already."

"First, let me thank you for saving Soren Rockwell's pathetic life, truly. You actually saved *me* from a big, old, nasty regret." Not a damn word out of his mouth made sense. "So now I want you to thank him for me, and yes, it has to be you. It won't have the right impact coming from me." I frowned, but those words implied he'd free me in order to complete the confusing favor, so I kept listening, waiting for the hilarity to click. "I couldn't have imagined a more satisfying payback than when you thank Soren for murdering my grandfather and thank Oliver for murdering my father in the least dignified way imaginable."

I covered my mouth with my hand, symbolically trying to stop myself from vomiting when I'd just gotten clean. "You? You're the clan leader?"

Events outside of my control had led to Pierce Evansson inheriting the right to claim me. Nicole had been annoyed that Soren hadn't already staked him, so much so that the feeble old woman considered doing it herself. Now I was annoyed he hadn't done it. While I wanted to flee more than ever, this elf didn't consider his vengeance satisfied until I was his. If Soren still wanted me—as the real me—I would've stayed, but now I had to stay to keep Soren safe.

Even if I managed to stake this despicable creature, the truth of my existence was out there—with certainty in Lily and Allison. An active search would be underway with renewed vigor because they were no longer chasing a ghost story. No matter how much I wanted to live my own life, I would always be the last female elf.

"I know what you must be thinking," Pierce said softly. "But you don't have to be afraid of me. I've grown accustomed to this lifestyle that our ancestors would be ashamed of and that my clan doesn't agree with. I live in a house like a human, not inside the clan's walls, and I pay my bills on a paramedic's salary. Yes, I save humans for a living, and I enjoy it."

He was living the life he wanted, refusing the obligations that tradition dictated. Pierce was doing what he wouldn't let me do.

"As next in line, I am the rightful clan leader, and when I so choose, I'll step into the position. But without a queen at my side, I find the role of leader...empty. I've made a life out here, one in which I can do more for our kind than in there. So, I do understand why you stood up for yourself and your beliefs, and I respect that. I've also learned some hard lessons along the way, and I won't make the same mistakes with you. We're both immortal, Indie, fated to be mates. I'll always be here when you're ready to join our clans into one power."

My clan had been wiped out because of his. I rose and said dryly, "I need to go."

Pierce rose and settled the painting inside the heirloom box with care. "You were never my prisoner, and you never will be. I only needed you to hear me out. All I ask is that you stay reachable. Don't disappear."

I wasn't a prisoner, yet he'd imprisoned me until he told his tale, and in exchange for my freedom, I had to do him a favor. I exhaled at the hypocrisy or blind stupidity. Not being hunted anymore was a freedom, but all he really offered was a larger prison where I could delude myself with normalcy until he was bored with it. A larger prison, pretending to have a normal life with Soren, was better than anything else I had. "If I stay in the area, you'll leave me be?"

"That's all I ask," Pierce said.

"Then I want your word you won't harm Soren. Everything that happened in the lab...has not. Understand?"

Pierce's jaw ground with frustration. "We're square."

"I accept your deal. Now I must be going."

"Of course." Pierce allowed me to leave without resistance.

For the first time in decades, I spread my wings and lifted off the ground, immediately becoming invisible to humans. I hovered just above the trees and power lines, taking in deep breaths of fresh air and relishing the feel of the wind trying to tussle my sticky locks in desperate need of a washing.

I had peace and limited freedom for as long as the elf allowed. But it turned out I did have unfinished business.

34

Hero Hair Soaring

Indie

Cora was home. I was thrilled to see a familiar and friendly face, and even more so because Soren had my car and my keys, and I couldn't wait to reclaim them. I lowered myself clear of the power lines behind the tiny house that was my temporary home. When I was confident that no humans were looking or lurking, I landed silently on my feet, and became visible once more. I knocked on the door, and my roommate let me inside.

"Hey, honey. Dear Lord, what happened to you? Are you okay?" Cora stared in shock.

I had been certain, with the vervain on her dresser, that she wasn't a vampire, and I was now certain she wasn't an elf who'd been faking her compulsion. I was glamoured, so she couldn't see the real me. Her sweeping, horrified gaze led me to the gruesome scene on my clothes. The blood had browned with air exposure, so at least she wasn't panicking and calling for emergency services—which would bring the elf literally back to my doorstep.

"Oh, I guess this looks bad, but it's paint. I tried out this artsy event, but it wasn't my thing."

"I'll say. Shower's yours, and you might want to make it a priority because whatever paint they used—it stinks. I'm making a bite to eat, but I can make extra. Are you hungry?" Cora strolled back to the kitchenette. "Hot dogs and corn. Super nutritious, but hey, I'm not a chef." My roommate filled a medium-sized pot with water and set it on the stovetop.

"I'm not hungry, but thank you." And she was right. I did smell, which was fitting, considering I looked like the dead, and almost had been dead.

Cora had already done more than enough for me. Now that I was free to choose a place, I needed to get out of her hair, but first, I needed that shower. Allison had stopped me from fleeing, but that was after I'd panic packed my car, which I'd given to Soren so he and his sister could easily escape. Now I realized no one had returned it. Since it wasn't valuable to...anyone—why I'd chosen such a drab vehicle—every guess I thought of wasn't good. "Can I borrow a shirt and pants?"

Cora paused in her efforts to open the can of corn. She gestured with her head toward the meager bedroom. "You know where the closet is. Knock yourself out, but pick a dress. I don't think my pants would fit you, and I'm not in the mood for humiliation."

"You can't fight genetics," I said reassuringly and exhaled sharply at my own words. I'd tried playing human, and it didn't work. From now on, no more spells for me. I would own my feathers—although I still couldn't let humans see them.

I moved into her bedroom while she grumbled to herself about her grandmother. The dried vervain bouquet was still here. I didn't notice any sprigs missing besides the one I'd taken. Her admirer was probably a normal human, the choice of flower had been a coincidence, and the source of the flowers had been accidentally erased when her memory had been tampered with. I was usually so good at targeting the exact thing, but I'd been playing human for so long I was rusty at being an elf.

At least I didn't hit the power lines.

I drew open the rolling door and took in the options. A wet plop of corn landed in a pot, followed by the water running once more and a rattle of metal as Cora settled the second pot on the stove. My roommate had a decent selection, but with our size difference, the only option was a dress. I lifted a hanger free and admired the light blue dress.

I hunched low for the footwear. Being curled up, the concentration of my stink should've been stronger, but it wasn't. I called to her, "Can I borrow your wedges again?"

"Sure thing, honey."

The ticking of the gas stove igniter reached my ears. It needed a good cleaning for it to take so long. I hooked my fingers into the back straps of the wedges and inhaled deeply as I rose. My eyes widened. That stink had never been me.

"Cora, stop!"

A *vhoomp* of ignition came from the stove at the same time a head-scrambling explosion threw me deeper into the closet.

Soren

Today was my war. I'd deal with the fallout at another time. All that mattered was Indie, safe in my arms. Nicole and my sister had armed me with blood bags, black nightshade, and a fairly intimidating stainless steel butcher's knife. I didn't have anywhere to tuck it, so I'd grabbed a smaller steak knife and stuffed it into the back of my jeans. I headed out in Oliver's Mercedes. The fumes were still annoying, but I didn't want to waste time taking the containers out.

Indie's car had been left at the lab in Green Bay. Same as her keys, purse...and phone, which was why she wasn't answering my texts. And it took me far too long to figure that out. The flaming shitbag would've healed her and brought her to his house. But she wasn't there. No one was.

Trying to quell the rising panic, I dialed Cora while crossing the Interstate bridge into Menominee. The call went straight to voicemail. I rolled down the window for fresh air and strummed the wheel, impatiently waiting at the lights that always seemed to turn red when you're in a hurry. The flaming shitbag—eh, it stuck—would be raging about my escape, but knowing what she was, I didn't think the elf would physically harm her.

Many more things could happen than physical pain, and I knew the elf was capable of that.

After waiting in the long line turning left onto Tenth Street, I zigzagged around slower traffic. Just beyond a small discount retailer, I swung into the left turn lane. While waiting for incoming highway traffic to clear, I eagerly searched for Cora's car, Indie's car, or any lights on inside her tiny apartment house. Of those things, I confirmed the lights and Cora's car. Indie had to be here.

When the traffic cleared, I pulled into the lot and parked, happy to leave the pungent gasoline scent behind for a while. I didn't think Pierce was here—at least his SUV wasn't. So all I took with me was the steak knife. I climbed out and locked the car doors with the fob. I took one step toward the front door, and an explosion blew me off my feet.

I blinked. My ears rang. There was smoke rising into the evening's fading light. Why was I on my back? I folded up and shook my head. Oliver's car had a nasty dent in it. He was going to be pissed, but on the bright side, the full gas cans in the trunk didn't blow. What the hell happened?

While bones knitted themselves back together and gray matter un-squished in my skull, the ringing in my ears cleared. I climbed to my feet with a few grunts. Cora's apartment had flames licking around the shattered windows. The roof dangled precariously, as if only a few lucky electrical wires held it up. The lights were off. How long was I out for?

I dashed to the wreckage and tore the smoldering door off the hinges and flung it aside. Without hesitation, I pushed my way into the blinding smoke and sifted through the debris—both scalding and sharp. I yelled Indie and Cora's names and listened for responses over the crackling flames. While I didn't need to breathe to be undead, I did need it to speak. The more I yelled, the more I inhaled and the more...I coughed. The wood smoke wouldn't bother me, but the burning in my lungs wasn't right. I pressed on. The tiny house was...tiny.

"Indie!" I called and coughed. "Where are you?"

Each breath was like glass shards dragging along my lungs, slicing and bleeding as they pushed in and out with words. "Indie! Cora?"

I folded over, and now I knew what it was. Aerosolized vervain—less potent than the injectable kind, but still debilitating after enough exposure. Who the hell was making bombs with vervain? I didn't need many guesses on that one, but who would risk Indie's life was a harder one. To buy myself some time, I dropped to my hands and knees, trying to keep below the smoke. I moved debris around. Lifted pieces of furniture and avoided the curtain of flames. I stopped calling. No one was answering. I just needed to search.

Maybe this had only been a faulty gas line, and I was in here like an idiot, volunteering for a vampire barbecue.

If the universe wanted to be that cruel, so be it. I wasn't giving up. Crawling through shattered wood from a table, I caught a sharp edge in the hip. I sucked in a burning breath, coughed, and persisted. A shape resembling a human sprawled near the sink, but after a beat of focusing my eardrums, I realized the body was Cora's, and there was no pulse.

I flipped her over my shoulder and rushed straight out. I settled her on the parking lot. Onlookers approached, and I ordered them to help her. EMS sirens wailed in the distance. I dragged in some fresh air and dashed back inside.

Indie

The clatter of metal on metal had always stirred my curiosity, much to my father's dismay. Skirting out of Birgitte's sight, I dashed off to Mother's chambers and found my mother almost completely wrapped in armor. I marveled at the glinting metal. Adoration spread from my lips.

"Mother, may I join you on this day?"

My long blond hair was pulled back with several small braids, just like hers, and as she lowered herself onto a knee to meet my gaze, the locks slipped over her shoulder. I brushed them back for her. Armor was constricting and heavy, but I still wanted it.

"I need you to tend to your studies. One day, Indiara Niskatar, you shall be the leader we all need, and great leadership begins with knowledge."

Those were the most disappointing words I could've heard. My pout had been legendary.

"Fear not, my child." Mother tapped my chin up. "Your day shall come. I'm sure of it."

"But if I'm going to be the clan leader, what of Reku and Kalevi? They're older than me."

Mother smiled, an image—now faded—I held sacred. "They are left wanting, Indiara. While they dutifully take up the sword and march on like proper males, your curiosity and righteousness serve you better. That head of yours shall take you farther than they could ever hope for."

"This is our little secret. Promise?" Mother's playful smile had me beaming with pride.

I nodded enthusiastically, but she hadn't mentioned the most important role I was to assume. "But what of the heirs? Do I have to?"

Her radiant smile drifted away, and I never saw it again. "Your father upholds tradition above all. I don't see why the wishes of the deceased should triumph over the desires of the living. But a great leader needs support she can trust, so find a worthy male who makes you want to be with him, regardless of his stature. Follow your heart, Indiara, and everything you want shall come true."

Those were the words echoing through my mind as she faded away, and I coughed. I blearily opened my burning eyes to near-blinding smoke, and they stung. I squeezed them shut and rolled to my side, coughing uncontrollably.

The explosion.

I looked for Cora, but I couldn't see but a foot in front of me. Over the crackles of flames and groans of the roof above, I could hear shuffling. "Cora!" I called desperately, trying to pinpoint where it came from.

Another smaller explosion rocked the tiny apartment, and burning chunks of wood fell from above.

"Indie!" a hoarse male voice called and coughed.

"Soren?" I coughed. "Is that you? I'm over here."

At once, arms scooped me up. With a whoosh of burning hot air and searing flames, I was on the hard asphalt parking lot, coughing and dragging in a fresh breath. Smoke billowed up out of the roof, which collapsed into another puff of fresh flames and smoke. That was close.

Sirens were approaching, and bystanders huddled nearby, focusing on something in the parking lot. Soren appeared above me, sooty and burned, but his injuries were healing. His voice was still hoarse. "Are you okay? Indie, talk to me. Are you okay? Is Pierce here? Was he in there?"

I thought I had answered him, but I must not have. "I'll be fine. Cora?" I lifted my head and the burning ruins, but Soren pushed me down.

I never should've forced her to harbor me. I'd known selfishly using Cora would get her hurt. She was such a sweet woman who deserved the world. Tears filled my eyes, a tiny reprieve from the burning smoke.

"Cora is being tended to, but you can't move. You have a piece of the table impaling you, and we have witnesses."

I focused on my glamour. Wide-eyed, I asked, "Did you—did they—see me?"

"No one saw anything. It's okay." Soren held my hand and gave me a teary smile.

"Pull it out. Then we can erase their memories."

Soren shook his head, and his voice was still gravel. "We're too weak. Let the ambulance come, and we can slip away."

I tried to sit up, but Soren stopped me. "I can't go in an ambulance. If they knock me out with their drugs, they'll see."

"Indie," Soren said calmly. His shaggy hair, gray with ash, fell around his handsome, sooty face. "I know the meat wagon drivers. One's an okay dude. He won't hurt you. The other...well, let's just say as long as I'm by your side, no one will hurt you."

The same promise he'd given me when I had only been a terrified human. I was now an elf wanted the world over, and he'd still keep me safe.

"I never should've wasted a second doubting you. I knew you wanted my help in saving my own sister. Everything else was not your fault. I knew the risk of returning, but I went back with eyes wide open." Soren gave me a lop-sided grin. "There was one small thing that caught me off guard. I don't think I've ever been speechless in my life, but like then as now, I was willing to do anything, absolutely anything, to have you in my arms. I'm so, so very sorry. Will you forgive me for all the terrible things I'd said and for not believing you?"

"There is one thing you need to know—" I sneezed, and a blinding flash of pain sparkled across my vision. A stab of pain, as if someone had a grip on my insides, made me want to curl up, but every moment—even breathing—felt as if I were still inside that fire.

Soren's smile slid away. Worry filled his brow, and he looked up at the traffic for a little too long before returning to me. "Indie? Hang in there. The meat wagon is almost here. Breathe softly, evenly. Don't move."

"I need to tell you..." I started. Soren shushed me. His worry had me worried, and I had to get this out. I squeezed his hand, and he leaned closer so I didn't have to speak so loudly. "None of it was an act."

Soren stared. He exhaled, and his brows tilted in relief as happiness took over. "It wasn't for me either."

"Kiss me," I asked quietly.

Soren assessed my abdominal impalement that I refused to look at, as if he were trying to decide if it were a safe idea. "Indie, I don't want to hurt you."

That meant it was as bad as it felt. "Distract me," I demanded softly.

He hesitated, but he came closer while bracing himself against touching me. With a flinch at the searing pain, I reached up to the nape of his neck and made him close the distance. His lips found mine, and after a sweet second, his hands moved behind my neck and into my sticky hair. I felt those lips and mouth on mine, and I forgot absolutely everything. There was only him. His gentle care and respect meant so much to me. His promise to keep me safe drove me to those arms where I wanted to stay forever. Tears flooded my eyes. He was the equal my mother had always wished I'd find. I bet she wouldn't even mind his fanged status.

While the pain was still gone, I gently pushed at Soren's beautiful face, and he backed up. "I have one more thing I need to say." Soren collected my hand again and held it against his cheek. "I love you."

With teary eyes, Soren kissed my knuckles. "I love you so much. You're going to get through this."

I focused on the warmth of those words and those beautiful green eyes while I gripped that hunk of wood and ripped it free. I folded, eyes wide, and I exhaled at the shocking pain, but now that it was out, it was just a little better—a very tiny bit better, but the increased bleeding wasn't.

"Indie, no!" Soren pleaded and uselessly pressed his hands over the wound. "Why did you do that?"

I gave him an apologetic smile. He couldn't bear the thought of my harming myself to save him. I knew he couldn't bear the thought of harming me himself, so I took that burden from him. "So no one else felt guilty for causing me pain."

The ambulance lumbered into the parking lot, and two men—one I fully recognized and one I didn't—rushed to my side.

"Indie, what happened?" Pierce asked, wearing a healthcare worker's uniform. With Soren, he shared a glare I could only describe as murder.

"Gas leak. I could smell it." A stupid accident of all things, but at least it was simply over. No new battle or hunt or vengeance had to be triggered. It was just...over.

"No more questions. She needs healing now. Yours won't work, Kevin," Soren said. The very young man frowned and focused on me, as if trying to figure out what I was, and I focused on him, wondering why he couldn't help. Even stitches from a human would be useful. "Can I trust you, Pierce?"

The brute elf I despised glanced at Kevin and leveled a serious gaze at Soren. He looked at me while he said, "I would never hurt her."

He would never hurt me in a way that caused physical pain—that I believed.

"Too many people are looking. Get her in there now," Soren ordered.

Soren had splinters all over his left side like a dog who'd sniffed too close to a porcupine, including a large one in his hip. "What about you?" I asked, still holding his hand while the pair lifted me onto a stretcher. "You need help too."

Soren looked down at himself as if finally noticing. A reassuring smile spread across his lips. "Harmless toothpicks. Let's go."

Kevin and Pierce lifted and pushed me into the back of the ambulance. Soren climbed up beside me, but rather than my healer, Kevin followed. Pierce closed us in and took the wheel.

The young man with buzzed hair and dark brown eyes looked like a teenage human to me. So youthful, spirited, naïve. But looks were certainly deceiving. "I'm Kevin Fontaine. We're going to park out of sight of the witnesses. So that means I get a few minutes with you, the legendary Indiara Niskatar."

"How do you know me?" I asked, struggling to place him.

Soren reached out and took my hand, squeezing with reassurance—not defensiveness. Soren trusted this young man with my identity, but my love focused on my blood loss. I was avoiding it.

"When word spread of a conflict, I made a habit of...lingering nearby. I was there when the humans marched to your gates. I never saw what became of you, but your ghost story has spread far and wide. Many people thought you were held captive. Others thought you were slain but buried so no one would know. Imagine my surprise to see you alive and...not exactly well, but the elf will take care of that shortly."

I studied the healthcare worker. He didn't have glamoured wings like me, but I'd had a fully effective spell shielding me. "You're not an elf?"

Kevin cackled. "Vampire."

It was deep into twilight, but he'd been on shift in daylight...this town really did break all the rules. I frowned. "What were you doing at the battle?"

Kevin shrugged. "War is always fraught with easy pickings. That night wasn't so tasty. No offense."

Then, as now, I couldn't fault a vampire for surviving. "None taken."

The sirens cut out, and the movement stopped. The driver's door opened and closed. In a beat, the elf climbed in through a side door.

"You sure get around," Soren said to Kevin, and the not-so-young vampire shrugged.

Pierce sat next to me. "I have to touch your skin, if that's okay with you."

"Of course," I said, irritated at everything the elf had put me through up to and including making me wait in excruciating pain. "Get on with it."

The elf rolled up my destroyed blouse, exposing the gristly damage and blood pooling and spilling rapidly. He didn't need to wipe it away. He placed his open palms on my abdomen and concentrated. His emerald eyes glowed a shade of sea foam green.

Healing as an elf wasn't an easy thing. To expedite the natural healing process of another, the energy needed had to come from somewhere, and since elves weren't witches who could draw from the earth, the healer had to relinquish part of himself, sharing a part of him, giving away a piece of him for the sake of another. And only copious sunlight and time could replenish that lost energy. It was in a way a temporary self-sacrifice. Until fully restored, he'd be weakened by an amount relative to healing required.

The gentle warmth of the heal felt like a warm blanket on a cold winter's night. It was relaxing, and as the pain eased, it brought out almost a floaty drunkenness. And it left no trace but the fresh stains.

Pierce Evansson healed me twice in as many days now. Not a gesture to be taken lightly, and he must have been very weak by now. The elf's eyes returned to their normal dark brown, and he covered me the best he could with the tattered fabric. "You're all set."

"I had every intention of killing you for what you've done," Soren said darkly to Pierce. "I'm fully stocked with black nightshade and blood for myself if you fought back. Check this out. I even got this here." Soren brandished a kitchen steak knife. "Don't look like much, but I'm motivated."

Pierce stiffened, but he didn't make a move. If Soren wanted to end the elf, he could easily right here, right now. But Pierce had already agreed to drop his grudge. He was backed into a corner of submitting or being killed.

"But I have a problem," Soren continued with a captive audience. "See, I'd promised to keep her safe, and now I know exactly what that means. Someday, like now, I might need you. So if you're willing to grant me a truce—a real one with no more potshots—I'll heed it."

Glaring in silence at Soren, Pierce frowned. I suspected it was a demonstration of strength—that he wouldn't surrender so quickly to his enemy. But I wanted the elf gone, and I wanted Soren to exact his vengeance so rightfully owed, but I had a deal. If my love destroyed this elf, the next one might not be so...generous.

"Done," Pierce replied evenly. He looked at me. He wasn't warm or cool, just a neutral stranger. "Your apartment is toast. Where would you like us to drop you off?"

My car was in Green Bay, but that was a big ask. So the only place I would want to call home...

"My house, please," Soren said before I could. We exchanged warm glances, and I suppressed my smile for everyone else's sakes.

After needing confirmation from me, Pierce respected Soren's wish, but I bet he was fuming inside.

I needed a shower—like, the literal kind—because I'd been nearly disemboweled twice in this outfit.

35

Dance in the Flames

Indie

Now I understood why Soren had smelled so strongly of gasoline just prior to faking our way into the dreaded lab. The pungent scent was nauseating as we rode back to Green Bay to pay the lab a visit. As much as I wanted private time with Soren, it was only right to include Della. Soren parked right next to my beat-up sedan—he'd never needed it, thankfully. I peeked through the windows, and none of my stuff had been taken.

Soren tossed the Mercedes' keys to Della. "If anything else happens to this car, Oliver will have your head. Not mine."

"I remember how to drive. It's not that hard." Della held the keys and looked at the trunk. "How do I open this?"

"You're not instilling confidence here." Soren showed her the right button on the fob, and she popped the release. While Della lifted out containers of fuel, Soren zipped around to my driver's door. He opened and closed it too quickly to guess the purpose. "Here." Soren tossed my keys to me. "But this doesn't change your moving in with me."

Nothing would keep me away from him ever again. I pocketed my keys and added with a playful smile, "But it does change who gets to park in the garage."

"This magnificent beast definitely gets priority over the Shelby—at least until Oliver comes home." He chuckled and took a gas can from his sister.

I still had my badge, and I'd use it to save time and effort, but if they'd kicked me out of the system—well, the three of us could figure it out. While darkness rolled across the skies, we marched through the parking lot, like soldiers heading to battle. We blew through the front door and found Chuck at his post. Before he sounded an alarm at our red gasoline cans, I closed the distance and compelled him to forget we'd ever been here tonight. He nodded his orders and returned to his station and his sandwich.

Just as they hadn't removed me from the system, they hadn't increased the security. Vervain wouldn't stop me, but they could've given him black nightshade, or told the witch to use a blocking spell. Perhaps Lily, now seeing a chance at her own freedom from the elf chains, had a change of heart. Or they, like everyone else, had simply underestimated me.

Some lessons were learned the hard way. "As we move through, prop open as many doors as you can. Fire moves easily with a clear path."

"This comes from the University of Indie and her library adventures?" Soren asked.

"Not down here, but living in my car is cold in the winter, so I'd warm up in libraries."

Soren gave me a short look, but we stayed on task, moving as swiftly and as quietly as possible, opening doors along the way, and breaking a few in the process. Baseball Bat was at his post, and Soren compelled him to allow us to pass without incident.

Naturally, he did.

"Shoe," Soren added. "Give me your shoe."

Baseball Bat did as ordered. Soren took it and smacked the human upside the head, knocking him clean off his feet. He exhaled in satisfaction and pressed the button to open the airlock door. As Della and I strolled through, Soren wedged the shoe under the door.

At the last door—the only thing standing between us and the misery behind it—I gripped that knob with metal-crunching strength and ripped the door off the hinges. That felt like the equivalent of a few months of therapy. Then I reminded Soren and his sister of the plan. "Clock starts when the camera sees us. Squeeze the fire suppression lines. Destroy all traces of the serum, and clear every room. No one is getting left behind. I need to get something."

The two of them splashed gasoline all over while moving from objective to objective, and I headed to my office. There was a lot of history, knowledge, and power inside this room. Power that had the ability to protect me from my own kind. What if someone else in my position needed that very same help? Could I remove that protection—that safety—from another in need?

I collected the last grimoire I'd browsed—the one with my notes as a bookmark. Gripping it firmly, I closed the door to this vast library gently, securely. The books were likely to survive, but that was all I was willing to do for them.

"Any prisoners?" I asked Della as she emerged from a prison cell empty-handed.

"No," Della said. "Not sure if I'm relieved or disappointed to be the last, but I know what helps." Della resumed dumping gasoline and knocking everything off the countertops. Even tipping over chairs. She had her own therapy to work through, and I wouldn't object.

Soren groaned as he buckled the suppression lines in his fists and then headed for Lily's office. While computer equipment crashed to the floor, I stopped at the refrigerators. With one sweeping arm, I brushed the trays of full test tubes onto the floor. Shelf after shelf, everything was kissing the tile floor. Glass shattered all over, but nothing in these refrigerators could harm me.

Soren appeared at my side, holding a small black device. He tore the lid off to expose a shiny disc inside. He let it drop carelessly onto the floor. It hit hard and bounced. "Oops." He jabbed his heel against it. "Oops again." He repeated the jabbing and apologizing, and I watched with amusement. "I seem to be having a seizure. I just can't stop—" He jabbed. "Oops. I don't know what it is about this hard drive filled with data intent on destroying my kind." He jabbed. "Oops. I'm almost compelled." I laughed, and he stopped and closed the distance between us with a warm, glowing smile. "There's something special about seeing you hanging on my arm, teasing my ear while club music bounces off the walls. But...this is the best date ever."

"It will be," I said, pushing him back. "There's glass all over, and I know a paper cut never hurt you before, but it could now. Stay clear, okay?"

Soren took my pleading arm and wrapped it behind him while closing the distance. His thumb brushed my cheek. "You don't have to worry about me."

"Are you a thousand years old?" Then maybe I wouldn't.

Soren pressed his lips thin as if realizing his inadequacy. "Hundred and eighty-ish," he said sheepishly. "I must be such a child to you."

"We're breaking all the rules of nature. What shall we do about it?" I added playfully.

Suddenly serious, Soren said, "I'll show you." His lips found mine, and I took his empty gas can and tossed it away. It thumped and bounced around the lab, hopefully taking more fragile things with it. Soren's hands found my throat and the back of my head. His fingers buried in my short hair as he walked us backward.

When we bumped into the countertop, I set the impeding grimoire down and wrapped my arms around him, holding him closer. He was never close enough. I needed more. His hips pushed firmly against me, and my breathing quickened. As always, I was lost in his arms, and I'd never let go.

I hopped up onto the countertop and wrapped my legs around his hips. He pressed harder, his soft groans leaving me aching for more. The throbbing down low—so heavily teased over and over—was screaming for release. Soren's mouth found my throat, and his breaths sent a shiver of need through my body. I grabbed the front of his jeans.

"Uh, gross?" Della said in lighthearted disgust.

Hands freezing in place, I blinked. Soren released my throat and rested his forehead against mine. We shared a not-so-secret smile. "Can you give me, like, a minute before you release me? I think we traumatized my little sister enough for one day."

I laughed. "I'll stay right here until the clock runs out."

Soren mouthed the words 'thank you' to me and rested his forehead against my shoulder. The tumbling toss of another empty gas can turned my head.

"Since you two have somewhere you'd rather be, how about we light this place up?" Della flicked a lighter and held the flame. Her brow lowered in devious challenge.

Soren reached into his back pocket, scrolled around on his phone screen, and set it on the countertop next to the grimoire. "Do it, Della. Then get out of here. I need a few more minutes."

"Just get out of here before you turn to ash, all right? Oh, and don't forget to smile for the cameras." With a beaming grin, Della looked straight into the camera and tossed the lighter. She vanished using hyperspeed. The gasoline ignited with a *vhoomp!* But this time, I wasn't worried.

The flames glided along their given path like an elaborate curtain before the show. Soren tapped on his screen, and a gentle melody rose from the tiny speakers. Soren backed up and offered his hand. "How about you make good on your promise?"

"Thanks to your sister, I can only do half of it. Is that okay?"

Soren exaggerated his consideration. "I'll accept half now and half later."

With a steamy grin, I took his hand and stepped into his embrace. He let the rhythm guide the swaying while his body pressed against mine. Our feet shuffled until silently settling on a simple box step, and with each landing of a foot, glass crunched. Flames rose along the walls. Every prison cell glowed. Soren cupped my cheek. The firelight flickered in his beautiful eyes. And while the lab of horrors fell to its knees, Soren said quietly, "Actually, this doesn't count."

I grinned at the prospect of a repeat. "And why not?"

"I never agreed to a timer." As the growing flames danced along with us, Soren's hair fluttered in the heat. Flames covered the walls, brightening the lab, but smoke formed faster than it could escape. He grabbed his phone, stopped the song, and pocketed it. "We need to go. Grab your book."

I pressed the thick tome to my chest, and Soren gripped my hand. We headed for the door. "One last thing." He paused, and I watched as he raised an arm and then a purposeful finger toward the camera. Soren's hair and shirt shifted with the heat, but he held steady—long enough for the voyeur to get his message. "Eat that." Soren coughed and pulled me through the doorway.

We rushed to the parking lot, unimpeded. Della had already gone, so we strolled to my unfortunate car—just the two of us in the quiet night with streetlights guiding our way.

"I've had enough fire for a while," I said and tugged at my shirt to cool myself off.

Soren held my face in both of his hands. "Indie, let's go home."

"My boxes are going to cramp your legs," I said, feeling shame for the first time.

His arms slid around my waist. "I think I can manage one hour of cramping. Besides, they'll be unpacked in our house tonight." Soren kissed me again, and his searching hands moved into my pockets and freed my keys. He released me and dangled his prize. "I'm driving."

"It's my car," I protested.

"Tonight you couldn't possibly drive fast enough." Soren dropped into my driver's seat, made a noise of frustration, and moved the seat back.

I climbed into the passenger seat. "Your skills can't magically improve the car's abilities."

Soren gave me a challenging grin. "We'll see."

Soren had opened up his life for me. Not only was I going home, but he was my home forever.

"Indie?" Soren asked while peeling the car out of the parking lot.

Dreamily, I answered, "Yes?"

"Use those beautiful eagle eyes of yours to find any cars in the ditch." Soren gave me a knowing grin and held my hand. He brought it to his lips and kissed my knuckles. I squeezed back and kept an eye out for Della.

Indie

Unpacking was not happening tonight. While I'd been tasked with watching out for Della and her rusty driving skills, I'd taken Soren's hand and brought it to the lovely package between his legs that I so desperately wanted inside me. He'd nearly crashed into a mature maple while swinging my car around to the side of the garage. Climbing out, he moved straight to me and took my hand—as if I wouldn't go with him.

He brought me into the bed-and-breakfast, where his sister and niece were chatting on the couch. Nicole gave me a sly grin as Soren and I headed straight upstairs. At the top of the steps, out of sight, he turned to face me. His eager hands removed my shirt in a quick swipe. I kicked off my shoes and headed toward him. He walked backward, shedding layers. First his shoes, pulled free and kicked aside, followed by his shirt. His hair became a wild mess, and I wanted to reach into his and guide his face just right. But we were still on the move. I grabbed those jeans and tried to unbutton them. His mouth on my throat tipped my head back, and I stumbled on the next step.

Soren captured me, and I wrapped my legs around him. He brought us to the long-awaited destination, and reluctantly, I had to let him go to take off my jeans. I unbuttoned in a hurry and wriggled my hips free of the remaining restrictive material. Soren followed suit, revealing his sexy shape and his intense desire. He was lean, but not sharp and hard. Soren knew his way around the gym, but a layer of softness helped hide the intense strength below, and a dusting of dark hair had me almost whimpering in need.

Soren scooped me up as he dove for the king-size mattress. I was caged beneath him. Intense, glittering eyes gazed at my face. "You're not really going to break me in half, are you?"

I grinned. "I could."

"Some ground rules then. One, no breaking me in half."
I bit my grinning lip. "I personally enjoy the function of my
spine, and pretty soon you'll fully understand why."

"Fair enough," I said.

"And two—no breaking the furniture or cracking the
walls. Nicole doesn't need more work on her hands, and I
don't want to hear a different kind of nagging."

"Three, Nicole's half deaf, but keep the screaming to a
minimum."

I chuckled. "There's a lot of confidence in that rule."

Soren winked. "And four...Well, there is no four. We won't
need protection. We're safe together."

I liked the sound of that. "Has anyone ever told you that
you talk too much?"

"Of course. How else do you exercise your tongue?" Soren
mischievously grinned at me. His mouth found my throat,
and his kisses trailed to my breasts. That tongue of his flicked
on my nipples. The throbbing had been teased for so long, I
arched my back upward and a sharp, gasping yelp passed my
lips.

Soren grinned self-satisfied and gave me a playful
chastising sound in return. "Watch rule number three."

"You're just loving this, aren't you?" I asked breathlessly,
panting with need, and about to flip him over and ride that
hard, teasing cock.

"Every single second." Soren continued his way down,
and I stuffed my hands in his hair as if I were going to ride

him. That saucy mouth of his found my inner thighs and kissed and caressed the sensitive area, and I was frustrated to bursting with his delays. I whimpered. My hips rocked, begging, pleading for the release I so desperately needed.

With a soft chuckle, Soren finally put that tongue to good use. I gasped. I rocked—carefully—and he put his whole face into the effort. Like bobbing for apples, he went down, and he didn't surface until I broke rule number three. Very loudly.

Soren gave his face a quick wipe in the sheets and climbed over me. I wrapped my arms around him and flipped him underneath me. I heard a crack, and I pressed my guilty lips together. "Was that you or the bed?"

Soren squinted with his internal assessment, pressed his lips together, and waited a few too many beats before saying, "I'm good."

As Soren liked to say, oops. So, I gently straddled his hips, found that soft-covered hard cock of his, and I seated myself fully in one slick motion. Soren tipped his head back and groaned. I gripped those mounds of pecs, and now better in control of my urges, I started slow with long hard thrusts, rocking the bed against the wall.

Deaf or not, this wouldn't do.

"One second." I unseated myself. Soren's eyes widened with the sudden chill. He watched me as I climbed to the foot of the bed and dragged the whole bed away from the wall—with plenty of space to spare. Soren's eyes were wide for a different reason.

My turn for a smug smile. I climbed back onto his lap. "Now, rule number two can be followed."

I gripped those pecs and resumed my long, slow strokes. Soren's hands explored my bouncing breasts and stroked my thighs as I kept moving. I thrust faster and faster, gaining momentum as my own mountain peak was within reach. The thrusts became harder, sharper, with a solid grind. There were more cracks involved, but unless there was a protest, I kept going. I rode him until I crashed over the side, my thighs tightening, my breath catching, and I broke rule number three.

We couldn't all be perfect. Soren had bragged he could go all day and all night—whatever I wanted. I met that challenge. I rode him hard, even when his hips rose and his muscles clenched with his own release. His cock throbbed with his release, and when he could catch his breath again, he cried out my name while panting.

Then I took that cock in my mouth and finished him again. Only after we were both spent, I draped myself over his naked body under the sheets. His fingers traced around on my arm, and he whispered, "You broke all the rules."

I smiled against his chest. "You're welcome."

36
Deal's a Deal

Indie

Soren had emptied all the boxes out of my car and brought them up to his room. I'd unpack after the nagging curiosity was settled. At a luxuriously long dining room table in Soren's B&B, I gently opened the grimoire I had rescued and freed my notes.

Soren approached, wearing a devilishly handsome suit jacket over a dress shirt and pants. There were just slightly too short on him. He kissed the top of my head. "I've got staffing issues to handle, so I'm heading to the bar, but feel free to visit if you get lonely. Seltzer water will always be on the house."

"I might have to take you up on that."

Soren kissed my lips—a hungry reminder that I was his. He whispered, "I love you."

I said it back, and the sexy vampire left for work—as normal as TV shows had led me to believe. I was home.

Smiling with a warmth filling my chest, I lifted my pencil and finished adding the legible marks to my page. With a little deciphering of the runic language—now known as Elder Futhark—by erasing and trying again until the words made sense, I dropped the pencil. I stared.

I read the spell to myself.

Instructions
for a punishment fitting for a beast.

Under the new moon,
bringeth thy blessed water, scorching fire,
bitter cold earth, and soft breeze.
Calleth to the spirits as set forth:
"Water of life, absorb thy shadows of the full
moon's night.
Imbue the receiver with a thirst so cruel,
guilt shall drageth him toward the light."

I covered my gaping mouth with my hand. The impossible was possible.

Allison

I sipped from the offered drink—an ordinary craft beer—fighting back a cringe at the lumpy couch in his bland living room. Pierce lowered himself next to me, nearly spilling my drink, and he set a small wooden box in his lap.

I marveled at it while my excitement grew. "Is that it?"

"Things didn't go the way they should've," Pierce said with his hands on top of the box. He didn't sound disappointed, but he obviously wasn't satisfied.

Needing the contents of that box, I argued my case. "I delivered your elf to the bar, but you didn't go get her."

"I was at work. I couldn't get away, but I knew she wasn't leaving until she got what she needed."

"And I was going to give it to her after making her jump through hoops with Lily. As if I'd need another witch to help with a spell." I swallowed down a sip and continued. "And I gave you the idea of putting in cameras—you're welcome. So because of me, your elf was stuck here for a while and under surveillance. When your elf was getting too close to the vampire, I deleted him from her memory to help discourage her."

"That didn't work."

"Who would've thought that slimy vampire could be charming? Are you sure about Indie? Because I'm judging hard."

Pierce gritted his teeth. "I'm sure."

I shrugged. "Cora sounded the warning alarm for me, and I convinced Indie to stay for him. And that did work. You even managed to catch that vampire thanks to me. All you had to do was end him while convincing her you had nothing to do with it.

Pierce's gaze darkened.

"I'm just trying to explain how much effort I put into this. I had Cora's apartment destroyed, so Indie had no choice but to run into your safe arms. I couldn't have guessed she'd go..." At the increasing warning in Pierce's gaze, I deigned to speak his name again.

"Don't ever put her life at risk like that again."

"She wasn't supposed to be there. On the bright side, she promised to stick around. Now you have time to win her over the right way..." I trailed off again, this time to let him stew over the option. "Or do it my way." I held out my hand expectantly.

Pierce opened the lid of the box, freed the valuable talisman from its protective velvet, and gently placed it in my palm. I marveled at the round, antique bronze medallion with a symbol for the Other Side carved into it. A delicate chain tinkled in my palm, and I grinned in anticipation.

"You do know how to use it properly?"

I frowned. "Of course, I do."

"Have a safe trip."

I gripped it tight and pocketed it. Now I could take a trip beyond the veil, because there was someone with unfinished business just dying for the ultimate vengeance.

To be continued...

Dear Reader,

Dive into the next chapter of Indie and Soren's trilogy in **Vampire's Destruction (Immortal Protector Book 5)**, where Soren's worst nightmare becomes a reality. And don't forget to check out the prequel to Indie and Soren's trilogy, **Elf Bound**, the dramatic war-torn backstory of Indiara Niskatar, showing who she's meant to be, and who Soren needs to step up and impress.

As an indie author, I'm thrilled you shared your time with me, exploring the crazy worlds residing in my head and keeping me up at night. Your reviews are very important to me, so if you enjoyed this book, please consider leaving some stars for the first installment of Soren Rockwell and Indiara Niskatar's story, **Vampire's Demand (Immortal Protector Book 4)**.

If you found any typos or errors, I blame my cat. Rat her out at: support@stephanieflynn.com.

Thank you for your support!

Also By Stephanie Flynn

Find my catalog at StephanieFlynn.com

Immortal Protector series

0.5 Vampire's Distraction

1 Vampire's Deception

2 Vampire's Secret

3 Vampire's Promise

3.5 Elf Bound

4 Vampire's Demand

5 Vampire's Destruction

6 Vampire's Conquest

Immortal Protector Side Tales

Deer Holiday

Depths of the Heart

Matchmaker in Time series
0.5 Minutes to Live
1 Seconds to Act
2 Hours to Arrive
3 Days to Hide
4 Years to Savor

Pirates in Time series
1 Pirate's Prize
2 Pirate's Treasure
3 Pirate's Plunder

Time Travel Romance Shorts
Fateful Time
One Crazy Time

If you like your urban fantasy without the romance, too, check out Stephanie Flynn's other name, Marie Flynn!

About Stephanie Flynn

Stephanie Flynn writes action-packed paranormal romance filled with adventure, suspense, and danger. She lives in Michigan, USA, with her husband and kids, and she spends her writing time surrounded by a herd of normal cats who bat everything off her desk, including her coffee. Check out her website for more books: StephanieFlynn.com

9 781952 372360